WOOING MISS WILBRAHAM

"Miss Wilbraham. Frances. What are you doing here? You know you should not be here. I never expected to see you again." He stayed by the chaise longue, as if hoping the distance between them might calm his reaction to her.

"I know. Nor should I expend any effort in clearing your name. I should simply leave you to rot and suffer the punishment you so richly deserve." Fran smiled and went up to the earl, holding out her hands. "But I could not. I was here on other business, and the temptation was too great. I had to see you."

"What about your reputation?" He took her hands and drew her close, gazing into the depths of her dark eyes.

"I shall not be about long enough for the biddies to destroy it."

"You are rash and impetuous and foolish to come here. But I am so glad to see you, darling Fran." He raised her hands to his lips and kissed each one. "You are a source of perpetual fascination to me. What you say, what you think, what you feel. I want to know all of the answers to these question̲s̲ ̲ ̲ ̲ ̲ ̲ ̲ ̲ject under the sun. I've ̲ ̲ ̲ ̲ ̲ ̲ ̲ ̲ ̲ ̲ ̲ ̲cret of another human b ̲ ̲ ̲ ̲ ̲ ̲ ̲ ̲ ̲ ̲ ̲ ̲. I cannot tell whether ̲ ̲ ̲ ̲ ̲ ̲ ̲ ̲ ̲ ̲ ̲ ̲ne and singers wail, but ̲ ̲ ̲ ̲ ̲ ̲ ̲ ̲ ̲ ̲ ̲

Fran w ̲ ̲ ̲ ̲ ̲ ̲ ̲ ̲ ̲ ̲ ̲ ̲ ̲er arms about his neck. ̲ ̲ ̲ ̲ ̲ ̲ ̲ ̲ ̲know no better than you what love might be, but I believe that this is the closest one can be to love. I do not know how or why I have come to love you, but I do . . ."

Books by Madeleine Conway

SEDUCING SYBILLA

THE RELUCTANT HUSBAND

THE ERRANT EARL

Published by Kensington Publishing Corporation

THE ERRANT EARL

Madeleine Conway

ZEBRA BOOKS
KENSINGTON PUBLISHING CORP.
http://www.zebrabooks.com

One

Grievously wounded peers of the realm were not Dr. Roundell's common run of patients. But on a mild afternoon in September 1823, he was faced with the difficulty of disposing of Earl Lazenby of Edenbridge, who lay unconscious in The Crown with a broken arm and crushed leg following some accident with his curricle. Both Bloxham, the innkeeper, and Roundell were in agreement: The Crown Hotel was not a suitable venue for an invalid to remain above a night, even under the supervision of Roundell's increasingly competent assistant, Mr. Balham. Roundell's own house was full to the brim with grandchildren and was not, in any case, grand enough for an earl.

"There's no help for it, Bloxham, I shall have to ask Miss Wilbraham. Dysart House is not secluded but it is the best house in town, and she has servants aplenty to assist in nursing the poor fellow."

The doctor spoke with more decision than he was actually feeling. The sensible course would be for Miss Wilbraham to refuse entirely to house a complete stranger, still less a male stranger of uncertain reputation. But there was no other house in town which would provide suitable accommodation for an earl and it was clear that Bloxham was neither willing nor able to care adequately for the injured man.

"Cramming his cattle, no doubt, Dr. Roundell. His horseflesh are in a sorry way, nervy, and unsettling all my mounts. See if you can find a home for his bays as well as the earl. Miss Wilbraham won't notice them eating their heads off, but I've a business to run and books to balance." The innkeeper turned brusquely away, busying himself with polishing his tankards.

"I shall go now to Dysart House and try to persuade her to take in our waif. If only Lady Tollemache were not staying with her, I should be much more sanguine."

"If you can speak alone with Miss Wilbraham, we shall have this fellow off our hands by nightfall." Bloxham considered the situation briefly before smiling. "I have it, Doctor. The haberdasher received a delivery this morning. I'll direct my boy Timothy to run over and tell the household. Lady Tollemache will be in Parry's before you can say fine as ninepence."

Bloxham's reading of Lady Tollemache's interest in the latest materials and patterns from London was accurate. Dr. Roundell had time to drain a tankard of ale as he watched Miss Wilbraham's sister coming down Churchyardside toward the Square and into Parry's Haberdashers. As soon as the shop's bell had ceased its jangling, he traced her steps back to the Dysart buildings where the Wilbrahams had lived for nearly two generations. He rang the bell and Reed opened it immediately. The butler looked baffled.

"We did not summon you, Dr. Roundell."

"No. Is Miss Wilbraham at home?"

Reed nodded and led the doctor upstairs to the first floor drawing room. He knocked, entered, and then ushered the doctor into the pleasantly airy room. Miss Wilbraham stood to greet the doctor and invited him to sit by the windows which commanded an excellent view across the street to St. Mary's Church.

"An unexpected pleasure, Dr. Roundell. I was expecting the ladies of the parish when I said I was at home to any callers. They'll be here presently to plan for the Harvest Festival."

"Miss Wilbraham, I have come to beg a particular favor."

"Name it, Dr. Roundell, and I will tell you whether I can oblige." Miss Wilbraham's voice was low and creamy. It was a puzzle to the doctor why no young buck had swept her up years ago, for she was a most restful female on both the eye and the ear.

"I have a new patient this afternoon who is causing me a little difficulty."

"Go on."

"He is a gentleman not of these parts. An earl who has been quite severely injured in a carriage accident. He is at The Crown, but his travelling companions depart tomorrow to catch their boat to Ireland and Bloxham is reluctant to let him stay on at The Crown. And I must confess, I think it a most unsuitable place for a sick man."

"Why?" enquired Miss Wilbraham.

"It is the best inn in Nantwich and consequently, it is the busiest. There is no one to spare any time to watch over a patient, it is noisy and it is not so very clean."

"I see. But there are other places he could stay, surely? I know in my father's day we would have taken him in instantly, but Lady Tollemache is forever telling me that what was acceptable then is no longer *comme il faut* in a single lady, however advanced in years."

"Advanced in years! Poppycock! Except that if I speak to you of your youth, you will think more about the impropriety. But there is no impropriety when a man may have to fight for his life. I would send him over to Lady Dorfold, but it is too far. What if I undertake to ride over there myself and ask her to take him as soon as he is fit to be moved? Until such time, I do want him easily accessible."

"Farr could care for him. From what you say, there seems to be no valet."

"No valet, but he does have a tiger and a pair of bay horses."

"I daresay Bloxham wishes to shed them also. There is plenty of room in the mews for the groom and the horses. There is really nowhere else you think suitable?"

"Miss Wilbraham, you are the only person in Nantwich able to release staff to care for a sick man full-time. If he were infectious, I would never ask such a favor, but it is a matter of someone watching him and keeping him in clean, well-aired accommodation, which is fit for an earl. Yours is the only household to fit all these criteria."

"You are persuasive, Doctor Roundell. You may walk up to The Crown and arrange for earl and horses and all to be transferred here within the hour. But if you see Lady Tollemache, simply tip your hat to her and leave me to tell her that we have a guest. Will he need a great deal of nursing, do you think?"

"I fear he may, Miss Wilbraham. I shall send Balham round with the earl, if it is not inconvenient. I should like Balham to stay with the patient for tonight certainly, and possibly tomorrow night. His leg is terribly mangled and I fear infection will set in unless he is carefully supervised."

"Balham is most welcome."

"You are very good, Miss Wilbraham. There is also the question of Tarbuck, your stableman. He is known as the best horse doctor in these parts. The earl is not a horse, but perhaps the man will be able to assist us in dealing with this leg. Everyone knows how well Tarbuck managed farmer Vaughan's mare when her leg was bad."

"Tarbuck will be delighted. He will never let you or Balham live it down if the man keeps his leg. By the by, does your earl have a name? If I know, it will keep Kitty occupied in finding out all she can about him."

"His name, according to his travelling companions, is Earl Lazenby, of Edenbridge, which I believe is in Northamptonshire. He arrived in the company of a Lady Ormiston of Hatherley, in the same neighborhood. She was joined by her husband, Viscount Ormiston. They told me they were travelling to Ireland and were booked on a boat leaving Liverpool tomorrow. They have urgent business there, I believe, and are reluctant to rearrange their plans."

"It sounds a little havey-cavey, doesn't it? Still, I daresay Kitty will know all there is to be known of such exalted folk. Speaking of Lady Tollemache, you had better leave before she is back from Parry's, or we will have no end of delay explaining everything to her."

Dr. Roundell thanked Miss Wilbraham and headed off at full speed to avert any chance of an encounter with Lady Kitty Tollemache. His timing was well enough and he was safely back at The Crown, reporting to the viscount and his wife that the earl would be removed to Dysart House imminently by the time Lady Tollemache left Parry's followed by her maid, Potter, bearing several packages.

Lady Tollemache was not pleased to find the household of her sister in an uproar over the arrival of an earl. She had hoped for a comfortable hour or more displaying her bargains to Fran, but her sister was instructing Maria to air the sheets, and Farr to turn the mattress in the guest suite, and Mrs. Cooper to start preparing the gruels and broths suitable for invalids. It was most exasperating and just like Fran to invite some stranger into the house with a calm acceptance of the imposition, not to mention the danger. What Arthur would have to say about these goings on she did not like to think. What was acceptable in a country gentlewoman was not acceptable to a lady connected with one of the great families of the land, even if that connection was only by marriage. Even if the invalid was an earl.

But what an earl! Everyone knew that Lazenby was most disreputable. There had been that business with Lord Moberley, who had threatened him with a whipping down the length of Piccadilly, or was it Pall Mall, if Lazenby so much as set eyes on Lady Moberley again. But that was what came of immuring oneself in the provinces where no one had the least idea of anything.

There was no time for Lady Tollemache to talk sense into her tiresomely independent sister before the earl himself arrived. At least, a litter arrived bearing the unconscious man. Somehow, between an ostler from The Crown, Mr. Balham, Farr, and Reed, the earl was borne into the house and upstairs to the guest bedroom. He did not come round. Naturally, Miss Wilbraham was there to see him into the house.

This was only the second earl Miss Wilbraham had encountered, the first being the elderly scion of the house of Tollemache, the Earl of Dysart. He had attended Kitty and Arthur's wedding, even though Arthur was only a nephew and merely a knight through his own efforts, and so, Kitty was always saying, quite beneath Dysart's touch. Although she could not claim in all honesty that she had met Earl Lazenby, since he had not come round as he was brought into the house and carried aloft to its second story.

In Fran's eyes, he looked much more impressive than Dysart, even in his senseless state. Lazenby had a profusion of hair, a considerable improvement on Kitty's in-law. He was young, a further advantage, for Dysart, pretend though he might to less than sixty-five, had seen many summers go by. Lazenby also had a rather dashing profile, as far as Fran could make it out. Certainly she noticed a fine straight nose and a definite chin with a small dent in it. His mouth was rather wide, with finely sculpted lips and he had elegant eyebrows. She had time to notice all this as she accompanied Balham up the stairs and to the guest-room, where she checked that everything necessary had been supplied for the comfort of both invalid and the young man keeping vigil over the patient. Roundell also inspected the room, asked for some boiled water to be sent up with clean cloths, then dismissed Miss Wilbraham.

"We must clean up his leg now. He may rouse and cry out a bit, but we shall strive to keep him quiet with lau-danum. I shall report to you on the likely outcome, but at the very least, your bed linen will be damaged beyond repair."

"I had instructed Maria to put our tattiest sheets on the bed, earl or no earl. If I can be of further assistance, I hope you and Balham will not hesitate to summon me. I am not in the least squeamish and would be happy to relieve you of at least one watch by his bedside."

"We shall see, Miss Wilbraham. That may be most use-ful. Harvest is always a busy season for the medical profession and if Balham can be spared during the day, I may yet call on you." It was clear that the doctor wanted her out of the way, so she left the room, only to bump into Kitty on the landing.

"What are you thinking of, Fran?"

Miss Wilbraham was tempted, very tempted, to remind her sister that this was not Lady Tollemache's home, but Fran's own, that Lady Tollemache might be married to a knight, but she was still Fran's younger sister by two years, and that if Kitty wished to remain welcome at Dysart House, she would kindly refrain from trying to instruct Fran on her conduct. But Fran was a good sister, eager to keep the peace. She obediently followed Lady Kitty downstairs into the parlor.

"I repeat, Fran, what are you thinking of? To allow a known rake, a libertine of the most low and immoral propensities into the house!"

"Kitty, the Good Samaritan did not pause to see if his patient was received in Society. This is a sick man. What would Papa have said?"

"Papa was too kind and allowed all sorts of rag-tag types to take advantage of him. I should be most dismayed to think of you following his example. People will say you are eccentric and odd. You will never find a husband."

"I shouldn't think you want me to find a husband. If I die without marrying, everything comes to you."

"How can you be so callous? All I want is that you should find some degree of happiness as I have done with my Arthur." Kitty reached for her handkerchief.

Fran silently cursed her rash tongue. Kitty was about to turn on the waterworks and it was unquestionably her own rash words that had sent Kitty to the brink of trembling lip and delicately poised teardrop. But Kitty was so infuriating. The only other person in the household ever to see through her had been Mr. Wilbraham, but he was two years gone now, leaving his capable elder daughter to deal with Kitty's fits, with no leavening of paternal wisdom to dilute her heights of fancy and puncture her pretensions.

A robust defence of their guest was impossible: she did not know the man, and it was all too likely that he was beyond the pale socially. Kitty was a dedicated tuft-hunter and if she did not care to know Earl Lazenby, he must be truly disreputable.

"Kitty, I would save Beelzebub himself from the tender attentions of the Bloxhams. Besides, he is unconscious and even if he recovers, he will be confined to a bath chair or crutches for months. I hardly think he will be able to pounce on either you or me and have his wicked way with us."

"Does Roundell fear for his life? I do not know what is worse, admitting this man under your roof in the first place or allowing him to die here! Really, Fran, you have no sense."

"None," admitted Fran dryly. "It is too late, Kitty. Earl Lazenby will remain here until Dr. Roundell pronounces him fit to be moved or until he wishes to go, whichever occurs first. You may as well accept it."

Kitty flounced from the parlor muttering dire imprecations and vowing to write to Arthur's Tollemache cousins, who would back her to the hilt. Fran wondered if she might actually pack her bags and leave, but the truth was that Kitty had nowhere to go other than to her in-laws. Sir Arthur was too busy making his fortune to have provided a home for his wife. If she chose to stay with the Tollemache family, she would find herself with infinitely less freedom than if she remained at Dysart House, which had been her childhood home.

Fran had visited her brother-in-law's family only once, but she remembered all too vividly the chaos of the Tollemache household. Sir Arthur's father, one of the earl's numerous younger brothers, had little income and no inclination for hard work. He had opted for the church of all the avenues open to him, and accepted a modest living from his brother. He had been feckless enough to marry a wife with as little fortune as himself and had compounded his folly by producing eleven children, of whom Sir Arthur was one of the eldest, and certainly the most ambitious. The Earl of Dysart had taken pity on his nephew and put him in the way of preferment, finding him a post as one of his private secretaries. Then Arthur had come to Nantwich to inspect the Dysart buildings, a development of townhouses sponsored by the fourth earl some generations back, and to attempt to buy back Dysart House.

Of course, Mr. Wilbraham had stood firm against the offer made by the Tollemache family, but Arthur had been able to sway the old gentleman's mind where it concerned his daughter. Arthur and Kitty had been married nearly three years now, and he was busy using her dowry to create wealth for himself, investing in ventures in both East and West Indies and collecting for himself a knighthood in the process. He had spent more time apart from his Kitty than with her since their marriage. In her crueller moments, Fran did wonder how the couple would fare when the time came for them to spend more than a few weeks between voyages together, but Kitty was certainly very happy to be married, especially into so grand a family.

Miss Wilbraham was not so eager to give up her own name. Her father, despite a scholarly, otherworldly air, had been both warm in the pocket and canny in his investments. He had no heirs other than his two daughters, for after Kitty's birth, Mrs. Wilbraham had been pronounced much too delicate to endure once again the dangers of childbirth. Although he had spent the next seven years cosseting his wife, she had died before Fran's tenth birthday and he had never had the heart to remarry. Fran provided him with companionship and Kitty with amusement. In addition, Fran had mastered the art of running her own household with few restraints. It would be hard, she thought, to give up such liberty to take on the running of someone else's home.

Mr. Wilbraham had not found Sir Arthur entirely to his taste: the man was significantly older than Kitty, had no discernible sense of humor, a great sense of consequence and a publicly-voiced interest in pounds, shillings, and pence which struck Mr. Wilbraham as bordering on the vulgar. However, it was clear that Kitty did care for him and for the possible entrée into *tonnish* Society which he offered.

As a father, it had been his duty to point out that there were warmer men than Tollemache who might yet offer for her, but at twenty-one, Kitty had been convinced she was on the shelf and that a rising man of thirty-five was her best hope. When she married, it was made clear to her bridegroom that she would receive all she could hope for from the estate as her dowry, with Fran receiving her share, including the title to the family home, on Wilbraham's death. None of the family had imagined that a winter chill would carry him off the following year.

Before her father's death, Fran had ventured into Cheshire society quite happily, but had never met a man who could make her laugh or think or argue even half so much as her father. She was charming, pleasant, and slightly distant, frightening off all but the most persistent of suitors who soon enough found themselves at the mercy of Mr. Wilbraham's dry tongue if they called. She was a beautiful girl, true enough, but it was the somewhat untouchable loveliness of a grave angel from an Italian painting, all elegance and solemnity. The only person who might disabuse the world of this erroneous impression was Kitty, who knew her sister to be mischievous, provoking, and liable in private to making jokes that were generally incomprehensible to anyone other than their father. But Kitty, although she gave her sister suspicious looks when Fran went off into fits of giggles at trifles, had a considerable sense of family loyalty, and would never disclose to anyone, even her own husband, her sister's more freakish starts.

In the two years since Mr. Wilbraham had succumbed to pneumonia, Fran had found in the management of her father's affairs first some relief from the pain of his passing and then considerable freedom. She was now a rich young woman, past the first blush of youth, which protected her from the fortune hunters who tended to be more interested in naïve heiresses out of the schoolroom. The future stretching before her seemed empty and she was casting about for some interesting and useful occupation to fill the hours which she had once dedicated to assisting Mr. Wilbraham in his scholarly endeavors.

Like a magpie, Fran had picked up a great deal of information from ordering her father's notes, copying out passages from the books he was reading, and from his translations of Greek and Roman literature. It was not a passion for her, though. Her brain wanted occupation, she was aware, but none of the questions which her father had found so consuming seemed to her of particular moment. Some of the stories Sir Arthur told of his travels in the West Indies had shocked her into sending for tracts from the Anti-Slavery Society, but her power to effect change was limited in a comparative backwater such as Nantwich. If she were to take up reformatory activities, she wished to do so with zeal and active participation. This would mean going to live in London, which raised great questions such as whether it would be best to close, lease, or sell Dysart House.

Even if she did not take up a cause, Fran was determined to travel. She wanted to see Italy and, if possible, Greece, distant lands which her father had visited as a young man, but which she knew only through books. Once Arthur had returned and taken responsibility for his own wife, Fran would be free to leave for Rome. There had been talk of his return from Jamaica these two months, but no sign of the man just yet. Fran would have found this most exasperating but Kitty seemed to accept the uncertainty of her present life quite calmly.

A husband did not figure large in any of Fran's plans. Mr. Wilbraham had been charming but demanding. Judging from the comments of her acquaintances in Nantwich, he represented the best a husband could be. On the whole, men appeared to drink too much, smoke too much, and require more attention than they warranted. More seriously, any hope of autonomy would vanish with a husband. Although Mr. Wilbraham had explored alternatives and arranged trusts, the law of the land decreed that a wife's assets became her husband's on marriage. There would be no jaunts to the Continent, no choice of charitable works, and a need to order a household to someone else's whims entirely.

Fran had heard of women who took lovers, of free-thinkers such as Mary Godwin. They were whispered about, never mentioned before young ladies, but people were starting to regard her as a spinster rather than an ingénue. She kept her mouth closed and her ears open when the ladies took tea and Kitty held court, describing in detail the *louche* goings on of London society to the eager sheltered circle of Cheshire provincials.

Fran did not affect to despise her neighbors, as Kitty sometimes did, knowing only too well that Lady Tollemache tended to exaggerate her own intimacy with the good, the great, and the mighty. But she listened wistfully as she heard of salons where the talk was all of books and pictures and the latest operas. She was not so entranced by the prospect of an endless round of balls and soirées, but she was conscious that there were thinkers and doers out in the world, while she remained in Nantwich. Now that she was coming out of mourning, now that she was reaching an age where she was less answerable for her actions, now that Kitty might soon have a home of her own, the prospect of true freedom shimmered before her.

A rough, anguished cry resounded through the house. The here and now beckoned. Upstairs lay a peer of the realm who would need considerable attention for the next few weeks, it was clear, and a sister who needed at least an hour of placatory soothing. Fran sighed and left the parlor, hoping that Kitty would prove amenable to reason, for she was firm in her resolve that the earl should stay as long as Roundell thought it necessary.

Two

When Roundell descended from the bedroom where Earl Lazenby lay, he went straight to Miss Wilbraham's parlor. She was, to his relief, alone.

"Would you care for some refreshment, doctor? You have had a wearing time of it, I gather."

He nodded, assenting to both her questions. He and Balham had been as gentle as they could in cutting away the earl's clothes, setting and binding his arm, and cleaning his leg, but inevitably, they had caused their patient considerable pain. They had dosed him with as much laudanum as they dared, but inevitably, there had come a point at which the patient had been roused by the pain they were inflicting on him and he had howled in agony. He had passed out once again almost immediately, but the fact remained that when he came round again, he would be in considerable torment. Miss Wilbraham must be warned.

"We did not disturb you earlier?"

"When the poor fellow cried out? I heard, but it did not disturb me. He will have a hard awakening, Dr. Roundell."

"I have supplied Balham with sufficient laudanum to last two nights. But I hope to be back tomorrow morning. I am most concerned about his leg. We cleaned it as best we could, but there are still splinters and the bruising is so severe I could not tell if any permanent damage has been done."

"Has Tarbuck seen it yet?"

"He has. He shook his head and said it needed someone with better eyes than his to clear the splinters. He suggested . . ." The doctor hesitated and evaded Miss Wilbraham's eye as he continued. "He suggested that we ask you to look at it. He said you had a steady head and a steady hand and he'd trust a horse with you over any of the grooms he's had these ten years."

"What an encomium! I have a strong stomach, and all the embroidery Miss Pinsent made me do has given me a fine eye, I suppose. I could take a look at his leg under Balham's supervision, if it would help."

"Miss Wilbraham, it is a very ugly sight. But if you have good nerves, a light touch would be ideal."

Fran took a deep breath and stood. "I'm ready, doctor." He followed her upstairs.

For some reason, Fran had expected to find the guest-room plunged in gloom, the curtains still drawn to hide the sun, as if the light might further injure Lord Lazenby. But Roundell had ordered the curtains thrown back and the windows opened. Balham was tidying up the remains of the earl's trousers and boots: the first task of doctoring had been to cut these free from his body. The patient's coat and jacket were draped over the back of a chair and the whole room was full of sun and breeze. The earl lay motionless, draped only by a sheet with a cage arrangement protecting his leg from even so light a pressure as the linen.

Roundell explained Miss Wilbraham's job to Balham. "It may seem unorthodox, but I've seen her needlework. She has a delicate touch where you and I have already proven to be cack-handed. She may be able to save the leg."

Roundell brought a chair over to the bedside while Balham lit a candle and heated a pair of tweezers in the flame before handing them carefully to Fran. As she sat, Balham brought a basin over to her and Roundell gingerly drew back the sheet from the earl's leg. The doctor had not bandaged it, preferring to leave it lying on a thick wad of lint. It was a terrible mess, the flesh shredded and gashed, studded with fragments, the bone nearly exposed, ligament and muscle torn. Fran nearly retched, but closed her eyes and summoned up the grit to re-open her eyes and focus carefully on the task at hand.

By gazing intently at only a tiny area of the leg, it was possible to forget that this was a man's leg and think only of seeking out the fragments of dirt and wood and fiber that lay embedded in the skin and raw muscle before her. It needed a steady hand and a systematic eye to do the work, particularly as the poor man flinched even in his unconscious state when she probed too far into the trembling, mangled tissue.

The two medical men stood by her, silent, steady, periodically rinsing the leg off with more lint when she took a brief pause from the task or offering her the candle to reheat the tweezers with which she worked. For some time, the only sounds in the room were the occasional involuntary whimpers from the wounded man on the bed. Finally, Fran dropped the tweezers into the basin, whose base was now covered with a fine layer of grit, splinters, thread, and even leather. She arched her back and rubbed it, stretched and stood. "I can see no more, Dr. Roundell. If you wish me to try again tomorrow, I would be happy to assist."

"Miss Wilbraham, you have the most delicate hands I've seen in any medical man and you have been working steadily nearly a full hour. If we can keep the leg clean and cool, I hope this unfortunate man will escape infection. It will be in no small part due to your care if he does so."

"How long before you know whether infection is likely to set in?"

"Two days, perhaps a little less, a little more. We must keep a close watch on him. The leg will start to swell, he'll have a fever and the skin will start to streak."

"He is welcome to remain here as long as necessary, as is Mr. Balham."

"You are very good."

Kitty did not agree with Dr. Roundell. Fran did not see her until suppertime. Kitty had sent for one of her Tollemache relatives, one whom Fran had never met, but had heard a great deal about.

"I have written to the Honorable Lionel Tollemache, who has some understanding of what is right and what is wrong. I have sent for him. He will make you see that Lazenby must not be allowed to remain at Dysart House."

"How will he do this?" asked Fran as she calmly took another spoonful of carrots with her pheasant.

"He will make it abundantly clear to Lord Lazenby that he is not welcome under the roof of a young woman with ample protection from one of the finest families in the land." Kitty continued more coyly. "And who knows, Fran, if you can bring yourself to behave like a woman of principle, Mr. Tollemache may remain in Nantwich a little longer than is strictly necessary."

Fran winced in horror. The Dysarts had decided that if they could not reclaim Dysart House through a simple purchase on the open market, they would try their hands at acquisition through matrimony. Clearly, she was not good enough for the Earl of Dysart's heir, but she was entirely suitable for a younger son. She could not remember Lionel Tollemache from the wedding, for he had been abroad, travelling in Italy at the time of Arthur and Kitty's nuptials. Whether this meant he had been sent abroad on a repairing lease or had chosen to enrich his cultural horizons, Fran could not tell, but assumed it would be clear enough should he arrive in Nantwich as Kitty had requested.

Lady Tollemache went on to extol the gentleman's numerous fine qualities which resided chiefly in his dress and deportment as far as Fran could tell. Unfortunately, Kitty noticed Fran's distinct lack of enthusiasm for this kinsman of Arthur's and there followed a diatribe about Fran's toploftiness, her unfortunate tendency towards independence, rashness, lack of judgment, and general unsuitability. Fran sat at her embroidery, stabbing at the canvas with uncharacteristic carelessness, desperately trying to control her impulse to stab Kitty with the needle. It was no good telling herself that she would have to unpick all the work she had done this night, she had to contain herself somehow and her innocent handiwork served admirably as a substitute for her sister.

Finally, she could stand it no longer. "Kitty, why is this Lazenby so unsuitable? Does he prey on innocents? Pray, explain to me, insofar as a married woman may when speaking to a maiden, why he is so unacceptable."

"It is indelicate of you to enquire. But the truth is that I am in greater danger than you from this *roué*. He makes it a habit to dally with married women, the more recently married the better. It is as if he is deliberately trying to show that all women are false and that young wives are falsest of all. Now do you see why we must bar him from the house?"

"So it is not my chastity you fear for, but your own. Why Kitty, I never knew you were so susceptible! But if you keep to your rooms and avoid any contact with him, particularly once he is convalescing, surely there can be no harm in his prolonged stay with us."

Kitty did not dignify this teasing with any response. Tossing her abundant dark curls, she withdrew for the night, leaving Fran to rue her impulsive tongue, for on the morrow, she would have to make amends.

As it turned out, she had no opportunity to apologize to her sister. Balham was called away by ten the following morning, for a hayrick had combusted, burning several farmhands severely, and Doctor Roundell had already been called to the bedside of a consumptive some miles out of Nantwich.

Balham had hesitated to desert the earl's bedside, but since the man was still unconscious and looked likely to remain so, Fran shooed the young fellow away. He was clearly needed more urgently elsewhere, and nursing the earl seemed straightforward enough: it was simply a question of checking him for fever and giving him regular doses of the draught Roundell had made up. The solution to their difficulties was for Fran to sit with the invalid while doing her household accounts, with Farr standing by to assist in delivering the prescribed medication. Tarbuck, once he had completed his duties in the stables, would take over the afternoon shift.

The guestroom, as with all four guestrooms at Dysart House, was handsomely equipped. It was one of the last rooms Mrs. Wilbraham had decorated before her death, with furniture in the Grecian style, including a matching dressing table, cheval glass, and chairs clustered under one window near the head of the bed. The bed itself was high, with a pair of Sheraton chests on either side. On the opposite wall was the fireplace, besides which were arranged a chaise longue and a commodious desk with an upholstered chair.

Mr. Wilbraham had allowed his wife and then his daughter a free hand in everything except for his insistence that, given the steady stream of scholarly visitors, every guestroom must have a reasonable working space. Fran was grateful for this luxury on this morning, for she had plenty of room for the arrangement of her books and ink and pens.

The household books at Dysart House were complicated by Fran's encouragement of her servants in entrepreneurial endeavors. She knew they did not have enough to do in caring for her and Kitty, so she encouraged them in various projects, from breeding goats to producing prints and *trompes l'oeil* for sale through Jackson, the bookseller. She had arranged for the purchase of materials and stock to be repaid from any profit the business might earn. If a venture became too successful, she sometimes lost her staff, as had happened when a footman had proved so skilled a cabinetmaker that rising demand for his wares led to him establishing his own workroom, complete with an apprentice. But by and large, her people remained with her, quite satisfied to make a little extra on the side and to continue in the security of her service.

"It's all very well," said Fran, laying out her work. She found it impossible to settle to it immediately. Under the guise of checking the pulse and general welfare of the patient, she went to his bedside and inspected him more closely than she had been able to on his arrival.

From what she saw, he was a tall, slim man. It was as well that the bed had no footboard, for it would have cramped him, although she supposed he could have lain diagonally across the bed. He looked to be in at least his thirtieth year, possibly more. He had fine skin, a mass of curling, light brown hair and now, the faint shade of stubble on his chin. Although his face was in repose, he looked as though he smiled and laughed a great deal. But there were also two faint frown lines marring his smooth forehead, perhaps indicating discomfort or worry.

It was odd to look on this man as one might look upon

a painting in a gallery. Fran had seen enough portraits of long-dead ancestors, madonnas, and martyrs collected on Grand Tours to wonder whether the models had been truly virginal or truly saintly, and to consider how much truth one could really read into a composition of lines and shades that one called the face. Here lay a man who seemed like other men and yet different to Fran. For no other man had made her heart speed up from a simple examination of his features.

There was no sign of his libertine propensities. He seemed in his unconscious state vulnerable and harmless. Yet, if Kitty were to be believed, this man who was not unreasonably, heart-stoppingly handsome, had jeopardized the well-being of countless women, mostly married. It seemed ludicrous that this man, whose face still held traces of the boy he had been, could be so dangerous and immoral. Surely so definite a quality must leave traces. But no, here was a man in his prime, who appeared innocent of all sin, clear of all guilt.

Fran returned to the desk and settled to her accounts, in which she managed to lose herself for nearly a full hour. She was shaking sand over a page when a low moan came from the bed, startling her out of her seat. She hurried over to the bellpull and tugged at it, hoping that Farr was standing by below stairs. Then she went over and as Balham had advised, dipped a sponge into some clean water and dribbled it between the earl's dry lips. He seemed to crane his neck toward the source of liquid, so she poured out half a glass of water and gradually trickled it into his mouth.

By the time the glass was empty, Farr was standing beside her. She instructed him to prop up the patient while she measured out the correct dose of medicine. She poured out more water and mixed up the draught, dropping in four careful drops of the laudanum, stirring it and then feeding it to the injured man as she had fed him the first glass of water. She put the glass down and waited, her hands clasped tight, her shoulders tense, as Farr eased him back down into a prone position.

As Balham had instructed, she monitored the earl's pulse and breathing. Once he seemed to be settled again, she returned to her accounts. It was past noon by the time she had finished and she knew she could not linger much longer in the sick room avoiding her sister. However, there seemed to be no sign of Balham. The only solution was to summon Farr to sit with the patient.

Once the footman was installed, Fran prepared herself to face Kitty's barrage of complaints and carping. Fortunately, she escaped an encounter with her sister who had eaten her lunch early and left to pay some calls that afternoon. Whatever she might think of Kitty, Fran acknowledged that her sister was fiercely loyal to her family and would neither voice nor brook any criticism of the Wilbrahams outside the home. This simply meant that Fran would be all the more tempting a target when Kitty did return home. After a light luncheon, it was time to turn her attention to the continuing management of the household. She was just about to meet with Mrs. Cooper when she heard a wild cry from upstairs.

"Miss Fran, Miss Fran, his lordship!" Farr sounded unusually panicked, so Fran hurried up to the guestroom. There she found the footman standing by the bed, holding a sodden flannel to Lazenby's forehead. The stranger was trembling so uncontrollably that the whole bed was shaking. Beads of sweat started from his brow and his skin was clammy and pallid. She pulled back the sheet covering his leg and, as Roundell and Balham had described, the leg was swollen and red.

Striving to remain calm, Fran issued her orders. "Go

down to Mrs. Cooper. Fetch me some of the water she has boiled and cooled down and plenty of clean cloths."

When Farr returned with the water, she sent him to track down Roundell or Balham. "Tell them he has a fever and the leg has signs of infection. I will bathe it as they showed me, but I would feel far easier in my mind if one or other of them were present. I am sure between us, we can care for him, but I am at the limits of my knowledge and I want some instructions should his condition worsen."

"I understand, Miss Fran. I'll be back as soon as I can and it won't be without one or the other in tow. But I take it you'd prefer Dr. Roundell?"

"I don't think it matters. They both strike me as men of sense and both know better than I do what to do in such cases. Just hurry."

The next couple of hours passed by in a flurry as Fran tried to cool Lord Lazenby's fever and to keep him as still as she could. She draped a cool cloth over his forehead, periodically rinsing it in the cold water Mrs. Cooper had sent up. Then she took up the lint that Mrs. Cooper had cut into small squares and bathed the leg, carefully dropping the used cloths into a separate bucket. She did not stop, sending down for fresh supplies of water and cloths from time to time.

Finally, Roundell appeared, still dusty from the road, flushed and flustered. He went to the window, removed his coat, shook it out and hung it over the back of a chair before rolling up his sleeves and washing his hands. Then he examined his patient.

"Miss Wilbraham, I need some moldy bread. If you have none, send to my wife. She will know what to bring."

Fran looked blankly at the doctor for a second or two, then did as she was bid. Fortunately, there was moldy bread in the kitchen and it was brought upstairs in min-

utes. She watched in amazement as the doctor laid it on
the earl's flesh, moistened it slightly and bound the leg.

"You have done a remarkable job, Miss Wilbraham,
and I must ask you to do more. We need to change this
dressing every few hours, every four or five hours ideally.
Could you ask Tarbuck to help? It requires no medical
skill, simply a steady supply of bread in this condition."

"Moldy bread?"

"It must have mold on it. I do not understand it, but I
learnt this in the Peninsular Wars. Some Irish women
swore by it and in some cases, it can stop gangrene where
it is beginning to take hold. Not always, not if the infection
is established, but sometimes."

"Let us hope that this is one of those instances." Fran
was more amazed than revolted and promised the doctor that she would ensure that the earl's leg was properly
treated during the course of the night. She was fasci-
nated by the treatments that Roundell prescribed to his
patients, but somewhat apprehensive about Kitty's reaction to any increased attention for their inconvenient
patient. Although, it was only Kitty who seemed remotely
inconvenienced by the earl's stay at Dysart House.

The most sensible course of action was to alternate
shifts with Farr and Tarbuck. One or the other could sit
with Lazenby for the next few hours while Fran took the
opportunity to refresh herself and strengthen herself for
the ordeal of dinner with her sister. An ordeal it certainly
proved: not having seen her sister all day, Kitty had
stored up her grievances like a squirrel hoarding its nuts
and burst into Fran's bedroom just before they were due
downstairs.

"Really, Fran, I do not understand you. I have made it
perfectly clear that this man is a libertine, a cad, a dastard,
and yet you persist in exposing yourself to him. You really
have no care at all for our name. How will I explain this to

Arthur? Have you no care for your sister? Have you no care for your own reputation? You will never find a man prepared to marry you once it is common knowledge that you have spent hours at this creature's bedside." She paced the room, wringing a handkerchief like Mrs. Jordan enacting the woes of Desdemona.

Fran could not bear this tirade. She dropped her hairbrush on the dressing table with a clatter and stood up, her arms crossed in an attempt to control her rising ire.

"Kitty, you do not seem to understand that I am perfectly happy as I am. You go on and on at me about marriage without considering once my position or my interests. I have no desire to be at the beck and call of a husband. I am fortunate enough to be in possession of a fortune, which I propose to enjoy. As a married woman, I must give up my money and my freedom. Leave me be. If it aggravates you so to be in my company, you should find another home while Arthur is absent on his adventures, but I will not be harangued at every opportunity because you have taken it upon yourself to order my life when I do not wish it to be ordered."

"You will lose any respectability if you carry on in this way. You need not look to me to reestablish you in society should you wish to rejoin respectable company." Kitty was defiant, her chin jutting, her lips thin as she continued, "Our Papa was regarded as quite eccentric enough, Fran, and you are in a fine way to following in his footsteps. People are beginning to talk, you know."

"Who is beginning to talk? Nantwich society? I can well survive the disapprobation of our neighbors. The ones who are worth anything will never cut me and I have no interest in the petty gossip and malice of the rest. I am tired of country dances and hunt balls." As usual, Fran regretted her intemperate words almost as soon as she had spoken them.

"You will regret this arrogance when even Lady Dorfold bars you from her home. I know you believe she is your bosom-bow and would never treat you with anything but fondness, but if you go beyond the pale, even she will give you the cut direct, and precious little you will be able to do about it. She cannot jeopardize the future of her girls if association with you might taint them."

Somehow Fran stoppered up her often ungovernable tongue and did not speak the harsh words about Kitty's sad want of charity, generosity, and compassion which whirled about her brain. It was unbearably tempting to give way to one of the explosions that had marked their girlhood, Kitty needling and needling at Fran until the latter could contain her anger no longer and was provoked into injudicious wrath. Today, Fran felt her fury might carry her past the injudicious towards the irreparable. It was frustrating to see Kitty coming the matron with her and assuming all sorts of prerogatives simply because she had been foolish enough to marry the first man who had offered for her. But Fran did not want a total rift with her sister, however much they might madden each other. She excused herself, omitting to mention that she intended to go upstairs and check on Earl Lazenby's dressing and relieve Farr at least until midnight. Fortunately, Kitty regarded herself as having triumphed in this encounter, so she descended grandly to the dining room without further comment. Fran found it next to impossible to eat anything and excused herself as soon as she was able.

Upstairs, all was as before, the man still lying unconscious, Farr sitting quietly in the chair beside the bed. The room was calm and quiet.

"I changed his dressing half an hour ago, Miss. He didn't stir. I added more of the mold and moistened it just as the doctor showed us. I've been giving him water every quarter hour by that clock there." He nodded at a small walnut travelling clock on the mantelpiece. "I can manage if you want to turn in now."

"No signs of restlessness or fever?"

"He's hotter than he should be, definitely, but it hasn't worsened any."

"Go down and get something to eat, have a little rest. Send Tarbuck to me as soon as you can. He can keep watch until the early hours, provided you can relieve him between two and three in the morning."

"Very well, Miss Wilbraham. Thank you."

Fran settled in a seat by the fire, with an oil lamp beside her and started unpicking the poor work she had done the previous night, during her earlier brangle with Kitty. It was, she acknowledged, ridiculous to feel more at ease in the company of an accredited libertine than in the presence of her own respectable sister, but so it was. There might be some justice in Kitty's view that she was becoming eccentric and arrogant. But that simply made it all the more important that she find some productive use of her time and money. Some position in the world where she might do good, learn humility, and usefully occupy the time which hung so heavy on her hands at present.

There was a soft tap at the door. Tarbuck came in.

"How is he, Miss Fran?"

"Hot and a little restive since Farr left. Have you arranged for Farr to relieve you?"

"Aye, the lad will be here by half-past two. If you don't mind, we'll break up the watches a bit different tomorrow unless the doctor or his man are back. Shorter is better as far as I am concerned." He went over to examine the patient who was twitching occasionally.

"You and Farr must decide things between you. It is you

who have work to fit in around this business. I am at your disposal. Dr. Roundell has simply left us instructions on how to care for the leg."

"His ribs and arms will be giving him trouble too. But I don't hold with too much laudanum, so I am afraid the earl will suffer a little."

Fran wanted to ask Tarbuck about gossip in town, but now was not the time. If people were going to raise their eyebrows at the arrival of the earl at Dysart House, Tarbuck would be the first to hear of it. He had a well-established network which had uncovered some of her wilder misdemeanors as a young girl. He had given her more than one dressing-down for pranks which had gone awry, but which her father had never heard of. If anyone could protect her reputation, it would be the stableman.

Three

A haze. In the leg. Rawness, throbbing. Shoulder. Arm. Heat. Hot. Then moisture, cooling moisture on the forehead, moisture between dry lips and still that pounding, agonizing heaviness in the leg. What had happened? The horse, a shot, a flurry of petticoat, a splintering, creaking, crashing sound of rending wood. What next? More drops of water easing between his lips, someone trying gingerly to raise him and a swift draught of something which made the pain go and the light go and all thought cease . . .

Dr. Roundell's consumptive revived, allowing the doctor to return to Earl Lazenby's bedside, by now extremely concerned that this most noble of patients might yet slip through his fingers, leaving his practice and his reputation sadly tarnished.

Consequently, there was no further need of Fran in the sickroom. Roundell and Balham came and went as they needed for several days, one or other always on duty, assisted by Farr and Tarbuck. This meant that Fran was at home to visitors when Lady Dorfold did call, the third morning after the earl's arrival.

Lady Dorfold was not someone Fran had expected to become a friend. She had come to Nantwich as a young bride some twenty years ago, and had seemed to a child of six an elegant, sophisticated young woman. Now, the twelve years between them had dwindled from a great gulf to a bridgeable stream. Despite bearing eight children, of which five survived, Lady Dorfold had kept her figure and a lively interest in society and all its goings-on. Her family was not her sole interest, and she still insisted on an annual visit to London to meet with old friends and relations. She was very much *au courant,* and rather more measured and experienced than Kitty.

Unaccompanied by any children, Lady Dorfold settled herself in a striped armchair and gazed around the room approvingly as she drew off her gloves and arranged her shawl.

"This scheme is very fine, Fran, just the thing. You were right not to paper the walls in the same stripe as the chairs."

Fran smiled at this opening gambit. It was ever the way of her friend to come at things from an unexpected angle. She did not disappoint. "I hear you have an arbiter of taste in your home even as we speak."

"Really? Kitty did not know so much of him. But he is in no state to pass judgment on my décor. He is very badly off, I am afraid. Dr. Roundell seems extremely pressed."

"The word is that he won't survive. Poor man, a carriage accident, I hear?"

"Yes. The lady appears to have escaped unscathed."

"There was a lady?" Lady Dorfold had not heard this.

"A viscountess. Very exalted. She and her husband were on their way to Ireland. Lord Lazenby was accompanying them or meeting with them and went to fetch assistance when a fallen tree blocked their way in Rockingham Forest. Or so I heard from Roundell, who heard this from Bloxham."

"The Ormistons, perhaps. Lazenby's land marches alongside theirs. Or rather, Dacre's land. Ormiston is Dacre's son, you know, the resolute widower. I believe Dacre and Lazenby are firm friends and both notorious for their liaisons. But surely he was travelling with a manservant of some sort?"

"According to the tiger, the manservant was in Crewe. I have sent for him, but he has not yet arrived." Fran waited to see how the gentle probing would proceed.

"You are very good, my dear. I suppose you have Kitty as chaperone and she is most exacting in her standards. But you cannot feel easy about so famous a rake making a prolonged visit beneath your roof."

"I confess, I am not easy. But I am not sure what I can do about it. His injuries are very severe. It will be some weeks before he heals sufficiently to be moved at all, and I doubt that he will be strong enough to travel far even then."

"Perhaps we can contrive something." Lady Dorfold pondered for a moment. "I could send the elder girls away, then he could come to us for a time. Sir Richard, as you know, is concerned only for a man's bottom on the hunting field and a little conviviality in the drinking of port. The girls are due to visit their grandmamma next month. If I brought that forward by a week or so, it would not signify. And it might relieve you of a difficult burden."

"If Dr. Roundell agrees, that would be very kind of you. But won't you be at risk?"

Lady Dorfold's smile was broad. "It is good of you to suggest that my looks are sufficient to attract the attention of such an expert in feminine loveliness. However, Lazenby appeals only to the sort of women who believe everything they read, particularly if it is of a romantic nature. You have tried me on poetry, you know it makes me laugh rather than swoon, and I daresay you are much too sensible for him also, but Kitty is not. And Sir Arthur has been away for some time."

"She has summoned some scion of the Dysart clan to keep watch over us all."

"Who would that be?"

"The Honorable Lionel Tollemache. He wasn't at the wedding."

"I've never met him. So he has returned from Italy? How interesting! Where is he to stay?"

"At The Crown, not here. Kitty wanted him in the house, but I said we had enough work on our hands with our current guest."

This proved to be true enough. Tarbuck and Farr were in continual attendance on the earl, generally assisting Balham. When Fran did see any of the three men, they spoke little and what they did say was indefinite and spoken in hushed tones, as though voicing the worry that Lazenby might not recover would lead to his demise.

On the fifth morning after the earl's arrival, Fran walked down the corridor past his room and found Balham slumped in one of the Chippendale chairs, cradling his head in his hands.

"Can nothing more be done, Mr. Balham?"

He raised his head, his eyes red-rimmed, a great beam on his face. "A great deal more needs to be done, Miss Wilbraham. The fever is broken."

"Mr. Balham, what a relief!"

"He is not yet out of the woods. He is still very weak and has opened his eyes only the once. He is sleeping now and we must watch him with great vigilance to see the fever does not return. But we have saved his leg and his life, I believe."

"He will be very grateful, I am sure."

"I would not presume to guess. He does not seem a happy individual. When in the throes of fever, our tongues and hearts speak unguarded. I do not believe that he has led a life in which he can take any pride. I would not, Miss Wilbraham, expose yourself too often to Lord Lazenby."

Naturally, such a warning was like presenting a mouse with a platter of Cheddar cheese. Fran could not resist asking Roundell if she might assist in the care of the patient now that he seemed out of danger. The doctor's request was strange.

"Would you read to him, my dear? I beg your pardon—not you, someone else. It is dull work to sit with a comatose body, but we do need to keep an eye on him and perhaps recall him fully to life. I am not sure that he is entirely with us."

"What reading matter do you suggest? Novels? Sermons? Poetry?"

"It really does not matter. I should not think our earl has ever been a great reader. But the sound of a voice may connect him more firmly with this world rather than the next."

"You still fear for his life, then?"

"The immediate danger has receded, as Balham said, but his condition is not good. He has, if I read the signs aright, led a somewhat rackety life and is weary of it. In so weakened a state, it would be all too easy for him to slip away rather than recover, thus avoiding the need to seek out or apply any remedy for his current mode of existence."

On his sickbed, Mr. Wilbraham's favorite work had been by Ovid. He enjoyed both the *Metamorphosis* and the *Art of Love,* although he had acknowledged that perhaps it was not entirely suitable to expose a young woman to the latter work, which was worldly and knowing. But Fran had come to love the works of the exiled poet no less than her father, and it was with the *Art of Love* that she began her work of reading to the Earl. It would be she who read to the earl. There was no one else readily available, neither Farr nor Tarbuck exhibiting any ability in this sphere. Besides, Tarbuck was anxious to return to his stables and inspect the earl's cattle. The rest of the staff had their tasks, and it was a useful means of escaping Lady Tollemache's strictures.

Fran did not read to Lazenby in the original Latin, but from a translation—perhaps not the best translation, by Francis Wolferston, which had always seemed serviceable enough. Wolferston, according to her father, was accurate, if not always beautiful.

So she seated herself at the man's bedside and started reading, smiling as the familiar, wry words of advice flowed from her lips. Get the maid on your side, but don't forget yourself so far as to dally with the maid instead of the mistress. Buy gifts for your beloved, but first write letters, interesting, witty letters, avoiding all tedious stories. Keep yourself clean and tidy for the woman in question. Trim beard and nails and never "let the hairs within your nostrils grow." Mundane, but as true now as in the long distant Rome where Ovid wrote and wooed. It had been all very well reading Ovid, but perhaps she had learnt too much about the way men went about their courting. Young men seemed so transparent and obvious.

"No wonder we try to keep the ladies separate from the classics." The earl's voice was hoarse and low from lack of use. Fran stood, the earl smiled and the book slipped from her fingers.

"Do you need the doctor?"

"Heaven defend me from the sawbones."

"He saved your life. And your leg."

"I wonder if it would hurt less if I had lost it."

"I'll call Dr. Roundell."

"Will you return and read some more to me?"

"Not before lunch."

"Afterwards then."

Fran nodded and fled. He was conscious and could no longer need a voice to tie him down to earth. Still, she did return after lunch, despite her doubts. She would simply skip over those indelicate sections of the poem which suggested ravishment and wantonness. She would simply follow the doctor's orders, she would simply ignore Kitty's dire imprecations, then she would avoid the earl thereafter. She had virtually promised to return after lunch and she would not break a promise.

The doctor visited Lazenby almost immediately. The earl lay quiet as his leg was investigated, his arm examined, and his ribs prodded and probed.

"Miss Wilbraham said you spoke."

"Only briefly. Her name is Miss Wilbraham?"

"Yes. She has been your hostess this week. She is keeping your cattle and has settled your account at The Crown Hotel."

"What account? I do not recall staying there. Whatever else has been damaged, I am confident my memory has not suffered as a result of this accident."

As far as Roundell was concerned, it was a shame that the earl had not forgotten substantial tracts of his life, for it seemed to have been largely frittered away on discreditable episodes, the memories of which hindered the patient's recovery.

"You were brought to The Crown Hotel by your friends the Viscount and Viscountess Ormiston. They left for Liverpool once you had been moved to Dysart House." Lazenby turned his head to avoid the doctor's gaze. He swallowed. The doctor continued. "Miss Wilbraham has been very accommodating. She is a kind lady with many friends."

"No need to warn me off, Doctor." He was about to make some light quip about warning her off Ovid, but decided that his credit was already too low with the saw-bones, who was more than capable of mishandling the changing of a dressing or binding of his ribs.

"Now, do you wish for more laudanum for the pain, or can you endure a little longer?"

"The pain is not excessive."

The doctor raised his eyebrows but departed without further conversation. The earl was left, conscious at last, alone with his thoughts. He had lied to the doctor. His leg was truly agonizing, although he realized that when he tensed his toes and his ankle, there was movement and no addition to the discomfort. His arm was strapped tight and any attempt to move his fingers did result in further pain. His back felt as if he were being fried like a freshly caught trout over an open fire.

The knowledge that he deserved pain was little consolation. He would have preferred his plan to abduct Viscountess Ormiston to have been successful, and at a pinch he would have preferred that if his plan had to fail, at least he might have remained uninjured. Instead, here he lay, in a gently bred woman's house, in her debt and likely to remain so for some weeks. The sort of woman, he recognized, that he had spent his life avoiding. Neither sophisticated nor wanton, she was the sort who had male relatives eager to parcel her off in an advantageous match. She was the sort of woman who had made him the man he was, canny, tarnished in reputation, jaded with easier conquests. And now he must endure such a woman reading Ovid in a mellifluous, faintly amused voice.

At least she was lovely to look at. She had no coquettish airs about her, which suggested that she did not realize she was anything out of the common way. Leave her loose in London for more than a night and she would realize that soon enough. Dark hair, dark eyes, exquisite jaw line, round cheeks, arching eyebrows, long eyelashes, an elegant neck, a narrow nose, neither snub nor equine, a high forehead and fine skin with an almost honeyed tone to it. A beautiful woman reading Ovid. Did she know the rest of the poem? Would she be brave enough to read it? It was really most indelicate.

She came back late in the afternoon. She was calm and steady-eyed. She was one of the most superb creatures he had ever seen. She was entirely out of bounds. Still, it was comforting to feel a surge of desire, surely a sign of recovery, even if it must be suppressed.

Fran sat down and opened her book. But she paused before reading, as though gathering her strength. Then she asked, "What did you mean about keeping ladies separate from the classics?"

"The man who allowed you to read the *Art of Love* wanted you to know all there is to know of men, with no illusions."

She smiled wryly. "A father's prerogative, perhaps."

"Ah! To what other works can he have introduced you? The darker sonnets of Shakespeare, I am sure, and the joys of Achilles sulking in his tent." It was odd to speak to a young woman and be so sure she would catch his allusions.

"Possibly. Do you think he wanted me to have a jaundiced view of my fellow men?"

"I am sure of it. You speak of him in the past. If he is dead, then his mission before dying must have been to equip you with an understanding that men are not reliable or charming, but brutish, deceitful, and full of seductive arts." The earl sounded startlingly matter of fact. Fran appreciated that he did not dance around her father's possible demise.

"In that case, he could not entirely succeed. I know simply from living with him that there are men who are not as you describe. There are men of honor and sense and good humor."

"Very few, upon my honor. What little I have left of that." Lazenby turned his head toward the wall and Fran bent her head to the book to take up her reading where she had left off.

Wise men mix kisses with the words they speak;
If they're not given, those ungiven take;
But she'll perhaps refuse and anger feign,
Yet wishes her resistance be in vain.

"You snorted there. I heard you, it was unmistakable. I take it that you never feign resistance."

"I shall continue reading." But Fran skipped forward, missing some forty lines.
"Too confident is he who doth expect
His mistress to ask first and him select."

"What a chunk you've missed, Miss Wilbraham."

"Well, it is nonsense. I have had this out with my father. Ovid is utterly wrong. There could be nothing worse to a woman than to be forced where she has no inclination, to have her nay read as yea. The poet clearly had no idea what it is like to be importuned and not to be believed."

"How vehement you are. I've had plenty of women tell me no when they meant quite the opposite."

Miss Wilbraham gave Lazenby a look that would have withered weeds in spring rain. He grinned back, waiting for her riposte. There would be one, he knew. She was refreshing. And whatever the surgeon had given him had loosened his tongue too far. He had overstepped the bounds. No doubt she would firmly repress him.

"Your plenty, my lord, is certainly another man's famine."

"What do you mean? That there are men who have

more experience than I with women, or that I have stolen women from other men? Indeterminate, Miss Wilbraham." But it stung that she should have reached either conclusion about him.

"It doesn't become you to ask in either case. Now will you let me read? You really aren't ready for extended conversation."

He suppressed the reply that she would never think him ready. He didn't want her to think too ill of him. Not just yet. That should be saved for when she became importunate. She would do so. All of them were, sooner or later. Somehow, the thought induced only weariness in him.

The opening of Book Two was safe enough, Fran saw, safe enough to send the earl into a doze. She reached the point where Icarus soared up to the sun and saw that the patient by now was soundly asleep. It was not sensible to read more Ovid to him. She knew the poem well enough and so did he. He seemed to have modelled himself on Ovid's cynical words, turned himself into a lover so used to using art that he had lost all grasp of what a woman might really desire. He did not respect the fairer sex, that was certain. As Kitty had said, although it galled to admit that she was right, a libertine. Better left well alone. But witty. And with such fine eyes. Blue, fringed with dark eyelashes so thick he seemed to have outlined his eyes through artifice. And such a fine voice. So deep, so measured, so rich. So weary. Too weary for a provincial lady.

She rose and left the bedroom and as she closed the door, she leaned back against it. He was, even injured and exhausted, the most potent being she had met. The sensible thing would be to avoid him. But just when Fran was planning to be sensible, Kitty inserted her oar, muddied the water and propelled her sister back toward the invalid. At supper, Lady Tollemache could not contain herself, reporting first that she had heard from the Honorable Lionel and he would be at Nantwich within the week, then declaring that it was entirely wrong of Fran to have visited the invalid this morning, let alone seeing him once again this afternoon. Really, he should be ignored and left to deduce for himself that the sooner he removed himself from Dysart House, the better.

The next morning, Miss Wilbraham did not bring Ovid. *Ivanhoe* instead, a book she had read in serial form and bought as soon as it was available in volume form. A book about knights and nobility and honorable individuals. An entirely modest book.

"Frightened, Miss Wilbraham? Or have you made your point and now feel safe in exploring your more romantic inclinations?"

"Dr. Roundell told me to read according to my inclination and this morning, I am not inclined to read Ovid." She opened the first volume.

"You must have an inclination to high drama, then."

"Not at all. I do not find the tale so very romantic." Fran leafed through the introductory epistle. "Ah, here we are, in that pleasant district of merry England which is watered by the River Don. I am in the middle of the tale, but if you do not know it, it would be best to start with Gurth and Wamba."

"Spare me the swineherd and the clown, let us progress directly to the ravaging Normans and the fair lady Rowena. I found her insipid, but Rebecca is a heroine with some spirit."

"For someone who seems to despise the book, you know it very well."

"I have enjoyed other books by Scott, although not his poems. Still, there are novelists I prefer."

"You seem very well read." Fran put a stop on her tongue but failed to conceal her surprise.

"I heard the rest of that sentence as clearly as if you had spoken it. I am very well read for a man of no reputation other than that of being a man with no time to read, so busy am I with my dalliances and my liaisons." The earl's smile was knowing. It was amusing to bait her. She had no wish to rise, but she was delightfully easy to provoke.

"Do you wish me to read, or shall we speak of you? I have heard that a man's favorite topic of conversation is himself, but I have lived a generally sheltered life."

"Read on, serpent-tongue, I fear you'll sting me more sharply if we continue to converse. Let us retreat to the time of King Richard."

Fran read two chapters of *Ivanhoe* without pause. The earl slipped in and out of a light doze but every time a deeper sleep was about to claim him, a sudden shift or movement would set him on fire again. Finally, Fran called a halt.

"Are you sure you do not want more laudanum? It would ease you, help you to sleep. Help you to recover." She sounded anxious.

"It's vile stuff. Clouds a man's mind, keeps him in thrall. The harshest mistress I've ever met; once she has her hooks in you, she does not release you."

"Your view of women is jaundiced, I must say, my lor—"

He interrupted her. "You were about to call me 'my lord' again. Would you call me Alexander? It would be much more restful."

"I should not." She caught his glance, mocking, slightly contemptuous. "Alexander." She spoke abruptly, in the tone used to scold a child. "Dr. Roundell left you with more medicine, I know. I am sure that he would not prescribe an excessive amount."

"Perhaps not, but whatever he has prescribed, I do not

wish to take it. Now, read on, I am longing to encounter the fair Rebecca. We have not yet had her description. At least Scott has an eye for a pretty woman."

"Do you dislike him so very much? I can bring something else if you wish."

"I preferred Ovid. I like poetry, both classical and modern."

They began a lazy discussion of the merits of novels and verse, Fran arguing for Scott, the earl announcing that the only novelists he'd ever enjoyed were Mr. Fielding and Miss Austen, both of whom had a clear-eyed understanding of how tiresome their fellow humans were. Finally, Fran rolled her eyes at his cynical view of human nature and returned to her book for a final chapter before lunch.

She did not return to the sickroom that day since Dr. Roundell did come round to inspect his patient in the afternoon.

"How long must I stay here, Doctor?"

"Where would you be going, sir?"

"Back to my home at Edenbridge. Or London. It makes no odds to me. But I do not feel I should remain too long under Miss Wilbraham's roof. I am returned to my senses, surely I'll be back on my feet within a week."

"Your estimate of your recuperative powers is optimistic. Your leg is very weak. You could put yourself in a carriage and cross the country, but you'll set yourself back considerably. The wounds to your leg are still open and liable to infection. The fracture to your arm was not straightforward and I would not recommend that anyone with broken ribs travel until those are set. I should say that the very earliest you could travel comfortably would be in a fortnight. But if you wish to put yourself at risk, by all means leave now."

"Surely I can be removed to some inn?" muttered the earl in exasperation.

"Here you have clean linen, decent food, and Farr available to nurse you. You would not be cared for half so well at The Crown and that is the only hostelry I could begin to recommend. Further, I understand that Miss Wilbraham has sent for your man. He will be able to nurse you and relieve some of the burden on the household."

This did not soothe the earl. Apart from the impropriety of remaining under the roof of a single woman, it was intolerable to be so dependent on the kindness of strangers. He was not unutterably proud, but it was uncomfortable to be beholden to a young woman for shelter and care. In practical terms, there was the doctor's bill, the sum it must cost to be keeping two extra horses, the summoning of Soames, his man, from Crewe and the general inconvenience. His pockets were pretty much to let until the next quarter's monies were due, most of which was already bespoke. He sighed. His ways were undeniably rackety. He was forever receiving letters from his steward and some fellow at Coutts called Lambert. If he did not find a way to turn things around soon, he must rusticate on the Continent. It would not be so great a hardship, he had travelled there before, in the days after Waterloo and the fall of Napoleon. Six or seven years ago now, but it seemed a lifetime ago.

Pinpointing the moment he had gone to the bad was impossible. There had been several slips, almost imperceptible. He had been war-weary, that was true enough. When at Oxford, he had kept to the straight and narrow. Then he had been offered the standard alternatives of the younger son: the church, a set of colors, a place at the Bar. Soldiering had seemed a reasonable option, but three years in a cavalry regiment had been enough. By then, his brother had died and he had become heir to the earldom.

After Waterloo, he had sold out and spent the next three years careering round Europe until there had been the letter informing him of his father's demise. He had not responded to any of the summons which had requested that he return home and learn his duties. Then it had been too late.

At last, he had come to grief and now was come to rest. First, while soldiering, he had fallen into the habit of straightforward lust. It had been a concomitant of battle and there had always been a plentiful supply of women. It had been as a young, gallant man that he had discovered that women could be fickle, faithless, and more interested in a man's purse than his personality. Then there had been the gambling. He could just remember the terrible nerves which had assailed him the first time he had wagered without having any reserves to pay his losses. Then it had become second nature to game and write notes and put off payment. There had been drink, a flood of fine wines as he toured France and Italy. There had been weeks of debauch when all he had wished for was a bed filled with ample, willing flesh. He had given way to every impulse, played every game, and now he was beached in a provincial market town, the girl he had theoretically given his heart to halfway across the Irish Sea with her husband.

It was not as if he did not know the right thing to do. Enough friends and relatives, even that roué Dacre, had seen fit to read him their lectures. He must mend his ways, find a good woman, cease playing at cards, running horses, buying wine, seducing wives, neglecting estates.

Alexander Ferrars looked back on the years to which he had laid waste and for once, for the first time ever, there was no distraction to draw him from contemplation of his errors and misdemeanors. A primrose path to perdition.

Of course, it was uncomfortable to contemplate one's own weaknesses, but there was within him a certain grit which now that he had gazed on the pathetic mess he had made of his life, prevented him from drawing his mind away before a solution could be found.

There were alternatives. He recognized as clearly as Roundell had that if he chose to turn his face to the wall, he might allow himself to decline to the point of death. But he had been wounded in battle, survived in circumstances far more challenging than this comfortable room, without any hope of treatment or even nourishment. It would not do to repay either the doctor or his hostess by dwindling away now. So he must mend himself and go on his way. Once he rose and was able to travel, he could return to Edenbridge and make some stab at setting his world to rights. On the other hand, he could simply fly to Europe, to some comfortable watering hole where no one knew him, where congenial company might distract him for another few years until he caught a disease or was destroyed by angry debtors. In the meantime, the decent thing would be to discourage the lovely Miss Wilbraham from spending any more time with him.

Four

Resolutions are only satisfying when we are called on to keep them. But Lazenby was not required to see very much of his hostess, for the day after she visited him to read *Ivanhoe*, Soames reappeared. As usual, he said little about Lazenby's condition, although the valet made his disapproval of the circumstances that had led to that condition quite clear through a generally stern demeanor. However, his touch with his master was gentle, earning the approbation of both Roundell and Balham, and he took over the reading of Scott and other authors to the invalid, his soft Lincolnshire accent soothing the earl into uneasy but necessary sleep.

Lazenby was in equal measure relieved and piqued by his hostess' absence. He had always been drawn by unavailability. Her intelligence and forthright demeanor were an added attraction. Soames might be intelligent, but he was taciturn under normal conditions, and his general disposition only intensified when irked by his employer. Their association was lengthy, close to twelve years. While Soames's familiarity with the earl did not appear to breed contempt, it certainly aroused no desire in Lazenby to probe the man's innermost recesses. Each man needed a little distance from the other. Consequently, Lazenby was left to his own thoughts, which aroused in him an uncomfortable combination of boredom and shame.

Miss Wilbraham's absence was due largely to the appearance of the Honorable Lionel Tollemache. He was much less oppressive than she had feared. A tall, slender man of fair complexion, he had a dry wit and keen eyes which took in more than one expected. He had Kitty's measure within minutes, as far as Fran could tell, but it was more difficult to read his intentions towards her, or indeed, whether he had any at all. He arrived in Nantwich late in the afternoon and put up at The Crown Hotel, but did not call until the following morning. His demeanor was calm, even as Kitty fluttered about him, offering him cushions, tea, biscuits, a footstool, and generally making much too much of him.

Fran asked him about his travels in Italy, to which he responded fully and with enthusiasm. He was not a languid, world-weary traveller, displaying instead considerable enthusiasm for the country where he had sojourned for far longer than he had expected. Neither did he fall into the trap of denigrating his own homeland and finding nothing but fault in his native shore, as Fran had encountered in other seasoned travellers. He was an engaging raconteur, telling stories about his own mishaps with language and luggage, painting vivid and attractive pictures of the sights he had seen. It seemed churlish to fail to invite so charming a visitor for dinner, and then at dinner, Mr. Tollemache displayed such curiosity about the locality around Nantwich that Kitty insisted on getting up an expedition to show him the finer aspects on the morrow.

The next day dawned fair and Kitty insisted that it was a perfect day to venture as far afield as Comber Mere. Fran had planned to complete several household tasks as well as visiting her invalid, but was forestalled by Kitty's vehement insistence that both sisters must attend this important Dysart connection. Naturally, Fran masked her reluctance as she climbed into the open-topped landau, and since there was no help for it, gave herself up to enjoying the drive and the company.

Entertaining Mr. Tollemache was no hardship. He was undemanding and appreciative of Cheshire's soothing landscapes and abundant woodland. He enjoyed the gentle amble along the edge of the mere, wandering happily through meadow and glade, occasionally recalling the verses of Thompson and Gray, which delighted Kitty. Fran found him perfectly companionable. He seemed to relish the picnic which Cook had assembled and his manner at no time indicated that he was the son of anyone particularly elevated.

On her return home, though, Fran was glad to retire to her room and a little solitude. As soon as the conversation had flagged, Kitty had jumped in with some further gambit, and in all courtesy, Mr. Tollemache had had to reply and Fran to participate in what seemed like ceaseless and inconsequential chatter the whole day. Silence seemed a precious commodity. Soon enough, though, there was a knock at the door, followed by Kitty peering round and bounding into the room.

"What do you think of Mr. Tollemache? Is he not the most charming gentleman, Fran?"

"Very pleasant indeed, Kitty."

"Such bearing, such address. All the marks of true nobility." The implication that Lazenby lacked any such qualities was unmistakeable. But Fran merely nodded in agreement. Kitty settled herself in the easy chair opposite the chaise longue where Fran sat and began extolling the manifold excellencies of the Honorable Lionel. She did not notice that her sister scarcely murmured in response.

Eventually, Kitty withdrew to make her own toilette before dinner. Fran readied herself, then left her room. Her footsteps took her past Lazenby's room, but she did not enter. She wanted to. But she did not feel equal to warding off Kitty's inevitable reproaches. Besides, now Lazenby had his man, any need he might have would surely be tended to without interference. It would be better to leave him to mend sufficiently to be transferred to Dorfold Hall.

So Lazenby remained isolated from the household. Soames did encounter the ladies of the house, for Miss Wilbraham summoned him to discover if there was anything he required. He returned to his master's side in a thoughtful frame of mind but said nothing. Finally, Lazenby gave way.

"You have been here several days now, Soames. What do you make of the household?"

"Interesting."

"Good heavens, man, is that all? No acerbic comments to make about the organization of the kitchen or the running of the stables?"

"No. Miss Wilbraham is a good manager. Looks after her troops. Looks after her guests. Little more to be said." Soames continued checking the earl's clothing.

"There is a great deal more to be said. What do you find so interesting?"

"You could marry her. She's warm enough in the pocket. She's easy enough on the eye. She'd sort out Edenbridge in a trice and you'd get yourself heirs. But you won't make a push for it. I've seen you shy away from the good ones before, and I reckon you'll do it again even though the opportunity is there." He shook out a clean pair of stockings.

"And you'd get your back wages and a decent amount saved. God knows why you stay with me. Enough men have tried to poach you." Lazenby watched his man closely, but Soames remained impassive, taking a seat at the desk where the necessities for a job of darning were laid out.

"I have my reasons. Same as you have for racketing about as you do. I don't question your reasons, and I don't see why you should question mine."

"What of the sister? She'd slip belladonna in my morning tea before she'd let Miss Wilbraham marry me."

"How do you know? You haven't met her. Lady Tollemache. You're right, though how you've worked it out confined to a bed and scarcely a soul to visit you, I don't know."

"Farr the footman has let the odd word slip. Is he alone, or do none of the servants think much of her?"

"Pretty is as pretty does, I reckon. They see through her. She'd like to be a real lady and swank about London ballrooms, but she'll never manage it. Miss Wilbraham is a different matter. She'd make a fine duchess if a duke were on offer. But she isn't one to marry for rank." Soames was busy darning.

"A woman of integrity."

"No need to sound so scornful. She's no London flibbertigibbet, that's certain." Perhaps feeling he might have gone too far with this compliment, Soames clammed up and no amount of provocation would bring him to speak further about the inhabitants of Dysart House. Lazenby began to feel very sorry for himself. His wounds itched, which all three of his persecutors (as he now saw his doctors and Soames) pronounced to be a promising sign of healing, his ribs continued to ache, and his arm was still too weak to hold a pen or a book.

As with so many male invalids, once he grew restive, Lazenby grew snappish as well, so when Fran did visit him once again, he was irritable and pettish.

"It is good of you to visit me." His tone was waspish and it was clear he felt she was anything but good. He could hardly admit how much her appearance affected him. She wore a simple dress, but it was in a sumptuous blue with subtle lace insets. Connoisseur as he was of milliners' bills and ladies' finery, Lazenby found the blend of modesty and luxury quite piquant.

"I've brought draughts. I think chess would make you too feverish. Cards would be too complicated to hold or deal. Do you play draughts?" Clearly his opening comment must be ignored. Invalids needed to be humored.

"Not since I was in the nursery. What about *Ivanhoe*?"

"Your man Soames told me that he had been reading it with great interest. I did not wish to disrupt his enjoyment of the book."

Soames appeared then and rearranged Lazenby so that he was sitting propped by pillows, able to reach for the draughts with his uninjured hand. The manservant then retreated to the desk while Miss Wilbraham set out the game on a small side-table by the bed.

"You don't mind playing draughts, do you?"

"Even if I did, it would be churlish of me to say so now you've set them up."

"I shouldn't think that would stop you. You must be in dire need of distraction. Let us ask Soames to toss a coin for us."

The valet stood and tossed a shilling piece. Fran called heads and won, so she twisted the board round and considered her first move. She did not seem to reflect for long before shifting her first man, and Lazenby responded similarly swiftly. He soon found that although she seemed scarcely to think before shifting a piece, she was clearly playing a strategic game without any signs of demonstrating mercy to a new opponent. He immediately upped his concentration, determined to prove worthy of her aptitude. Nonetheless, she won the game easily enough.

"Another match?" asked Lazenby.

"Certainly. Shall we make it the best of three?"

"Yes." The earl hesitated. "I don't suppose you'd care to make a small wager on the final outcome?"

"I don't bet on certainties. I shall win, and you will then owe me money that I do not need but will make you feel uncomfortable."

"You seem very sure of your abilities." Lazenby smarted at her condescension.

"If you were not dosed with laudanum and still experiencing some discomfort, you might well turn the tables on me, but as it is, I believe I shall best you and make the most of the opportunity to do so."

So saying, she set up the board again, and proved the truth of her words. Although Lazenby's pride was dented by her supremacy in the game, he enjoyed their match, for it provided an opportunity to watch his hostess in thought, a beguiling sight to any red-blooded male, however grievously injured. She displayed an almost masculine force of concentration, both when planning her own moves and when watching his. She made no conversation. Finally, when she had quite defeated him a third time, he asked her why she was so quiet.

"I have been in company constantly. I find it quite wearing. I enjoy the pleasure of new acquaintances and old friends, but at times, I like nothing better than silence. One finds oneself speaking with such inconsequence, we jabber on simply to fill the void." She sat back in her chair, depriving Lazenby of a rather fine view of her bosom. The way to ensure another glimpse was to engage her in conversation.

"You have had visitors?"

"Kitty—Lady Tollemache's—cousin, Mr. Lionel Tollemache, is visiting Nantwich. I believe he hoped to reacquaint himself with Sir Arthur, my brother-in-law, but he has had to make do with us."

"I'm sure he doesn't consider it making do. I don't believe I know him."

"He has been in Italy until very recently. He has many fine tales to tell about the lakes and the palaces there. It sounds very lovely." Miss Wilbraham's eyes were distant as she contemplated all she had heard.

"You sound wistful. Do you long to visit Italy?"

"I would like to travel. I would love to see all the great cities and the landscapes of Europe. My father used to ask me to read travellers' tales to him. It has made me very restless." She smiled and reached for the draughts to set them back in their box.

"Why don't you go? Surely you could leave Lady Tollemache to look after your home and head off whenever you pleased." Lazenby began helping her put the pieces away.

"I don't believe I could. Not just yet. When Sir Arthur has returned and settled on a home and Kitty is safely established, then I shall consider it."

Just then, their fingers met and entangled as they reached for the box simultaneously. A rare but unmistakable jolt afflicted the earl. He looked up, his hand withdrawing, but Miss Wilbraham's eyes were downcast. Either she was a better actress or a more accomplished flirt than he had imagined. She certainly concealed any reaction to his touch most effectively. This only tempted him to touch her again. But he did not give way to the temptation. She looked up.

"Shall I leave the draughts here? We could play again tomorrow."

"Yes. I shall know I am truly recovered when I am able to trounce you as thoroughly as you have trounced me." His voice was light.

Miss Wilbraham left, bidding farewell to Soames as well as to Lazenby. The earl fell deep into contemplation. His reaction to her could simply be a sign of his physical debility. His defences were weak. The last time a woman had so affected him with a mere touch had been in Lisbon, the winter before the hard campaigning to seize Ciudad Rodrigo, Badajoz, Salamanca. Lord Ferrars had been a foolish young captain, the lady had proved false, and war had worn away at the remnants of the romantic boy he had been. His next winter in Lisbon, he had started his own campaign to taste the favors of every willing wife he could find, determined to prove to his own satisfaction that all women were false.

But this young woman was no bored wife repenting an over-hasty marriage to a man who had looked very fine in uniform, but absented himself ten months out of twelve to fight the scurvy French. It might be that Miss Wilbraham had been impervious to Lazenby's glancing touch. She had felt no shiver of awakening desire.

The earl called Soames over. "This Tollemache. See what you can find out about him."

"He's putting up at The Crown with his man. I'll do what I can." Soames was careful to conceal his pleasure in this instruction to investigate the competition. He had said too much about Miss Wilbraham already, and it was his firm intention that Lazenby should not leave Nantwich without a betrothal in the offing. He had watched this young man grow up at Edenbridge, made sure that he should not have to grub about the Peninsula eating acorns and weeds like other officers, and followed him in and out of danger, but it had been beyond him to ensure that the man who had fought beside him and saved his life more than once could find lasting happiness.

It did not take Soames long to strike up an acquaintance with Tollemache's valet, who was a starchy fellow in his fifties. He had been taken on in London, just before

Tollemache set off for Italy, and ascribed his master's enjoyment of that country solely to his own ability to shield the honorable gentleman from all manner of hazards, from banditti to excessive garlic and grease in the food. While he lacked any knowledge of Tollemache's conduct and family in England, he was garrulous enough on the subject of his master's manifold virtues.

"He does not drink, he does not game, and there were no women in Italy," reported Soames.

"He is entirely chaste?" asked Lazenby incredulously. "No whores, no mistresses, no masked encounters in Venice?"

"Apparently not. No men, either." The valet's countenance was impassive.

"What's he made of? Milk and water?"

"Seemingly so. He is on the prowl for a bride with a dowry. Being a younger son and all. He is very prudent, apparently."

Lazenby caught Soames's eye and they both grinned. Soames had invested the word "prudent" with a pained disgust which made a mockery of all the lectures he had ever given the earl on the virtue of prudence.

Whether it was the challenge of a competitor or simple recovery, Lazenby soon sought Roundell's permission to attempt to rise from his sickbed. The doctor did not see the point in objecting, well aware that the earl would do as he pleased. The best means of returning the invalid to his bed was to allow him to find the limits of his own strength.

It was a slow process. The first day he found himself struggling simply to stand. Once he was upright, everything was agony—his left leg, his right arm, his ribs all seemed to ignite. It was, although he was not prepared to admit it, a relief to return to the horizontal. But the next day, he tried again and managed to stand for a little longer. Within a week, he had managed to move from the bed to a chair by the bedroom window and was able to take in the view of the rear gardens of Dysart House. These were not extensive, but provided some entertainment, for beyond the formal lawn and flowerbeds one could see the kitchen gardens, a run for chickens and the orchard. Two pretty maids came daily to feed the hens and pick apples, pears, and quince from the laden trees in the small orchard. Miss Wilbraham also conferred every morning with her gardener, collecting fresh flowers for the house. Small pleasures, but a considerable improvement on the unchanging vista of bedroom walls.

After a damp start, the month was proving warm and sunny, and it was far more comfortable to sit in a nightshirt by the open window than to lie abed. It also made it easier to play backgammon and draughts with his hostess. Her visits considerably accelerated his progress toward health. Time spent in her company seemed to evaporate. She made him laugh with her wry retelling of the foibles of her neighbors.

The workings of her mind were increasingly fascinating to him. She was clear-sighted, not cynical, forgiving of folly where it was matched by kindness, and implacable in the face of cruelty. She could discuss Marcus Aurelius and Montaigne, then turn the subject to London fashions and seem equally absorbed. Most compelling of all, she showed little personal interest in Lazenby himself. She asked no impertinent questions about his estate or his history. If he gave an opinion, she would weigh it and consider it, but she did not alter her own views to chime with his, and if she thought his views ridiculous, she would make it plain without undue discourtesy. She did not seem to judge him in any way. It was a considerable novelty to a man all too used to being courted for his title and position and spurned for his loose morals.

Roundell neither praised nor condemned his wayward patient for his impatient advances. But once the earl had been three weeks at Dysart House, the doctor asked Miss Wilbraham if he might speak with her and Lady Dorfold about the invalid. Kitty was wild at being left out of the conference, but Frances reminded her that poor Mr. Tollemache must be kept amused. So it was with ill grace that Lady Tollemache took her cousin out just as Lady Dorfold stepped down from her carriage to confer with her dear friend and the doctor.

"Does he make good progress?" she asked Roundell as she was pulling off her gloves and reached for the tea which Fran had poured for her.

"He does. His ribs are nearly mended, his arm appears to be knitting well and the wounds to his leg are also healing, although the tendons were badly torn. I would still be unhappy for him to take to his carriage and jaunt about the countryside before he can walk with some semblance of normality."

"He cannot take to his carriage. That is irreparable. But I might offer him the landau if he wishes to return to his home." Fran wished to be as accommodating as possible.

"I would not advise it until his arm is fully recovered and he is able to walk without a crutch. He is far weaker than he is prepared to admit or understand. The fever he suffered was not mild."

"But he is strong enough to come to Dorfold Hall, do you think?" Lady Dorfold stirred her tea.

"I think that would be an excellent solution. Miss Wilbraham has been more than generous, but now that he is on the mend . . ." Roundell coughed delicately.

"You think that a rake of his caliber should be removed from a household of women?" suggested Fran. "I've seen him every day this week. He does not seem ready to ravage any stray woman that crosses his path." Naturally she did not mention that strange, brief mingling of fingers which had occurred nearly a week before. It was negligible, it meant nothing.

"I daresay not, but he needs space in which to recover without setting your house about its ears every time he ventures from his room. Imagine, dear Frances, how Kitty will fly into the boughs if the poor fellow dares to set foot in the front parlor. And you have too many stairs in these narrow townhouses. We can set him up in one of the ground floor rooms where he may stretch his legs and take his ease without negotiating any stairs at all."

Fran could not object to this sensible appraisal of the situation. Kitty's constant complaints must be silenced if the earl were to leave the house, and certainly, Dorfold Hall would provide the room for him to roam about and regain his strength. She was surprised to find that she did not want the earl to leave, but after all, Dorfold Hall was not barred to her. There could be nothing strange in her visiting the patient, let alone the friends whom she saw three or four times a week. But a sense of flatness overtook Fran as she agreed to the plans for the earl's removal from Dysart House.

Five

The question of moving had of course to be agreed upon by the earl himself. It was Roundell who broached the matter with his lordship, and did so with tact and delicacy, making it clear that this should be viewed as an experiment to test Lazenby's strength and ability to return home to Edenbridge rather than the eviction of an inconvenience from Dysart House. His argument was strengthened by a visit by the Dorfolds, extending in person their invitation to the Hall. Sir Richard was shrewd and direct, while his wife was elegant and kind. All overruled Lazenby's vague mutterings about returning to Edenbridge, and Lady Dorfold consulted with Soames on the best way to transport the earl to Dorfold Hall so that the earl found himself being readied for the brief trip within a day of agreeing to the change in domicile.

On the morning of his departure, Miss Wilbraham came to his room bearing the backgammon set. "I am here to occupy you while Soames packs."

Lazenby was sitting in his customary wing chair, his left leg propped on an ottoman, wearing his nightshirt and a heavy brocade dressing gown with navy frogging. He seemed unusually somber.

"I must thank you for your kindness to me, Miss Wilbraham. I have been most handsomely cared for under your roof and I appreciate it fully."

She smiled at this formality, but played the game. "We are delighted to see you so much better. But you or your people will still have dealings with us. Your horses remain in our stables for the moment. I suspect my man Tarbuck of self-indulgence, for they are superb specimens and exercising them is giving him a great deal of pleasure."

"Once I am able to write again, I will ensure that your inconvenience is recompensed." Lazenby tried to remain formal and detached. But Miss Wilbraham looked a little stricken.

"I had thought we were on a more friendly footing, my lord. I believe Soames has settled with Roundell directly, so you owe us nothing here. You have provided us with a good deal of interest and excitement, more than enough to recompense me for the occupation of a room."

" If your only excitement is playing at children's games with an invalid, excitement must be in short supply in Nantwich."

"Not just any invalid. A noble invalid. I am the envy of all Nantwich." It was clear from Miss Wilbraham's tone that she did not think Lazenby merited any particular honor for his nobility, whatever the rest of Nantwich might think.

"Will all of Nantwich now envy the Dorfolds?" Lazenby fiddled with the counters laid out on the board before him.

"Not if I reveal how very prickly a guest you are."

"I am surprised my reputation has not gone before me."

"The errant earl? Of course it has. But it only makes you more alluring, for no one seems to know of what sins you are truly guilty. Great tales abound, but my sister has done her utmost to quash the more outrageous accusations levelled at you."

"I am astonished to hear of such a defender."

"She is concerned for the Wilbraham name. She may

not approve of you, but she will not allow you to be slandered while you rest beneath our roof."

"You, I take it, have fewer qualms."

"I have heard nothing against you at all, my lord, so I can neither defend you nor disparage you. The most I have been able to say is that you are a most restless invalid and it is just as well that Sir Richard and Lady Dorfold are taking you under their wing." Fran threw down the dice decisively and moved her counters with her customary swiftness of decision before directing an interrogative glance at the earl as he sat motionless.

Lazenby sighed in resignation. Miss Wilbraham would not indulge him further with speech now the game was on. Still, it was worth venturing one last query.

"Will you still visit me at Dorfold Hall?"

"I will visit Lady Dorfold, of course. If she happens to be sitting with you, I daresay our paths will cross."

So they were to be chaperoned and hemmed about, No more quiet afternoons of idle discourse over some game of strategy. Disappointing, but not entirely unexpected. Certainly the safest possible outcome for her. Soames would be discouraged by this setback, but what good was it setting out to court a young woman who had seen him at his lowest ebb? A man had his pride, and as far as Lazenby could see, there was precious little advantage in arousing interest through pity.

Skilled enough at concealing her feelings from Kitty and the busybodies of Nantwich, Fran had no intention of allowing Lazenby to see how dismayed she was by his departure. Amusing, sophisticated, well-read, he had livened up her days considerably, despite exacerbating the ongoing wrangles between Kitty and herself. At least his presence had given them something of substance to wrangle over, rather than Kitty's customary litany of petty grievances and longing to interfere in the running of the household.

But now he was going, and Kitty would crow, and she would have no one to share her thoughts with once again. Of course, one could hardly compare the loss of her father with the removal of the earl from her home. But for the first time since her father's death, Fran had caught a glimpse of the possibility that there might be others who shared her outlook on life, her pleasures and her dislikes. Of course, Lady Dorfold stood as her great friend, but Lady Dorfold was a busy woman with considerable calls on her time. However fond of Fran she might be, her obligation lay with her family. Besides, Lady Dorfold was a woman. It had been a pleasure to converse once again with a masculine mind. She had suspected at times that the earl was ready to embark on a flirtation, but then they would share a joke or he would seek to persuade her to accommodate his point of view and any coyness or risqué badinage faded away and he spoke straightforwardly, without condescension or ulterior motive. She would miss him.

The earl's removal from Dysart House was accomplished easily enough by Soames and Farr, who carried him downstairs in a chair with extreme caution. The earl was not a substantial man, and his sickness had further reduced his weight. Despite his best efforts to conceal the twinges of pain, it was clear that excessive jolts and shudders did affect him. The short carriage trip to Dorfold Hall, less than two miles from the center of Nantwich, proved so wearing that Lazenby retired immediately, unusually docile to Soames's pronouncement that bed was the best place for him.

True to their word, the Dorfolds had installed the earl in a comfortable bedroom on the ground floor of their home. It was clearly a room intended for honored visitors.

There was an elaborate Turkey carpet covering the highly polished parquet, a very fine intaglio cabinet, several gloomy paintings depicting the more gruesomely martyred saints, including one of the Catherines and a Sebastian, matched in attention to detail by a vivid Flaying of Marsyas, a magnificent bed with red brocade swagging and canopy, and a ceiling across which sported a forestful of naked nymphs and cherubs. French windows led onto a terrace overlooking the gardens. It was a peaceful, secluded place, sheltered from the bustle of the main house. Lady Dorfold came to see her guest settled.

"Soames and I have spoken already, Lord Lazenby. For the moment, we have agreed that you should have meals served to you here in peace, but as soon as you feel strong enough, please join us in the dining room. If there is anything we can provide, you have simply to ask."

She was a charming hostess, and came to visit him at least once daily. She seemed to judge to perfection the appropriate length of a visit, depending on Lazenby's progress, which was by no means even. The move to Dorfold Hall wore him out more than he expected. Although such weakness astonished him, he was quite relieved to retire to his bed for an entire day after the change in his domicile. Soames was privately concerned by the docility shown by Lazenby in submitting to the doctor's suggestion that bedrest would be the most effective cure for even so brief a journey as two miles. The young campaigner who had gone weeks without sleep, who had fought on despite wounds major and minor, appeared to have vanished.

However, it seemed that the earl had simply regrouped, the better to move forward with his campaign of recovery. His breathing eased as his ribs ceased to hurt, he was gaining movement in his right arm with every passing day, and he even began to be able to exert some mild pressure on his damaged leg. His old resilience seemed to be returning. Within a week of settling in at Dorfold Hall, the earl made his way gingerly, on crutches, to the dining room to join the family for dinner. There, he was introduced to the three younger children in the family. Master Richard Dorfold, heir to Sir Richard, and the third of the Dorfolds' children, was a pleasant youth of some fifteen summers, late returning to Shrewsbury for the Michaelmas term because he had inconveniently caught the chicken pox from his younger siblings, Matilda and Walter, who at fourteen and twelve respectively were just emerging from the schoolroom and consequently on their best behavior.

Lady Dorfold watched the earl carefully over dinner to see that the children did not bore him or overtire him. She found him surprisingly unstuffy. He spoke of fishing and shooting, which were the chief interests of all the menfolk about the table, but was also able to discuss drawing and the latest songs in London's drawing rooms, which drew a response from Matilda, who was the chief pianist in the family.

"Do you play the piano, sir?"

"No, but I do sing."

"Would you sing for us after supper?"

"Matilda! His lordship is scarcely off his sickbed. Show some consideration!"

Matilda bit her lip, but Lazenby came to her rescue.

"I cannot claim to be in good voice, but I would be pleased to test my recovery with a song or two. Roundell has not forbidden it, at any rate."

The earl was pleased to find that singing did not strain his ribs unduly, and the Dorfolds were delighted by his clear tenor and his unfussy style. Matilda established that Lazenby knew most of the family favorites and they all sang together, first cheerful folk songs, then more gentle ballads of love and loss, rounding off with "The Ash

Grove," a Welsh tale of a love defeated by death. The earl then excused himself and retired.

Soames was waiting up for him, carefully concealing any anxiety he might be feeling on behalf of his master. Lazenby hummed as he undressed and accepted Soames's ministrations before sitting in a chair before the fireplace, his leg propped on an ottoman, the lamp on the sidetable glowing, a recent novel by Amelia Opie beside it.

"What tune is that?"

"You know it. 'The water is wide, I cannot get o'er.'" A favorite of theirs from campsites all over the Iberian peninsula.

"Funny how one forgets." Soames too started to hum the mournful tune, then recalled the words and began to sing. Lazenby's tenor blended with his man's baritone as they recalled the words ruefully of the old ballad:

> *"Must I be bound, O, and she go free!*
> *Must I love one thing that does not love me!*
> *Why should I act such a childish part,*
> *And love a girl that will break my heart?"*

"My question is, which is the girl who'll break your heart? The one that's gone to Ireland, or the one you've met here in Nantwich?"

"Does it matter, Soames? I can have neither. Married or unmarried, they are both protected by stout hearts who consider me scarcely fit to breathe the same air."

"So you don't deny that Miss Wilbraham could break your heart?"

"You don't catch me out so easily. I have no heart to be broken, or so the world says. No heart, no conscience, no morals, no qualms."

"The world has been proven wrong before now."

Soames could see that his master was close to hurling a book at him, so left before the earl could take aim.

Once the door closed, the earl picked up the novel, then tossed it aside again. It was a dreary Quakerish tale which he had borrowed from Miss Wilbraham in an effort to ensure that she would visit him, if only to retrieve the volume. But she had not yet appeared. He levered himself up and went to the window, drawing back the curtain and looking out at the garden, dimly lit by the full moon. He wished he had a cheroot to smoke, but did not know where to look for such a thing. He had had some in his luggage, but where Soames had put them, he had no notion and no desire to hunt through drawers in search of tobacco.

Before his accident, he would have had no qualms about calling back the manservant and demanding that the cigarillos be found. He had changed. Before, he would have chased the Ormistons to Ireland if thwarted. Now, he acknowledged that such action would be fruitless. Lady Ormiston did not want him, would never want him, and it was not the action of a gentleman to press a lady, let alone attempt to abduct her. He could scarcely conceive how he had developed from a chivalrous cavalry officer into a cad capable of running off with the reluctant wife of another man.

Lazenby jerked the curtain back into place and heaved himself to the side table, maneuvering himself so that he could douse the lamp. Then he progressed to the bed and threw off the brocade robe which Soames had draped about his shoulders. He eased himself under the bedcovers and shifted about until he could settle in one position. He lay there, unable to sleep, gazing about the darkened room trying to make out the nature of the shadows.

In an effort to induce sleep, he tried to recall every detail of the painting which decorated the ceiling. There were the nude naiads and dryads, a group of three here, a pair there, listening in rapt enchantment at the young, muscled satyrs playing their pipes. In the distance, Daphne transforming into a laurel tree as Apollo chased her. More bloody Ovid. Elsewhere, Dionysos was sporting with Maenads, and about the edge of the central roundel, Cupid and small, rotund followers were smiling benignly on the scene as they prepared their bows and arrows. It brought to mind bacchanalian evenings he had spent, which now seemed to fade, undistinguishable one from another, in pursuit of willing women of every degree and rank, from street sluts to grand patronesses of salons attended by princes and dukes. It had been enjoyable, getting drunk and chasing lightskirts, but such pastimes had lost their appeal long before he had come to grief on the road to Crewe.

Did he have a heart to lose? Even if he did, the earl knew that he was equipped with sufficient morals, qualms, and conscience to ensure that any lady who might win it would be left in ignorance of the fact that she had conquered the supposedly unattainable goal of attaching his interest. He was not a reputable catch for a woman of good reputation. The only way to redeem himself would be to marry some antidote who had sat long on the shelf and was a stickler for moral purity. He must resign himself to lectures and Bible readings and prayer in the hope of mending his soul in the years remaining to him. Such women had been picked out for him by well-meaning relatives and he had rejected them unreservedly, but there was always another waiting in the wings, with heavy eyebrows, a po-faced demeanor, and drab clothes. Angels with swan-necks, soft smiles, and merry brown eyes were not prescribed for the reform of rakish cousins.

The fact that Frances Wilbraham's image came to mind every time he thought of his ideal woman was no proof that he had lost his heart. He had been infatuated before, and this was similar to that sensation. He thought of her constantly, he missed her presence, and yet found himself irritable and spiky when with her because he was conscious that she had calls on her time that took precedence over spending more time with him. Now, there was this Tollemache that her sister had dug up, a prime candidate for her hand in marriage. She had not yet visited Dorfold Hall since he had removed there, or if she had visited, she had not come to see him. There was no way he could ask the Dorfolds if she had been there.

Lady Dorfold, in any case, would have been obliged to tell him that Miss Wilbraham had not visited. A note had come from Dysart House, inviting the Dorfolds to dinner with the Honorable Lionel Tollemache, to which Lady Dorfold had replied accepting the invitation. She had also revealed that between Lady Tollemache and Mr. Tollemache, she had scarcely time to manage the regular routines of Dysart House, let alone come visiting. But this state of affairs did not prevent Lady Dorfold from speculating about a possible attachment between the earl and his previous hostess.

"Would it be so very bad?" she enquired of her husband as they prepared for bed some nights later. "He has not behaved in a gentlemanly fashion in the past, I will grant you, but he seems quite reformed to me."

"I daresay the world will wear it well enough. Neither is in the first flush of youth. She would be securing a title and he would be mending his fortune. It is just such a match as is made every day in the high Season." Sir Richard paused as he pulled his shirt over his head. "However, the only reason he is not rakish is because he cannot be, not with his body in tatters. No guarantee that he would not return to his ways as soon as he's mended."

"She could do much better if only she would go to

London and give herself a Season. But she will not turn Kitty off, and Kitty will not do, however she preens herself on her Dysart connections." Lady Dorfold sighed.

"Aye, it's a pity the woman has no home of her own. But it's to Fran's credit that she will not have a word said against her sister."

"I suppose so. Do you really think Lazenby is not reformed in any way?"

"Women like to believe that men can be changed, but it's not a notion I hold with."

Lady Dorfold's smile was swift and secretive. Sir Richard's memory was selective and it would be cruel to remind him of how much he had altered his ways over the years of their marriage. She watched him as he carried out his nightly rituals, folding his clothes, rinsing his hands and face, brushing his teeth, snuffing the lights in their room. Of course, one could ascribe change to factors other than feminine influence. He had changed physically since they were married, had lost that stringy lankiness of boyhood, and now his hair was graying, both on his chest and his head. Maturity, greater responsibilities, boredom all played their part in minimizing the attractions of strong drink, loose women, and deep play.

Certainly, there were hardened creatures who married and altered their ways not at all. But Lazenby was not that stamp of man. He had the air of a penitent about him. Lady Dorfold was sure that there was a fundamentally moral core beneath the careless façade, as sure of that as she was of her own good fortune in marrying a man of utter trustworthiness. She did not know the earl, he had not been in her house a week, but somehow, it was clear that here was a man who had gone wrong, but had the capacity to go right.

Of course, Fran had given no obvious indication that she cared for the earl, or could bring herself to care. But this did not deter Lady Dorfold from considering a possible match. Lazenby's reticence in speaking of his erstwhile hostess spoke volumes to the squire's wife. He had not held back when discussing other mutual acquaintances, amusing her with his piquant descriptions of unfortunate millinery choices, flagrant liaisons, and balls intended to be glittering. She wished to think the best of him, of course, because he had amused her, and it had come to her as she sat with him that he had probably amused her dear friend too, and how rare it was that Fran met with people who could amuse her. But he had not asked about Fran nor commented on her, nor on her sister. That spoke of some degree of interest, in Lady Dorfold's opinion.

There were obstacles, of course. Kitty. The earl's own reserve. If he were not the sort to bandy about the name of a lady, he would be even less inclined to court one. Wry asides he had made already suggested to Lady Dorfold that he was the sort to regard himself as unworthy of the attentions of a true lady, and also the sort to regard any woman who paid him any regard as no true lady. Tiresome, but not, she thought, insurmountable.

The more serious obstacle was Lady Tollemache. Until Sir Arthur returned, there was no hope of releasing Fran from the baleful presence of her sister. Kitty had always been a charmless infant, pushing herself in where she was not wanted, at once knowing and falsely modest about her pretty looks, convinced of her own rectitude, longing always to outdo her sister, and conscious that she never would. It was impossible not to be suspicious of this Lionel Tollemache she had dragged up. If she wanted Fran entangled with him, there must be something wrong with him. Lady Dorfold was looking forward to meeting this paragon. From the little that Fran had said, he seemed harmless enough.

But harmless was not what Fran needed. Since her father had died, she had retreated into herself. Lady Dorfold understood how and why, but she missed the light-hearted young woman who had happily danced till dawn at hunt balls. It was all very well being capable and generous with one's dependents but the mantle of responsibility which had come upon Fran seemed to carry with it all the disadvantages of matrimony with none of its pleasures. She had no opportunity to use her abundant wealth because she was bound to her home and her sister. In addition, Kitty's finicky notions of respectability were binding her sister into an ever-narrower path and sooner or later, she was likely to break out in the most spectacular way, unless something could be managed.

Fran was definitely a breaker-out. All the signs were there, the distant look, the wistful smile when she saw children getting themselves into scrapes, the slight frown of impatience swiftly concealed when taking tea with the biddies of Nantwich. Fran had the capacity to do something impulsive and irrevocable, like marrying a footman or running away to Italy. An attachment to an earl was a relatively mild form of rebellion, even if he was an acknowledged rake. Even if they ended by eloping, it would be a containable scandal.

Before they could reach that stage, they must be brought together. Fran had been surprisingly assiduous in her avoidance of Dorfold Hall this past week or so. That would change.

"You are plotting something, my dear, I can always tell. If you are inclined to meddle with Lazenby, let me warn you against it. He is not the malleable type."

"I won't meddle."

"You won't meddle actively, but you'll do your best to throw them together." Sir Richard settled under the covers and reached for his wife. "If Kitty Tollemache comes brandishing a tomahawk for your scalp, I'll defend you."

They laughed and Sir Richard dowsed the lamp by their bedside.

Six

Nearly a fortnight in Nantwich had left Lionel Tollemache in a state of some confusion. It had been a surprise to receive a letter from a cousin-in-law he scarcely knew, but his mother gave him to understand that Arthur's wife was of respectable stock and had come well-dowered. The sister had her own funds and, if the Countess remembered correctly, even better looks than little Kitty, who was charming enough to be sure. It had been all very well visiting Italy, and one's allowance certainly went further there, but it was time, the Honorable Lionel felt, to settle in England. The only way to do that without taking up some form of employment (not a congenial prospect) was to marry money.

Miss Wilbraham was a true bargain. Her income, so far as Mr. Tollemache could discern, was not tied up in tiresome trusts and so, on marriage would devolve automatically to a husband. She was more than pretty; she was considerably wiser than her sister and markedly less prone to put on airs. Of course that meant she was less impressed by his connections to an earldom, but that equally meant she was unlikely to be impressed by Lazenby's tarnished credentials.

Not that Lazenby appeared to be any great threat. Despite the somewhat agitated letter from Kitty Tollemache, Miss Wilbraham showed no signs of attachment. That was the problem. She demonstrated no interest in the Honorable Lionel either. One would have thought that the arrival in her orbit of an eligible, elegant man of some address was rare enough to have merited some reaction. But the woman was impervious. Pleasant, mildly engaged by his tales of Italy, but unmistakably, unshakably distant. She was not hanging out for a husband. She gave the distinct impression that even if she had been hanging out for a husband, the Honorable Lionel Tollemache would not have met her requirements.

So here he was, stuck in Nantwich, faced with having to discover the requirements of an old maid. An undeniably lovely old maid, but nonetheless, a woman fixed in her ways. It somehow went against all his principles to seek to attract a woman. He did not know how to begin. What did one do to entice women? At this very moment, gazing on his reflection as he adjusted his cravat and checked the studs of his shirt, the Honorable Lionel would have given anything for five minute worth of advice from the practised seducer who was ensconced in Dorfold Hall.

There had been women, of course, but there was the risk of disease and scenes. Tollemache feared the former and detested the latter, having taken on a ladybird just after coming down from university who enacted Cheltenham tragedies with a regularity and enthusiasm that left him with an entrenched horror of prolonged conversation with any female. Lighthearted flirtations conducted under the eyes of duennas proved quite sufficient for Lionel. Discussing the latest novel or the way a satin sash matched the blue of a girl's eyes were easy enough tasks, but he had not sought to go beyond that for many a year. In Italy, he had been regarded as a catch, so young women had made themselves pleasant to him.

As he walked through Nantwich, swinging his cane, on his way to dine at Dysart House, it came to Tollemache that he must make himself pleasant to Miss Wilbraham in the manner that ladies had made themselves pleasant to him. How had they gone about it? They had listened to his stories and laughed at his witticisms, they had complimented him on his appearance and his intellect, they had stored up those snippets of information he dropped so that when he met them again, they would have ready a new song in the style he liked, or a little picture he might be interested in. How novel it would be to be the hunter in this particular game rather than the prey!

Arriving at Dysart House, full of good intentions, Tollemache was dismayed to find that he must share Miss Wilbraham with the Dorfolds. Still, it provided a good opportunity to practise listening, a skill he had not often had cause to use. The first useful titbit he collected was that Miss Wilbraham had causes. He listened as Lady Dorfold asked after one of the causes.

"How is your Hannah coming along?"

"Very well. I have persuaded Kitty into one of her creations and with your support, I am sure that she will be dressing half of Nantwich by Christmas."

"You'll lose her. Mind you, she has younger sisters." Lady Dorfold gave a gleeful smile. "Parry will not like it. He has ensured that his family has provided most of Nantwich's finest ensembles these fifteen years or more."

"It will encourage him. Competition is a good thing, gentlemen always say so, do they not, Mr. Tollemache?"

"In matters of sport and economy, so I believe. I do think if it is a question of tailoring though, one ought to find the man who can fit one out to the best advantage and stick with him. Loyalty produces a more flattering result than the resentment borne of competition. Although Miss Wilbraham need not fear, she would grace any costume she chose."

"Prettily done, Mr. Tollemache." Lady Dorfold took

out her fan and watched her young friend, trying to gauge the effect of this compliment.

Fran was unreadable. She thanked her sister's cousin for his kind words, then excused herself to turn to Sir Richard, seated on her left.

Tollemache sighed and Lady Dorfold commiserated *sotto voce.* "She can be most infuriating. If you really wish to engage her attention, you must contrive to get Kitty out of the way. She will not consider anyone seriously until her sister is safely off her hands. You don't happen to know anything of Sir Arthur's movements?"

"I do not. I had not realized that the difficulty lay in that quarter. I thought it was simply that I lacked sufficient address."

"Mr. Tollemache, your address is more than sufficient, if only she would allow herself to acknowledge it. But Kitty has no home of her own, Sir Arthur is forever away, and it suits the proprieties that Miss Wilbraham should be chaperoned by her sister. Until this situation is resolved, I fear that she will hold all potential suitors at a considerable distance."

Having planted this seed in the Tollemache mind, Lady Dorfold was quick to turn the subject. She had been quite forward enough. She had not taken to the Honorable Lionel, she wished him to show his hand early and in so doing earn his dismissal from Miss Wilbraham. Perhaps, he might also be instrumental in encouraging the Tollemache family to take proper notice of Kitty.

The next challenge was to bring together once more Miss Wilbraham and the earl. This was a simple enough matter. Kitty excused herself as they left the gentlemen to their port, and Lady Dorfold was quick to invite Fran to Dorfold Hall to visit her goddaughter Matilda.

"She is in need of some feminine company other than her mother. I wish you would give her some advice, for she is entering that difficult stage of girlhood when whatever a mother says must be wrong."

"Advice? What advice could I offer her?"

"Oh, heavens, where shall I begin? She is developing the most florid taste in clothing, she wishes to throw herself in the way of the most tiresome of young men, and whenever we make an excursion, she is perpetually in search of possible flirts. My dear Fran, I am beginning to believe I can take her nowhere—and at home, our very guests are in danger! She is quite capable of making eyes at Lazenby, even though she regards him as positively grandfatherly."

"Matilda! Flirting? She's scarcely turned fourteen."

"She has elder sisters. Girls with elder sisters always mature more swiftly." Lady Dorfold sent a silent apology to all her daughters, but mostly to Matilda for exaggerating her flaws so extremely.

"Why do you not send her to visit me?"

"Are you avoiding Dorfold Hall for any particular reason?"

"By no means. I just feel it might appear a little artificial if I visit and you send me off with Matilda in a huddle."

"Bring her some new music. Or a book. You are always doing such things, and it would give you an ideal opportunity to speak with her."

It was agreed that Fran would come round the next day. The truth was, she had been careful not to turn up unannounced at Dorfold Hall in case she was accused of chasing after the earl. But now Lady Dorfold had provided her with a respectable reason for visiting, neither Kitty nor the other cats of Nantwich could comment or complain.

Kitty returned to the drawing room and the ladies passed the time until the gentlemen rejoined them in idly turning the pages of Ackerman's Repository and discussing which of the latest furnishings would be tolerable in the home. It was not long before Sir Richard and Mr. Tollemache entered the room, whereupon Mr. Tollemache discovered that the object of his intentions had a tolerable voice and good taste in songs. He took a turn about the room, noting its tasteful but somewhat outmoded appearance, observing the number of books scattered on sidetables and the neatly ordered chessboard, boxes of playing cards, and the backgammon set. He returned to Lady Tollemache's side as Fran finished singing.

"Who is the player of games?" he asked.

"My sister, not I. I can never remember rules, Fran tries and tries to teach me a game but I have forgotten the rudiments by the next day. Do you play, Mr. Tollemache?"

"A little chess, but whist is my favorite. Do the Dorfolds play?"

"I believe so. Why do you not sit for a hand or two? I have my embroidery and will be happy to watch." They exchanged a complicit glance. It would be a fine opportunity to extend the visit.

The Dorfolds and Miss Wilbraham were quite willing to sit down to a rubber of whist. Mr. Tollemache found himself partnered with Miss Wilbraham, which suited him well. Cards were always an ideal means of deepening an acquaintance, he found. He was a reasonably competent player and provided the play was not too deep, it was a straightforward enough matter to converse while engaged in the game.

Later, once they had bade goodnight to their guests, Kitty asked her sister what she made of the Honorable Lionel.

"He is well enough. Very keen to secure his trick, sometimes at the expense of his partnership." Fran was tidying up the decks of cards.

"Is that very bad?"

"By no means. It is a fairly common trait." Fran turned the subject. "I shall be going up to Dorfold Hall tomorrow. Lady Dorfold has asked me to visit Matilda. Do you wish to accompany me?"

"Will you see Lazenby?"

"I have no idea. Does it make any difference? My concern is my godchild, not the earl. She stands in need of a little guidance and is not inclined to follow a mother's hand."

Kitty could not argue with this innocuous request, although she did find the explanation suspicious. Still, she could not believe that Lady Dorfold would deliberately throw Fran in the earl's way, and it had been only a week since he had left in a state of considerable invalidism. It was unlikely that he would be up and about.

Of course, the earl was up, although not really about, since he was confined to a chair in the orangery of Dorfold Hall, where Miss Wilbraham was guided the following morning by one of the footmen. There also were Miss Matilda and Lady Dorfold engaged in reading to the earl from the latest edition of *The Spectator*. All were laughing at some wicked description the earl had given of one of his fellow lords, mentioned with considerable respect by the editors of the esteemed publication.

The earl did not mean to catch Miss Wilbraham's eye, but their gazes did meet as she was announced, and pleasure lit their faces in equal measure. Lady Dorfold noticed this even as Miss Wilbraham glanced away and made much of Matilda.

Her visit was a merry one. They discussed novels and Earl Lazenby lamented that he had been unable to enjoy the book he had borrowed from Miss Wilbraham, so serious and worthy had been the intentions of the author. Miss Wilbraham confessed that she too had found it virtually unreadable and much preferred lighter fare. They discussed songs and Miss Wilbraham drew out the sheets of music she had just received from London, two duets and a collection of new songs from Italy. It was fixed that she would return the next day, once Matilda had had a chance to study the melodies, and they would practise them, ready for the return of her sisters. They spoke of fashions and Lady Dorfold kept shaking her head over Matilda's wilder dreams of a cherry-red pelisse for the winter, while Miss Wilbraham spoke in her goddaughter's defence and the earl argued that cherry red was entirely suitable a color for a young girl.

At last, Miss Wilbraham left on her other errands, her return the following day quite settled and all parties delighted by the visit. As she sat in her carriage, Fran congratulated herself on the innocuous tone of the conversation and the unexceptional nature of the topics they had covered. It had been a pleasure to see Lazenby going on so well, and she would be able to report to Kitty that being clearly on the mend, it would be only a short while before the neighborhood was rid of his vexatious presence.

As she watched the barouche roll from Dorfold Hall, Lady Dorfold congratulated herself on the easy way that Fran's presence had been reintroduced into her home. She turned to find Matilda on the step beside her.

"I am so glad Miss Wilbraham is my godmother, Mama, she is the least stuffy of ladies. I am much luckier than Sarah and Caroline."

"Lack of stuffiness was not the chief characteristic that swayed me in my choice of godmother for you, my dear, but I am glad that you are able to appreciate your good fortune. She is charming."

"I can never understand how it is that no man has offered for her."

"You are treading on the verge of indelicacy, child, but let me assure you, more than one gentleman has offered for her. But she is, as you recognize, unusual and interesting, and accordingly, needs an unusual and interesting gentleman to interest her." Lady Dorfold guided her daughter back indoors and up to her dressing room. "Shall we look in my box for some pretty trimmings for your winter bonnet now?"

In the orangery, the earl was considering the Dorfolds' guest also. His heart had leapt when he saw Fran's elegant figure at the door of the orangery, and somehow it had not settled as she had talked. He had watched her constantly, compelled by her face and her lovely voice, unable to drag his gaze away. It had been disconcerting to react quite so enthusiastically to the arrival of a woman. It had not happened for years now. When she had risen to take her leave, dejection had struck, and only the knowledge that she was returning on the morrow had kept him from protesting that her stay had been too short.

On her return to Dysart House, Fran found Mr. Tollemache settled in the front parlor with Kitty. She was able to react with equanimity, although her heart sank somewhat when she saw him, she could not tell why. His address was unexceptional, he was pleasant enough, but it was something of a labor to sit with him. She always felt under scrutiny and he smiled a good deal. Not that there was anything wrong in smiling. It was just that when he smiled, she did not feel particularly like smiling back. There seemed to be some condescension, some air of superiority about him that she knew Kitty found compelling but that she could not approve.

Still, the knowledge that she would be back at Dorfold Hall the next day sustained Fran, and she found herself chatting quite amicably with her sister and her sister's cousin.

It was almost without realizing it that a pattern to the days emerged. Within a week, Fran had returned to her routine of visiting Dorfold Hall either daily or every other day and somehow, every time she visited, she seemed to encounter Earl Lazenby. These meetings were not significant. He was helping Matilda with her playing, or teaching the child some new game, and it eased Lady Dorfold's mind to know that the child was properly chaperoned. It was unfortunate that her governess had come down with chicken pox just as everyone else had recovered from it, but with Fran present, there was no harm in a little exposure to a rake. Especially since it was so clear to Lady Dorfold that the rake's real interest lay with the woman rather than with the naïve child.

It was not as if they conversed much with each other. Fran could report in all honesty to Kitty that Earl Lazenby had commented on Matilda's fingering, or tempo or lightness of touch, but had otherwise scarcely spoken. She did not need to mention that the earl's eyes had lingered on her, that he had kissed her hand as she arrived and departed, that he was standing only with the aid of a walking stick now, that although he moved slowly, he was no longer chair-bound. There was virtually nothing of the invalid about the earl at all. But Kitty need not know that.

One week stretched into two, the earl had been in Nantwich nearly seven weeks now, and the nights were drawing in, the air cooling almost daily as October approached November and Lady Dorfold consulted with Fran about Harvest Festival.

Mr. Tollemache was becoming impatient. He had done his utmost to beguile Miss Wilbraham. He had learnt new songs, sent for his sketchbooks from Italy, walked with her, listened carefully to discover her tastes in fashion, fiction, and foods, put up with the endless inconsequential chatter of her sister and still, every time he attempted to seek her out on her own or to draw her further into conversation, she sidestepped him. She was elusive and awkward. What was strange was that for once, he had not been deterred by this determined evasion. No. More than ever, he was fixed on Miss Wilbraham and her property and her money. He had expended so much time and effort on her behalf that to surrender now and leave Nantwich was unthinkable.

It did occur to Mr. Tollemache that even if he managed to get Miss Wilbraham alone and prepared to discuss courtship, she might put him off. So it suited him for the time being to remain in her presence chaperoned by his cousin-in-law or any other company that happened to be available. Even such uncongenial company as Lady Dorfold. That way, he would become so established a suitor that Miss Wilbraham would eventually have to accept him. It did not occur to him that a maiden lady with independent means might choose to remain so rather than acquiesce to a marriage against her inclination. But it did not prevent him from becoming impatient, particularly when assailed by those irritating missives from his man of business pointing out that his resources were stretched to their limit and no income appeared to be ameliorating the situation. The innkeeper Bloxham was also pressing for a settlement of at least his first month's account at The Crown.

Although she said nothing about the Honorable Lionel to anyone, Fran did find his presence increasingly irksome, not so much because he was in any way unpleasant, but more because he seemed always to be there. In those rare moments when she could be private and peaceful, Kitty would call up and say in flurried tones, "Darling Fran, our Mr. Tollemache has come calling." There would always be some little bibelot to admire or a tale to hear or an article from *The Times* that must be of interest. In an attempt to avoid Mr. Tollemache, Fran found herself taking refuge more often at Dorfold Hall, until she finally broached the matter with Lady Dorfold.

"Am I too often here? Kitty tells me so. I would not wish to push myself in where I am not wanted."

"How can you be so ridiculous? You were always at the Hall, day in, day out, before Sir Arthur left on his travels. We are simply reverting to our old ways. But do let Kitty— Lady Tollemache, I should say—know that she too is always welcome here."

"Where Kitty goes, there also goes Mr. Tollemache."

"Perhaps that is why we are seeing so much of you. It would be kinder to let him have his say and dismiss him once and for all."

"I have tried, and heaven knows Kitty has tried to encourage him to declare himself, but he holds back. His game is deeper than I can understand."

Lady Dorfold explained. "He is establishing himself so firmly as your cicisbeo that no other man will ever approach you and you will be so eager for attention that you will finally accept his."

"How can he be so foolish?"

Lady Dorfold looked at Fran, who sighed wearily and said, "Kitty. She will not understand that I do not seek any husband at all." The thought crossed Fran's mind that she should ruin herself with Lazenby and end Kitty's aspirations for her once and for all.

The earl gave no indication of wishing to ruin Miss Wilbraham. He was circumspect with her because he did not know what to do, a state of affairs he found novel and in its way amusing. Certainly it amused Soames, who said nothing and watched as his master recovered and seemed almost whole, although his broken arm was still splinted up. There was no more talk of Edenbridge, but neither was there any talk of Miss Wilbraham. It was as though the earl had placed himself on extended holiday, for none of his creditors knew his location, and none of his current companions seemed to worry about his reputation. The layers of cynicism and devil-may-care bravado that characterized his dealings with London friends had been stripped away by the accident and by the unquestioning assumption of his hosts that he would behave in a way that was acceptable and pleasant. Removed from the possible irritant of social disapprobation and gossip, the earl had no reason or stimulus to behave badly, and the trust and common sense of the Dorfolds and Miss Wilbraham did not allow for any lapse in demeanor.

This perhaps was the most effective cure for the malaise that afflicted the earl. For Soames, it was an unalloyed delight to see the earl enjoying, for the first time in many years, simple pleasures. One of these was Miss Wilbraham's company. Soames had begun to wonder whether the earl would be able to shed his rakish ways, whether the art of seduction and the habits of high play and heavy drinking were so ingrained that he would never change and must end by going to the devil or Europe, both of which were dismaying prospects to the manservant.

It was clear to any who saw them together how much the earl and Miss Wilbraham had in common. They laughed easily together, their tastes for certain poets and composers were similar, they found themselves fervent on the same questions of the day in the newspaper. In addition, Miss Wilbraham displayed a compassion and disregard for pettiness that allowed them both to forget Lazenby's worldly reputation. However, very few people did see them together—only the Dorfolds. So the deepening interest they took in one another went largely unobserved by Nantwich in general and by Lady Tollemache in particular.

Seven

When the doorbell at Dysart House rang on the Tuesday before Harvest Festival, Fran and Kitty were expecting Miss Reid to discuss the flowers and which of the deserving poor should be brought up to receive bounty from the altar the following Sunday. Since for quite different reasons, neither sister saw eye-to-eye with Miss Reid's selection of deserving poor, both were dreading the meeting. However, instead of the stick-like figure of the parish's driest spinster, a distinctly masculine figure stood behind the butler, notable for his bulk, magnified by a travelling cape and broad hat. Kitty leapt up with a cry of astonishment.

"Arthur! Can it really be?" The butler withdrew, Kitty ran into her husband's arms and promptly burst into tears.

"Hey, hey, puss, what's all this?"

"I'm just so happy to see you! It is so unexpected! Why did you not write of your coming? When did your ship come in?"

"I arrived in Liverpool last night and thought it quicker to come in person than to shilly-shally with letters and so forth. I knew Fran wouldn't mind."

"Of course not, brother. You are most welcome." And Fran came up to kiss her brother-in-law in greeting, genuinely pleased to see Kitty happy and Arthur apparently so eager to see his wife.

Sir Arthur threw off his cloak and hat as Fran called

for refreshment. He had arrived with only a small bag, but asked Fran for permission to send for his travelling trunk from Liverpool. "I could not wait to see my little Kitty and tell you both my news, but all my gifts are in the trunk."

"What news, Arthur?"

"Our fortune is made, my dear, and I need not travel again. We must find a house of our own, or have one built if you prefer. I thought to ask Miss Wilbraham's advice on whether there are any suitable houses for rent here or hereabouts, and then you and I can plan for the future."

"Oh, Arthur," squeaked Kitty. "A home of our own?"

"And a London Season for my little puss."

"This is truly good news, brother," commented Fran, not quite daring to believe that she would be relieved of Kitty's immediate presence without losing her entirely. "We must consult with Marsden and Farrow, my solicitors, and they will be able to advise us. If you wish, we can send for them today or tomorrow."

"No rush, no rush," said Sir Arthur. "Meanwhile, I understand my cousin is come to the area. It will be good to see Lionel once again; it is some years since we met. He and I were ever in scrapes as boys."

Fran found it hard to believe that the spruce and circumspect Mr. Tollemache had ever had a boyish scrape, but she smiled and withdrew to leave the reunited couple to themselves. She also needed to send a swift note to Dorfold Hall to explain her absence today—she could not go calling the very moment her brother-in-law arrived.

Lady Dorfold was sitting with her husband when Fran's excuses arrived. She opened the note and exclaimed, "I thought he'd never return! And she thinks he wishes to settle in the area. I daresay they will end by keeping that milk and water creature with them and the three of them will badger poor Fran more than ever."

"What milk-and-water creature?"

"The Honorable Mr. Tollemache, my dear."

"Whenever you call me 'my dear,' I know I have failed to follow the female mind and blundered in some mysterious way. I do not see that it is any of our business. In any event, there is nothing we can do to prevent or encourage it."

"Won't Lazenby confide in you? He must act, he must do something to rescue our poor Fran from her relatives."

"Of course he won't confide in me. We scarcely know each other. It would be the greatest presumption on my part to start interrogating him, and once again, my love, it is none of our business."

Lady Dorfold could have shaken her husband in frustration, but in justice, she knew he was right. There was no way of knowing the earl's intentions toward Fran. It would be deeply indelicate to probe. But it was obvious to Lady Dorfold that her friend cared for the earl, and she would have put money on the depth of the earl's affection for Fran. It was not cupboard love. He was not the sort to make up to a woman for her money. In fact, Lady Dorfold suspected that Fran's money might be an obstacle rather than an incentive.

It would be appropriate, she thought, to invite the Tollemaches to dine. If they all came, with Fran, perhaps the earl would see just how beset Miss Wilbraham was, and his innate sense of chivalry might propel him into declaring himself, simply to rescue the poor girl from her relations. Ideally, the couple needed another month of quiet meetings before either of them would be ready to admit their feelings, let alone act on them, but time was short and the pressure that the Tollemaches could bring to bear on Fran was increasing.

The Dorfolds' invitation came promptly in response to Fran's note. It was received by Kitty and Sir Arthur as nothing less than their due and by Fran as a profound relief. Lady Dorfold was careful to invite the Honorable Lionel also. As she had realized, Sir Arthur's arrival heralded an intensification in Kitty's campaign to marry Fran off to Lionel Tollemache. By inviting him, she could see how far their plans had progressed.

Now that Sir Arthur was in residence at Dysart House, Lady Tollemache's first move had been to request that Mr. Tollemache be invited to stay. Fran resisted this by pointing out that Sir Arthur's demands on her staff were considerable. He had a way of making requests that seemed mild and easy to comply with, but which ended by causing a good deal of upheaval and disruption.

First there was the alteration of rooms—what was suitable for a woman was not suitable for a married couple, naturally, so in addition to sending for Sir Arthur's luggage in Liverpool, Fran's people were occupied by shifting Kitty's things, then rearranging the disposition of the furniture in the suite taken over by the Tollemaches, then unpacking Sir Arthur's things, then assisting in his correspondence and business activities. There seemed to be a never-ending stream of minor errands to be run. Kitty's demands also increased, for she was eager to shower on her husband every luxury and delicacy that he must have missed while abroad and at sea.

Of course, Fran did not complain about the chaos visited on her household. Matters would settle, and her father had been just as capable of visiting equivalent uproar on Dysart House in his day. But when she did come calling at Dorfold Hall, the day before the Tollemaches were due to dine, she was subdued.

Lady Dorfold sent her through to the music room, saying she must quickly consult with her housekeeper before joining Fran there. Miss Wilbraham found Matilda practising a sonata and the earl leafing through a nocturne by John Field, the French windows ajar to make the most of the unusually clement temperature. He looked up from the sheets of music.

"Come for a turn in the garden. It is a beautiful autumn morning and we must profit by it before the days draw in." He stood and held out his right arm. Fran looked at him questioningly. "Your touch is very light and the arm really is feeling much better. I'm hoping to be able to play the piano again very soon."

The music room gave onto a terrace which led down to the rose garden created by Sir Richard's grandmother and lovingly tended by her two successors. Of course, there were no roses out. The bushes had been prepared for the frosts and storms of winter and the beds looked sparse and sad against the red-brick of the sheltering walls. Despite the warmth of the sun, Fran found the place curiously desolate.

"What is troubling you?" asked the earl.

"Do I seem troubled? I had not meant to. There is no reason. My sister is happily reunited with her husband and I shall, I hope, soon be free to go to London or wherever I please."

"You do not believe that. You fear that they will hedge you about and protest so greatly that any plans you make will involve a great deal of complaint and lecturing. You are too good to say so, but you are beset by your family."

Fran laughed at this accurate picture. "I must have been very careless to allow you to draw such wicked conclusions. "

"Not careless, but trusting, I hope." He nodded towards a nearby bench. "May we sit? My leg is still a little tender."

"You scarcely seem to use your walking stick."

They sat and the earl continued. "Miss Wilbraham—"

"I thought I was Fran."

"Fran. Frances." He reached for her hand and raised it to his lips. "I shall be leaving for Edenbridge soon. In a week or two. I have imposed on the Dorfolds long enough and my health is sufficiently recovered for it to present no excuse for lingering. I have a great deal to do when I reach my home."

"You've mentioned that you've neglected it, in your view." Fran was determined to remain cheerful and light-hearted, but it was difficult because his words had caused a sudden constriction in her throat.

"And in the view of my creditors. It is common knowledge that my affairs are a sorry mess."

"It may be common knowledge, but it is not really any of my business." Although she wished it could be her business. She wished that all his cares were in her keeping, and that he would propose and she could give him her money. But one glance at his resolute features told her that this was not a likely outcome of this conversation.

"I do not wish it to be any of your business either. That is why I intend to return to Edenbridge and investigate the true state of things. Once I know how things stand with the estates, I will be in a better position to plan for the future." The earl paused, then stood up. "Miss Wilbraham—Fran—I wish for nothing more than to include you in that future, but I cannot yet offer for you. Forgive me for being blunt, but there is little time and if I say nothing, you might take some irrevocable step. I know I have no right to say as much as I have said, it is not gentlemanly to speak so when I can offer you nothing and do not know whether I will ever be able to offer you anything. But will you wait a little?"

Fran gazed down at the ground and stirred a pebble with the toe of her shoe. She wanted to shout back that she would wait until the stars were put out and the sea dried up and the earth ended—but for heaven's sake, there was no need, she had more than enough for both of them. Suppressing this impulse took all her concentration. She looked up and met his gaze. He looked unaccountably fierce.

"What do you wish me to wait for?"

"I won't come to you with my life and accounts so mangled. I will go to Edenbridge for the winter and see how things are. If they can be mended and the damage repaired, I will come back to Nantwich in the spring and speak. Otherwise, I shall go to the continent on a repairing lease. It may be that matters have come to such a pass that I must sell."

"Aren't there entails?"

"I'm the last of the Lazenbys. I have no cousin waiting in the wings."

"Why could I not come to Italy or France, too?"

"Fran, if we were married, all your money must go to paying my debts. However cleverly your father may have tied up your money in trusts, we would have nothing to live on. I am not contemplating some fashionable existence in Paris or Naples, but a hand-to-mouth life on the fringes of society."

"Why should we get married? Why could we not elope and become lovers? There would be a scandal to be sure, but then we could lead a comfortable life on the fringes of society. The fringes are full of interesting people, artists and poets, freethinkers."

"The fringes are not nearly so lively and colorful as you imagine. Besides which, Fran, I could not be your dependent and even if I could bring myself to such a pass, what would become of any children?"

Fran grasped at one essential. "If women may become

mistresses, why cannot men emulate them? Why should I not have a lover in my keeping?"

"No reason on earth apart from your own pride. And mine. I have no wish to be your lapdog and I have no wish to see you become a tyrant. This is what I have seen in others." The earl smiled ruefully. "You know in your heart that we could never live that sort of life, Fran. It is not a question of respectability or acceptance in society. You know as well as I that the world is full of hypocrisy and if you were to take a lover, you are quite rich enough to withstand the scandal, because what matters more than morals are the guineas at your disposal."

"But?"

"But it is a life that would part you from all your principles and every precept by which you have been raised. You are an honorable woman, Frances, and I could not bring dishonor to you. I will not do it, however tempting the prospect might be."

He sat again and took her hand again, but this time he did not let it go. "Fran, I want to be worthy of you, not see you dragged down to my level. I don't know whether I can raise myself up again, but at least give me the chance to attempt it." Their eyes met and held. She nodded.

"I will wait to hear the outcome of your investigations at Edenbridge. I will wait until the spring."

The earl leaned forward as if to kiss her. But Matilda came out of the music room and called for them. "Come and listen. I think I have finally got it right now." He sprang back as though burnt, and the moment was lost forever.

As the carriage carried Fran home, she thought of that conversation and wondered if she could have changed the outcome at all. She thought not. She thought that if she had given any other response or if the earl had felt in any way inclined to take up her offer, they would neither of them have been the people with whom they had each fallen in love. For she had fallen, she finally acknowledged to herself. And the earl had fallen too. But love, she began to see, was not enough. Or more accurately, love was too much and required the earl to behave better than he had ever done before. Any compromise and he might return to his previous ways, because any compromise would mean a cheapening of his love. He was too ridiculously idealistic for his own good, and consequently, for her own good too.

Fran was not of a naturally pessimistic turn of mind, but she did not dare hope for the best in this case. The earl, she thought, would return home, find that his affairs were in such disarray that there was no possibility of retrieval and would decamp to some shabby corner of the Riviera. What would she do in this case? A tear trickled down the side of her nose and she wiped it away angrily. She would not remain in Nantwich to be harassed into some suitable match by Kitty and Arthur, that was sure.

This rebellious frame of mind stayed with her even as Farr handed her into the barouche the following evening, along with the three Tollemaches.

"I do not very well remember the Dorfolds. What sort of people are they?" inquired Sir Arthur.

"Sir Richard is very much the sportsman. He lives for his game, his hunting and his trout. I daresay we shall taste the fruits of his shooting tonight." Kitty paused. She found Lady Dorfold difficult. "Lady Dorfold is a woman of good principles but a little flighty in some respects. But you should ask Fran about her, they are forever in each other's pocket."

Fran smiled at Kitty's needling. It was borne of the irritation that while Kitty felt that as sisters they *ought* to be in each other's pockets, in reality, there was nothing she wished for less. She then answered Sir Arthur's unspoken question.

"They are a very old family, very well-established and warm enough, I understand. The girls will all have full London Seasons. Lady Dorfold is the daughter of a marquis, I believe, and very well-connected."

"Yes, she's the daughter of the Marquis of Yelland. I met her brother in Italy, a charming fellow, most unassuming." Mr. Tollemache continued, "I suppose she might have looked higher than a baronet, but she seems most content."

Having established the credentials of his hosts, Sir Arthur modified his behavior accordingly. He had heard from Kitty all about the Dorfolds' lapse in offering a refuge to the iniquitous Lazenby, but their importance in the county was not to be underestimated. They were a family of rank, to be cultivated whatever their fits and starts.

With an excess of men, Lady Dorfold had seated Kitty between Lionel Tollemache and Lazenby, who was by Sir Richard, opposite Fran. Sir Arthur was treated as the guest of honor and seated on her right, next to Fran. Lady Dorfold resigned herself to an evening of acquiescing to whatever the two gentlemen had to say, for she had noticed that each in his different way enjoyed laying down the law on whatever subject was raised. It had occurred to her to leaven the company with the presence of her children, but then she thought better of it, for neither Sir Arthur nor Mr. Tollemache struck her as the sort who would be indulgent to those of a younger generation.

Fran and Sir Richard had plenty to say to each other. They shared views on aspects of stewardship and commanded similar influence in the neighborhood, so there was always something to discuss when they met.

Kitty was placed in a quandary. Mr. Tollemache was occupied with his hostess and his cousin. This left her only Lazenby to talk to, a task she felt was fraught with terrors, even though her husband was seated opposite her. Strange to realize that she had not had one conversation with the roué while he was under Fran's roof! But the earl proved surprisingly tame. He answered her questions about his health with calm straightforwardness, he told her frankly that he had trespassed too long on his hosts and explained that he would be leaving the area in the next ten days.

"Sir Richard has prevailed on me to test his coverts and his river now that I am recovered, but my presence at Edenbridge is long overdue."

Lionel Tollemache turned his attention to Kitty and the earl.

"There's good sport to be had in your part of the country too, I hear."

"Indeed there is." Lazenby steeled himself not to rise at the condescension he heard in Tollemache's tone. "You have not had the opportunity to sample it yourself?"

"I'm not a sporting man myself. I prefer the gentler arts—music, dance, painting. I am counted a reasonable hand with watercolor, I fancy."

"What is your instrument?"

"I believe I can acquit myself with some credit on the cello. Do you play?" Tollemache clearly thought the earl an unlikely musician.

"The pianoforte and the violin. But I have not had much opportunity to play in recent weeks."

"Ah, yes, your injuries. I do hope you will recover the full use of your right arm."

"So do I. Roundell certainly seems to think that all will be well."

"These country doctors! I am surprised you have not

called on a London man. It would have been my first step."

With every new utterance, the earl seemed to hear Tollemache sneering at him, for reasons Lazenby could not fathom.

"By the time I was sufficiently conscious to think of such things, I was on the mend. It really did not seem necessary. I found Roundell a most thoughtful and well-informed sawbones, which is more than can be said of most of the charlatans of Harley Street."

"Mr. Tollemache, do tell us about the fabled lakes of Italy. I understand that you spent a good deal of time in the area of Lake Maggiore." Adroitly stepping in, Lady Dorfold prepared herself for a dull travelogue.

"I was in Stresa for some months, and I then toured the area. I found it most romantic and also very comfortable. There are some fine mansions there, exquisite settings. The palace of the Borromeo on Isola Bella is extraordinary, I must say. I was privileged enough to secure an invitation, although the Borromeo are very exclusive."

Mr. Tollemache was diverted for a time to animadvert on the characteristics of the Italian nobility, but he returned to his quarry soon enough. Addressing Lazenby, he asked, "Have you travelled much in Italy?"

"Not very much. I should like to return. I saw Genoa and Milan once, but I am more familiar with Spain and France."

Knowing that the earl had served under Wellington, Tollemache read this as a slight on his own position as a non-combatant. He bristled, but was saved by Kitty, who could see where the conversation might lead. She did not want him shown up before the Dorfolds and the earl.

"I have heard that Spain is a barbarous and primitive country."

"Only in those areas most affected by the war. There are oases of tranquillity and ease."

Sir Richard chimed in unexpectedly. "I'm not a great traveller myself, but my brother served there before he was killed, and his letters revealed a fondness for the place. He also thought a good deal of Portugal. Apparently the hunting there was very fine over the winters."

Sir Arthur began to discuss hunting in the Nantwich area, and then revealed a good deal about his own travels and experiences. As the most recently returned traveller and in some degree the guest of honor, it was only to be expected that he should have his say, and this fortunately prevented Lionel Tollemache from launching any further attacks on the earl. When the ladies withdrew, Lionel joined them swiftly, for he did not smoke and had little taste for port. This was a relief to Lady Dorfold, who preferred to avoid tête-à-têtes with Kitty, for she had the most unfortunate way of patronizing Fran when in the company of other married ladies.

When the gentlemen did rejoin the ladies, Tollemache continued his attempt at one-upmanship over the earl. Lazenby accompanied Fran in some folk songs, but Tollemache decried their simplicity. When the conversation turned to a new picture that Lady Dorfold had purchased on a recent visit to London, Tollemache insinuated that the earl understood nothing about art. When the earl returned to Miss Wilbraham her dull novel by Miss Opie, Tollemache ventured to praise the book in the highest terms and suggest that anyone who failed to appreciate it was an ignoramus.

It was Kitty, conscious that her chosen beau for Fran was exhibiting the worst aspects of his character, who suggested that the Wilbraham carriage be called.

"It is getting late, Lady Dorfold, and we all have much

to do on the morrow, I am sure. Will we be seeing you at the Assembly this weekend?"

"Certainly. Lazenby has consented to attend also, haven't you?"

"Indeed! My enjoyment will be limited, as I shan't dance, but it is always a pleasure to see a fine company enjoying itself. Lady Dorfold tells me that your dances are well-attended."

"Very much so, and it is an opportunity to see a good deal of finery, sometimes of questionable taste." A frown crossed Kitty's brow. "They are letting almost anyone attend these days. Perhaps we should ask the master of the hall to be a little more selective."

Before Lady Dorfold could comment, her footman announced that the carriage was ready to return to Nantwich, so the Tollemache party departed and the earl excused himself.

As he readied himself for bed, Sir Richard commented to his wife, "You were right about that Tollemache fellow. Milk-and-water mixed with a dose of spite. Fran will never have him, don't you fear."

Lady Dorfold felt that this was true, but she did fear that Fran would never have anyone. The earl had been most circumspect this evening and so had Miss Wilbraham. There was scarcely a sign that they knew each other, let alone cared for one another. Yet Lady Dorfold could have sworn that there had been something there. But it looked as though she must seek elsewhere for a suitable mate for her friend.

Eight

The Assembly Rooms of Nantwich had a dance every fortnight, and as Kitty had commented, these were well attended by most of the gentry in the area, all of the professional people, and as many of the families of those in trade as could afford the subscription fees. The gatherings were generally packed and had created a demand in the area sufficient to support two dancing masters able to instruct young ladies and gentlemen in the arts of the waltz, a range of quadrilles, and the mazurka. There had been great discussion about allowing the waltz, but when it was discovered that the Shrewsbury and Wrexham Assembly Halls permitted it, there could be no further discussion.

The party from Dysart House arrived promptly enough for Lady Tollemache had been button-holed by Mr. Harthill, the master of ceremonies, about opening the dancing with Sir Arthur, but the Dorfold Hall group was late. This was also at the suggestion of Harthill, who was somewhat concerned about precedence. Technically, Sir Richard and Sir Arthur were of identical rank, but only one couple might lead the dancing, and Harthill found it impossible to decide whether a baronetcy dating from Norman times outweighed a more recent baronetcy where the knight in question was nephew of an earl. Fortunately,

Lady Dorfold was generous enough to care very little who opened the dancing.

"What a squeeze it is this evening," commented Lady Dorfold, struggling to catch a glimpse of Fran or Kitty. Unfortunately, the first sight to meet her eyes was Lionel Tollemache leading Miss Wilbraham out for a set of the Lancers. Fran was looking most delectable in a russet velvet gown, with an amber aigrette in her hair. Lady Dorfold followed Sir Richard and Lazenby to a quieter area in the hall, away from the musicians and near the door to the card-rooms, and there she waited with Lazenby while her husband went in search of refreshment.

"Now, Lady Dorfold, the greatest pleasure of these events is to discover who is standing up with whom. As a native of the area, you must explain to me the most unlikely pairings and the most inappropriate pairings."

Lady Dorfold smiled and began to comment on the dancers and the guests in general. She voiced her surprise at seeing the Taylors, for it was known that they were short in the pocket, but she supposed with four girls to get off their hands, the subscription fee was a most economical means of introducing the young ladies to a wide range of potential suitors.

Of course, this was Nantwich's first opportunity to inspect the earl. As they chatted, both Lady Dorfold and Lazenby became aware that they were attracting surreptitious glances and gradually, as the earl's upright bearing, elegant dress, and neat features were absorbed, more brazen interest. He did look very fine for a man who had been at death's door only six or seven weeks before. He seemed significantly taller than most other men present, and also trimmer. Soames had had to take in his evening clothes for the fever had caused him to lose a little weight.

The Lancers came to an end, and Mr. Tollemache

handed Miss Wilbraham off the floor. Miss Amy Appersett and Miss Charlotte Farnham came over to Miss Wilbraham. They were the sort of girls to whom Mr. Tollemache had a particularly strong aversion, being healthy, giggly and animated. He excused himself to go in search of lemonade, leaving Miss Wilbraham at their mercy.

"The earl is very dashing, Miss Wilbraham. Is he really so wicked as they say?" demanded Miss Farnham.

"I've no idea, Charlotte. He has behaved with the greatest propriety both while under my roof and at Dorfold Hall."

"What is he really like? He reminds me of pictures of the Duke of Wellington, but with less of a nose," observed Amy.

"He looks nothing like the Duke!" exclaimed Charlotte. "He doesn't look like a horse presented with unacceptable oats. But what is he like, Miss Wilbraham?"

"Pleasant, but quiet. Not what you would expect of a rake. But perhaps that has been because he was so injured."

"Is he dancing this evening? I hope he does. One always learns so much by seeing a man on the dance floor." Miss Appersett opened her fan and fluttered it in what she hoped was a sophisticated manner.

"Really?" enquired a deep voice behind her. It was the earl, who had come in search of Miss Wilbraham when he saw that she was free of the Tollemache fellow. "Do enlighten a member of the species, what do young ladies learn about us?"

Miss Appersett blushed, then rallied. "Some men are generous and thoughtful, others approach the dance as if it were a massive hurdle to be surmounted, and then there are those who are careless and tread either on their partner's toes or on the hems of other dancers."

"Surely this simply tells you how well a man likes dancing?"

"Oh no. It is not just men. To be sure, there are men who are clumsy but well-meaning, and of course, there are men who dance exquisitely but have no other praiseworthy qualities at all, but you see, all of us reveal something of ourselves when we concentrate on doing something. If men cared to watch as carefully as women do, they would learn quite as much about their partners in the course of a waltz."

Fran looked at Amy in amazement. She had watched the young lady grow up, the daughter of a local attorney-at-law, but never realized what an astute judge of human nature the girl had become. "You are dangerous, Amy, you will be weighing us all and finding us wanting."

Amy smiled a secret smile, which Fran caught. The little miss had some hidden pleasure in the assembly other than the opportunity of flirting and wearing her newest dresses.

"I believe you are right, Miss Wilbraham. Such an acute observer of foibles and personalities will not long be able to restrain herself from setting down her observations in print, if she has not already done so."

Amy blushed again and said, "I could never own to it, even if it were true, for if it got out, people would be too careful before me."

"I shall be looking out for a tale of provincial dancers in all my periodicals now." Fran smiled and pressed the girl's hand. "If you have undertaken such a path, I wish you every success. Will you accompany your mother next time she calls on me?" She was determined to discover more of this intriguing young woman, perhaps assist her if that was necessary or possible.

"I shall, Miss Wilbraham."

Some young men came up to spirit away the two young ladies, leaving Fran alone with the earl.

"Will you take a turn about the room with me?"

"With pleasure. Are you dancing tonight?"

"I wish to, but I fear to. I think I must try my paces in private before taking to the floor in so public an arena. Only think if Miss Appersett saw me slip, I should be immortalized as a clumsy earl in her next novel."

"Next? You think there is one already?"

"I do, although I am not sure that she has yet found a publisher. You must see if you can get a glimpse of it, for I daresay you will recognize half Nantwich in it and it will cause you great amusement."

"Not if I am included in it."

"I daresay you are a model for the heroine, unless Miss Appersett prefers the incapable type who is perpetually at the mercy of a clumsy villain."

"You flatter me, I think, although I am not sure that I would wish to appear in anyone's novel either as a heroine or a minor character. I am not nearly interesting enough to feature in a novel other than as a distant and possibly smug Lady Bountiful." Fran sighed. "How I wish *I* were nineteen and writing novels."

"What is the source of your regret? That you are no longer nineteen, or that you do not write novels?"

"Neither really. Just a sense that life is passing me by and I have achieved very little, seen very little. Kitty believes the answer to all my difficulties lies in marriage." She left unspoken that the one man with whom she could contemplate marriage was beside her and unavailable.

Lazenby looked at Fran, so elegant beside him, so calm. It was illusory. She was not calm at all, but wound tight as a watch spring.

"What is worrying you?"

"I cannot speak about it, it would not be delicate." Fran shrugged off his inquiry brusquely.

"Tollemache. He is biding his time."

"I wish he wouldn't."

"If I press my suit a little, he may show his hand."

"Urged on by my sister and brother-in-law. It will be exceedingly uncomfortable at Dysart House."

"Leave them to their own devices. Announce your intention to visit Paris. Surely one of your father's acquaintances has a family which could usefully invite you for a visit."

Fran's face lightened. "I had forgotten! I do have friends to whom I could apply for refuge in such a case. Perhaps I shall follow your advice and decamp."

The earl felt an unaccountable pang at the idea of Miss Wilbraham disappearing from this environment in which he could visualize her once he had left Nantwich. It was all very well suggesting routes to escape the attentions of the Honorable Lionel, but what if such routes led her to encounter more suitable and attractive courtiers? He could not expect her to suspend her life and exist like some candied fruit preserved simply for his pleasure. Nor could he expect her to commit herself to him when the extent of his financial troubles was unknown. He would not marry her for her money.

Sir Arthur emerged from the card room to see his sister-in-law and the earl walking steadily round the edge of the ball room deep in conversation, their eyes meeting continually, both smiling and nodding, more intent on each other than anything that might be occurring in the room. Alarmed, he went in search of Kitty.

"My dear, your sister has been in conversation with his lordship for a whole set of dances! What's to be done? She should be dancing with my cousin, not flirting with that reprobate."

"She's promised to Mr. Tollemache for supper and the set of minuets immediately afterwards. I cannot force her to dance with him again and no one else has had an opportunity to ask her for a dance." Kitty stood in thought, tapping her fan in the palm of her hand with increasing velocity.

"Get Harthill to find some suitable gentleman. Surely there must be some. I don't suppose we can press Sir Richard into service, he don't dance except with Lady Dorfold." Sir Arthur steered his wife toward the Master of Ceremonies, who was at that moment engaged in a discussion with a young woman with dark hair and kittenish features. The lady looked round the great room and her eyes fastened on Lazenby. Kitty saw her smile at Harthill and gesture towards the earl. Harthill shook his head and gestured towards Sir Richard and Lady Dorfold who were dancing. She spoke a little more, then turned and left for the dining hall.

Marching up to Harthill, Lady Tollemache wondered who the woman was, but dismissed her in the urgency of her request for a dancing partner to remove Fran from the earl's presence. The Master of Ceremonies was most obliging, for he knew of just the fellow, a visitor from Ludlow, he believed.

While Harthill went in search of the gentleman from Ludlow, Kitty swooped down on her sister, determined to break up the tête-à-tête even if she could not send the earl packing.

"There you are, Fran! Mr. Harthill wishes to introduce you to a gentleman from Ludlow, I believe, just in time for the final set before supper. I do hope your lordship will excuse her. By the by, a young lady seemed to be in search of you. I did not think you knew anyone in these parts."

"I do not. I daresay she will find me if she wishes." The earl made a small bow to the sisters and excused himself promptly.

"At least he has the decency to withdraw where he is not wanted."

"Kitty, you are uncharitable. He has behaved with perfect decorum. We simply took a turn or two about the room because he does not dance. Surely it would have seemed far more peculiar if I had cut him after he spent weeks under our roof?"

"I suppose so," replied Kitty with ill grace, craning her head as she sought out Harthill and the elusive Ludlow man.

The earl wandered through to the room where refreshments were being served before supper. He stood in a line for drinks, wishing for something stronger than orgeat or lemonade. He felt a tug at his elbow and turned.

"Sally! Mrs. Featherton! What on earth are you doing here?"

It was the kitten-faced woman, her watery blue eyes steady, but her fingers trembling as they fastened onto his sleeve.

"I only just arrived and here I find you at a dance but not dancing. What have you been up to?"

He loosened her grasp with a wince. "That's the arm I've recently broken, Mrs. Featherton—a little lighter with your touch, if you please."

She dropped her arm as though burnt.

"Broken? And you're walking with a stick!"

"There was an accident with my curricle. But you have not answered my question. What are you doing in Nantwich? And a further question for you—where is Mr. Featherton?"

Sally Featherton smiled nervously. "I am here on my own." She lowered her voice. "I must speak with you privately."

"Not here. Can it wait?" Foreboding crept over the earl.

"I am at The Crown. Will you visit me there tomorrow?"

"I shall."

"Very well, I shall return there now. I do not wish to

cause you any embarrassment." Sally lowered her eyes as she spoke and Lazenby wondered whether for once she meant what she said. But she withdrew and he watched as she left the Assembly Rooms without further contact with its occupants.

Soon after, Lady Dorfold approached him.

"If you are tiring, we are quite ready to return home. Sir Richard has allowed me my dance and I have allowed him his discussions with the menfolk."

"I would be glad to see my bed."

"Very well, we shall call the carriage."

As the earl sat in the carriage, he tried to formulate a plausible excuse to bring him into Nantwich the following morning. He could not yet ride, so it involved calling out a carriage, although he could not see the Dorfolds resenting this in their visitor. It came to him then, that of course, he had not seen his own cattle in some while. He would tell a lie and say that Miss Wilbraham had invited him to visit her stables to inspect the pair of bays. He would go to The Crown and send to Dysart House to ask if it was convenient, then he could go there after seeing Sally.

Sally Featherton. His mistress, off and on for eighteen months now, and increasingly off, as she became more clinging. Mrs. Featherton had assured him that Mr. Featherton was a complaisant husband. A dull and dry lawyer with no interest in his wife or her passions. Sally was an opportunistic vixen with a taste for the high life and an enjoyable lack of scruples. All very well for letting off steam, never a long-term proposition. He had to give her credit for tracking him down. But she had looked drawn and nervy as a filly tonight. Something was badly wrong.

The next morning found the earl at The Crown before ten, calling for Mrs. Featherton, Bloxham noted. She was installed in a private parlor before a fire which snapped and crackled as a maid added more fuel. Bloxham ushered the earl through the door from the hallway, leaving it open. The earl waited, hat in hand for the maid to finish her work. She bobbed a curtsey as she left. He closed the door firmly behind her. There was a curtain which could be drawn across it to diminish the draught. He pulled it with a rattle of brass rings against the rail. There was another door across the room, leading, the earl assumed, to Sally's quarters. The curtain across that was already drawn.

"Good morning, your lordship." Sally was seated in a wing-chair by the fire. The earl strode over to lean on the mantel.

"Good morning to you, Mrs. Featherton."

She looked up at him. "You did not used to be so distant."

"Don't play games with me, Sally. I repeat my question of last night. What are you doing here?"

"I've come in search of you."

"So I gather. Why? Where is Mr. Featherton, what are you doing travelling the countryside unaccompanied? I want answers, Sally, no shilly-shallying."

"I—my husband—he . . ." Sally was unusually flustered.

"He's found out that you've been unfaithful?"

"Yes. But that's not all." She chewed at her lip and wrung her hands. Then she rubbed at her temples before standing and pacing the room.

"What more can there be?" Lazenby felt impatient now. All he wanted to know was when to expect the irate husband and whether the lawyer was the sort to challenge him to a duel. He stood, his arms folded, his face implacable, waiting for Mrs. Featherton to speak, to explain.

"Can't you guess?" Sally looked at him beseechingly

as if she hoped but did not expect the earl to lift all the burdens weighing upon her.

The earl met her gaze. For the first time, she looked him full in the eye, steadily, without wavering.

"You are carrying a child. My child." He spoke simply, as though he had heard this before.

"It can only be your child. It cannot be Mr. Featherton's." Sally swallowed. "He—we—there had been no relations between us for some months. There was only you. I swear there was only you."

The earl closed his eyes and suppressed the urge to curse at length and vividly before a lady. Before a woman who had not acted as a lady should, and was now paying the price. His eyes opened and he saw Sally watching him fearfully, tears welling, hands clasped tight together. "You do believe me?"

"Yes, my dear, I do believe you." At this, Sally sank back into the chair, convulsed with sobs.

"I'm so relieved. You'll look after me, won't you? I know you will. I know I've been wicked and careless, but I prayed and prayed I'd find you, then I did. He sent me away. He'd been watching me all the time, watching to see what sort of trouble I'd get myself into. I didn't realize. He came to me the night I discovered I'd missed two of my monthly courses. The very night, as though he'd been counting. He said . . ." Her face crumpled afresh. "He said it was one thing watching me act the strumpet, but it was another to raise my bastard. He said I must go and never come back. The very next day. That was a week ago. I went to Edenbridge. I saw your Mrs. Bytham. Your housekeeper. She told me where you were, said she'd heard from Soames."

The earl flinched. So all his people knew of this blunder. The whole county would know soon enough. Not that it was the sort of thing that could remain a secret.

"Why didn't you write? It would have been forwarded to me here."

"I had nowhere to go. Only a little money. I told you, he said I must go. I didn't know where to go. I thought, if I came here, if I saw you, you'd know what I should do."

Lazenby felt like repudiating the whole damnable mess, sending Sally away, disappearing himself, and pretending the affair had never happened. But he could not. No pretence could mask his guilt, no disappearance could assuage his guilt, and Sally must be cared for. He knelt down in front of her and took her hands.

"There, there, Sally. I'll make sure you're looked after. I would marry you, but that won't be possible before the babe is born, but I'll make a home for you and the child. I promise." As he spoke, he felt a great weight settling about him, a darkness descending, as though he were entering a cell and hearing a great wooden door close behind him, a key grate in the lock and bolts creaking into position. He pulled away from her. "I was planning on leaving for Edenbridge next week, but we'll go in a day or two, together. I'll hire a carriage and take you with me. I'm just going to check my horses now. Do you have enough money to stay here for another two nights?"

"Yes, I believe so. But you can't take me back to Edenbridge. Everyone will know, they'll sneer, I cannot stay there."

"I'll take you to London. We'll find you a house, some servants. Don't worry, Sally, I will take care of you." He paced the room.

"But you won't stay with me, will you? Even if you could marry me, it would never be a true marriage. You'll never touch me again. Lord, I've been such a fool!" White-faced, she stood up. "Go on then. Look to your horses. I'll try to be as little trouble as possible."

The earl took his hat, gloves, and stick from the table

where he'd laid them down in anticipation of a short, sharp visit, then came toward Sally.

"You're the mother of the only child I'm likely to have. You will always have my respect and support."

She looked up at him ruefully. "But not your love. I've never had that, and I never will now. Still, you'll be a fine father, I see that."

"Either I'll come and see you tomorrow, or I'll send a message to tell you when to be ready." He made for the door. Just as he was leaving, he turned and looked at her one last time. "I'm sorry, Sally. I was careless and you've endured misery because of it. I'll try to make sure you don't suffer any more."

"Until tomorrow then." By the time she had finished speaking, he was gone, the door closed behind him. She went to it, looked round the room, astonished that it seemed impervious to the great scene it had just witnessed, and went upstairs to her own room.

Seconds later, the other curtain was drawn back. Lionel Tollemache stepped into the empty room, from a small alcove. Rarely had he had so interesting a morning. He went to the fire and stirred up the coals in the grate, then sat in the wing-chair, contemplating exactly how he proposed to use the information he had just gathered so painlessly.

Nine

Lazenby walked out of The Crown Hotel steadily and walked as briskly as he was able down Churchyardside to Dysart House. He went round to the mews where the horses were kept and called out to a young groom.

"Is Tarbuck about?"

"I'll fetch him for you, sir."

The stableman appeared in minutes and showed the earl to the stalls where his pair of bays were happily feeding.

"They're doing well, and we shall miss exercising them. A fine pair. I've had them between the traces several times now and they show no signs of discomfort or worry."

"That's something. I had feared the accident would have unfitted them for future use as carriage horses. I have no doubt that their state now owes a great deal to your ministrations, and I thank you for it."

"No need." Tarbuck turned at the sound of footsteps. "Ah, here's mistress now."

Fran came into the stables, bearing secaturs and a basket. "Is that you, Tarbuck?"

"It is. I'm with the earl, inspecting his mounts."

Fran turned to Lazenby and smiled. "When you are finished, my lord, perhaps you'd care to join me for some tea."

"I have had a chance to express my thanks to Tarbuck,

so I can join you now, if it is convenient." Her smile faded as she registered his serious tone and solemn expression. She paused, then shrugged.

"Very well, accompany me to the glasshouses. I'm just going to get some flowers and fruit for the table this evening."

The earl followed Fran. It had not been his intention to speak to her today, but he knew that one way or another, he must tell her the truth. There would never be a right time to explain that he could never court her, that as soon as he was able, he would move to some quiet corner of Italy with Sally Featherton and their illegitimate child. He swallowed at the prospect of her reaction. Her petticoats rustled as she stepped through the door of the glasshouse. She turned to watch him closing the door. The air was heavy with moisture and heat.

"What is wrong? You look utterly beset."

Lazenby smiled ruefully. "I don't know where to begin."

"You need not speak of it if you do not wish." She turned and began testing some peaches and nectarines for ripeness.

"I do not wish, but I must. Fran, there is no hope for me. I shall never offer for you. It is my dearest wish to do so, but there are obstacles and I am not able to propose marriage to you." The earl leaned on his stick, afraid that if he did not, he would hurl it through a pane and into the garden.

"Are you able to explain why this is so?" Fran's tone was calm. Her back was rigid.

"I could, but I should not. It is an unedifying tale." The earl paused. "I will tell you because you have a right to know, and besides, I fear that the tale will come out one way or another. I would prefer you to know the exact truth rather than some garbled nonsense."

"It is something to do with a woman, I daresay. A

mistress." Fran put down her secaturs, twisted round to face him and leaned against a table of seedlings. "I have always known that your past was discreditable. I should have realized that it might catch up with you." She watched him coolly and it came to the earl that she was already withdrawing her warmth from him. He was horrified to find his chest constricting, his throat tightening, symptoms he had not felt since he was a boy, upset, distraught, weeping.

"Yes. It is a woman. But it isn't so simple . . ." Lazenby could not go on.

"Alexander, it is always simple. There is some hold, some call she has on you that you cannot deny. Is she with child?"

He did not respond, gazing downward at the walking stick, its ferrule grating against the brick floor. Finally, he raised his eyes to meet her steady gaze. He nodded.

"So you must marry her, clearly, and legitimize the child. But wait, surely she's like all your paramours. Surely she's married." Her hands gripping the handle of the basket, Fran kept going, knowing that she was piecing together a tale that was giving immense anguish to both Lazenby and herself. But she wanted him to hurt. She wanted him to suffer as much as she was suffering. She wanted him to feel as though someone was peeling away his skin and lashing at the nerves below, she wanted him to feel as though someone had punched him in the gut or the chest, she wanted him to be in pain. She released the basket and looked down at her palms, red with the imprint of the handle. "There's no question of marrying her. Which means that if you are taking her on, there will be a great scandal."

"She is married. Her husband has repudiated her. I must look after her. She is my responsibility. There will be a scandal, but she is not of great interest to the *ton*, being the wife of a humble lawyer. Still, I shall take her to the Continent."

Fran gave a wan smile. She drew breath and looked away, holding back tears. He would not have been the man she loved if he had not spoken those words, but they were the death-knell of her hopes. It was her turn to remain silent.

"I never loved her, Fran. I never knew what love was before I met you and now it is too late for me. But please, Fran, let it not be too late for you. Leave this place, leave your family, travel, meet people. There are better men than I, by far, and you could easily love someone much worthier than I could ever be."

"Of course I could. That's why I am a spinster in a provincial town instead of a wife and a mother, because I can love so easily and so lightly."

"Sarcasm doesn't become you, Frances."

"Remorse is a poor substitute for your affection." Fran shook her head, as if to clear the fog that had descended on it. "At least no one but you and I know of my great folly. You will go and I shall carry on, withstanding this suitor and that."

"Are you sure you will withstand them? What about the Tollemaches? They won't wear you down?"

"It is not your place to ask that sort of question, Earl Lazenby, but I shall answer. No, they will not wear me down. I could no more marry Lionel Tollemache than I could marry Billy the stable-boy. And sooner or later the Honorable Lionel will discover this for himself, and I shall have merry hell to pay with my sister and her husband." She sighed. "You are right, of course, I should leave here. Now that Sir Arthur is safely home, there is no reason for me to stay in Nantwich. None at all."

"I want to ask where you will go, what you will do, but I have forfeited the right to do that. All I can say, Frances, is

that wherever you go, you will always be in my thoughts."
Lazenby drew himself up, readying himself to leave. "You
won't hear from me again."

They looked at one another. Each wanted to ask the
other for some keepsake, some memento of their weeks
of friendship, each wanted this moment to last forever,
suspended in time. The earl took a step forward, then
backed away. Fran's eyes were large with longing, with
her unspoken question.

"No. I won't. It would make it even harder on us both.
If I touch you, it will hurt even more. Please, Fran, just
look away."

"Not even one kiss?"

"Not even one kiss."

"Very well." She bent and picked up the basket,
turned away and collected up her secaturs. The last sight
the earl had of her was her back, as she walked up to the
end of the glasshouse, gently pulling a gardenia blossom
towards her and brushing it against her cheek.

He left the glasshouse. She heard the snick of the
latch as the door closed behind him. Her head felt
woolly and clouded. She must not cry. She must give no
signs of distress, not now, not ever. Perhaps, if she was
very quiet, she might weep into her pillow at night, but
right now, she wanted to tear at her clothes and wail and
tug at her hair and sob until her eyes were puffed and
her skin streaked red and she could not give way to the
rage and the sorrow eating at her. She could have hurled
flowerpots at the head of the retreating earl, slapped
him, pummelled his chest and screamed at him like a
harpy for being such a profligate fool with his favors.
Instead, she must contain herself and maintain her self-
control. There was a tall stool by the seedling table. She
put the basket down, leaned against it, arms crossed
tight as though she were holding herself together. Then

she pulled herself together, picked up the basket, and returned to the house. She was astonished to find it was not yet mid-day. She went to her bedroom and sat at the writing desk there. Finally, she reached for her pen and ink and drew out a piece of paper. It was time to arrange her escape.

As for the earl, he walked slowly back towards The Crown, where the Dorfolds' carriage was waiting for him. He did not feel ready to enter its confines just yet, he certainly did not feel equal to returning to Dorfold Hall and making himself pleasant or explaining his need to depart the following day with a strange woman in his entourage, either to his hosts or to Soames. None of the parties in question would make any comment or pass any judgment, he knew, but they would all be disappointed.

He passed by the stationer's and entered, on impulse. The store was empty of customers so he was eagerly greeted by the proprietor. He asked for charcoal and paper. These were bundled up for him promptly and once again, he found himself heading back to the inn. The Dorfolds' coach was standing outside, the coachman waiting on the box. Lazenby looked up at him.

"I am going walking by the River Weaver. You may take the coach back to the Hall, I am ready to walk back without assistance. Please let Lady Dorfold know that I shall return sometime this afternoon, perhaps between three and four."

The coachman nodded in assent and the earl watched as he cracked his whip and set off for home. It was probably foolhardy to attempt to walk the miles to Dorfold Hall, but the pain was deserved and might prove a welcome distraction from the deeper ache which assailed Lazenby. He headed for the riverside, crossing the bridge and walking southward on the river's left bank. Once away from Nantwich, he sat down in the shade of a chestnut tree and unpacked his parcel from the stationers and started sketching. It was Fran's face that took shape on the paper, at first small rudimentary doodles at different angles, then a larger, more detailed portrait as though he were trying to engrave the image of her onto his memory.

He would have to leave England with Sally. He would take her to London, settle her there for a month and return to Edenbridge to put his affairs in order and then they would go to some quiet place where he could afford a house big enough to accommodate them both without having to encounter one another on a daily basis. He would offer Soames the opportunity of leaving his employ, he would cut all ties with home and he would see this child raised and provided for. As for Sally, any spark of attraction that had flared between them was now quite doused. How it would be, living with a woman he could not love, he could not imagine. Everything seemed desolate to him.

By contrast, matters had never looked so promising to Lionel Tollemache. He was not sure what use he would make of the information he had gathered while hiding in the alcove of The Crown, but he was sure that the information would be useful at some point. It certainly gave him the confidence to call at Dysart House and ask if Miss Fran was at home. He was admitted into the drawing room, where she joined him some ten minutes later. She was wearing a fetching ensemble of blue kerseymere, he noticed, that blue that painters seemed to use so often for the robes of madonnas, and she gave off an air of serenity to match the color of her dress.

"Mr. Tollemache, we do not usually see you so early. Sir Arthur and Kitty are out, viewing a house, I believe." She took a seat in an armchair by the fireplace, inviting him to sit opposite her.

"So they are determined to settle here." He crossed his legs and drummed his fingers on his thigh as he spoke.

"Yes, it is convenient to Liverpool where Sir Arthur's business takes him and it is Kitty's home, after all. There does not seem to be any great advantage in uprooting themselves to a new and distant part of the world."

He leaned forward, hands clasped together. "It will make you very happy to have them close at hand, I imagine."

"Of course, though I plan to travel a little once they are safely settled."

"Travel? Where to? With whom?" Tollemache was alarmed—this was not part of his plans.

"I am hoping to go to France and Italy in the spring. Friends of my father's go there every year, and I shall accompany them. I have written to ask their plans this very morning. They have often pressed me to join them, so I am sure we shall be able to come to some arrangement."

"Miss Wilbraham! It seems so precipitate. I was hoping that perhaps . . ." Tollemache's voice trailed off, then he rallied. "I was hoping that you would consent to a trip to Italy with me. A wedding trip." Tollemache stood up. "Miss Wilbraham." He knelt before her. "Would you do me the honor of accepting my hand in marriage?"

She looked at him. Slim, his coat beautifully cut, his linen exquisitely arranged, his hair brushed, his eyes intent, he was, she supposed, the answer to a maiden's prayer. But not her prayer.

"Mr. Tollemache, you do me a great and signal honor, but I cannot marry you. Please do not hope for anything more than friendship from me."

"Is your answer quite irrevocable?" He rose up and stood, brushing himself down as if her carpet were the dustiest he had ever knelt on.

"I am afraid it is."

Mr. Tollemache shook his head in disbelief. "There is nothing I can say to alter your disposition?"

"Nothing. It is not you, Mr. Tollemache, who is at fault. The fault is mine entirely." Fran wondered when he would start to understand.

"Your affections lie elsewhere?"

"They do."

"So I may expect to hear a happy announcement in the near future?"

"Mr. Tollemache, you are not alone in being disappointed in your expectations. You will not be hearing any happy announcements concerning my future. That is why I am proposing to travel." Fran deliberately failed to invite the Honorable Lionel to sit in the hope that he would take the hint and withdraw. But her words seemed to stun him into taking up his old position opposite her.

"Well. I see." He gazed into the fire for some moments. "There is no prospect that you might change your mind once you have returned from your travels?"

"None. I must be frank with you, Mr. Tollemache, I think it highly unlikely that I shall ever marry and it would be unfair to suggest to you that I might alter my intentions." It was very tempting to state bluntly that in the unlikely event that she should wish to marry, the Honorable Lionel would not be a strong candidate, but bluntness was not Fran's way. Besides, she did not wish to create ill feeling between herself and her sister's family. "Perhaps it would be best if we mentioned nothing of this to Sir Arthur or Kitty."

"Perhaps. They will find it very curious. Lady Tollemache has been so encouraging. I feel somewhat misled, I must confess."

"I am very sorry to hear it." Fran wished to wring her sister's neck. How Kitty could have fooled herself into believing that Fran would marry Lionel Tollemache, she did not know. "I know that it is one of my sister's dearest wishes to see me settled, but I had not realized it had gone so far. I must work harder to make her realize that marriage, even to so personable a gentleman as yourself, is not the summit of my ambitions."

Lionel Tollemache smiled wanly in acknowledgment of Fran's compliment. What he truly wished to know was the identity of her unattainable lover. Surely he could get her to let slip some information about the mysterious object of her affections.

"So we are both disappointed in love!" Tollemache shook his head. "It is a terrible business, is it not?"

"I do not propose to dwell on it. Distraction may, I feel, be the most effective medicine for this complaint." Fran was determined to be robust in her suitor's presence. She thought it highly unlikely that love had played any part in his offer for her, although of course, it would be rude to say so.

"It creeps up upon one so. Why, only a few weeks ago, I was fancy-free and now I am in the throes of unrequited fervor. Was it the same for you, Miss Wilbraham?"

"Not precisely."

"Ah, you have been nursing a passion for some time, then. But what strange creature could be so foolish as to ignore a woman as fine as you?"

"I would really prefer not to discuss this further, Mr. Tollemache." Would the man never leave? Fran felt increasingly desperate. Fortunately, her sister and Sir Arthur burst into the drawing room at this point.

"Fran, what good fortune to find you here. The most marvellous chance, a house has come up only a few miles away, and we are off to look at it this afternoon, unless you need the carriage. Otherwise, we can hire one from The Crown, I daresay. It sounds perfect, the old

Egerton place, the one that has been standing empty since he died. His heirs are in dispute about whether to sell it or live in it, and the whole tangle will take years to resolve, so they are letting it in the interim. Do you know the house?" Kitty was clearly itching to have her own household after all these years of living under Fran's rule.

"That is excellent news, my dear."

"Tollemache, my dear fellow, why don't you accompany us? And you too, sister?" offered Sir Arthur. "We could make an expedition of it."

"My morning has been somewhat interrupted and I am behind in my duties, so I will not accompany you, Sir Arthur, but Mr. Tollemache must see this place. It is a charming location, I know, and he will be able to advise you on all sorts of matters." Fran was quick to suggest the plan, desperate for some time to herself.

It was agreed swiftly enough that the Tollemache party would set out after a brief collation. Fran and Kitty withdrew to neaten themselves up before eating. Kitty accompanied Fran to her room. As soon as the door was shut behind them, she clutched her sister's arm.

"Fran, what has happened? Has he offered for you? He was asking me whether he should or not, and I told him to put it to the touch."

"Kitty, why didn't you ask me first? You could have saved us both a great deal of discomfort. He did make an offer and I turned him down, as I would have told you I should if you had only thought to consult me."

"You turned him down! But he's the son of an earl!"

"He could be the son of the Great Panjandrum for all I care. I will not marry without love, and I do not love Lionel Tollemache. I never will."

"Fran, how can you be so maddening! He is so respectable. He worships you."

"He worships nobody so much as himself. He doesn't have the slightest bit of feeling for me, not that it would do him any good if he did."

"What do you mean?"

"Kitty, I love someone else. It would be utterly wrong of me to accept an offer from anyone other than the man I love, and he cannot offer for me."

"Who do you love, Fran?" Kitty looked at her sister with increasing suspicion. "You didn't love anyone a few weeks ago. Who have you fallen in love with? If it isn't Mr. Tollemache, who is it?"

Fran stood silent and defiant as Kitty glared at her. "Who can it be? If it isn't Mr. Tollemache, who can it be?"

Fran made no answer.

"Lazenby. It's the earl, isn't it?" Kitty put her hands on her hips. "If you have anything more to do with that man, Frances Lucy Wilbraham, I shall never speak to you so long as I live."

"Sadly, Kitty, you will have the opportunity to speak to me at length however long you live, since nothing will come of this attachment. However, if you do choose to speak to me, I should prefer it if you would avoid this subject entirely." Fran felt her fragile control finally slip. "And Kitty, I should prefer it above all things if you never in future speak to anyone on my behalf about *any* matter. You had absolutely no right to suggest to Mr. Tollemache that I might entertain an offer from him. And while you were perfectly at liberty to invite him to Nantwich, you were not, nor are you at liberty to invite anyone you choose to Dysart House. I have had enough of your meddling and your carping and your general interference in my life, Kitty, and I will not have it any more. You may keep your opinions to yourself. I shall do as I please."

Fran's bitter words froze Kitty to the spot. Some degree

of her sister's misery penetrated Kitty's carapace of self-absorption.

"Fran? Fran, I only want you to be happy."

Fran was at the washstand, soaping and rinsing her hands, her back rigid, her shoulders firm, her jaw clenched. Kitty went to her sister and turned her around. Silent tears were coursing down her cheeks.

"Oh, my dear, what has happened?"

Fran simply shook her head. She could not speak yet. Kitty led her to a chair and sat her down, kneeling beside her and holding her hands. Fran's grasp tightened on hers and the tears seemed to come all the faster, but not a sound escaped her lips. Then she cast off Kitty's grasp and walked to the window, wiping her face, her body still shuddering slightly. She pulled out a pocket-handkerchief and blew her nose in a thorough and rather unladylike fashion, went to the washstand and rinsed her face with cool water and sat at her mirror to check how blotchy she had become. Then she turned to Kitty.

"Lazenby is embroiled in a scandal. We will hear about it shortly, so you may as well know now. He is planning to flee the country with one of his mistresses in tow. So there is no question of an offer or indeed any sort of honorable connection between us." Fran spoke the words carefully and calmly.

"How did you come to give your heart to him, Fran?" Kitty could not conceal her exasperation entirely, but there was some sympathy in her question.

"He has his own code of honor. It is a peculiar one, to be sure, but he does live by it and besides all that, he makes me laugh. He understands me. If I said half of what I thought, I should be forever explaining myself, but he does not need me to explain anything to him." Fran rubbed at her temples. "Kitty, make my excuses. I cannot eat just now. But you must go down, and I hope the house is all that you hope for. I'll be fully myself by dinner."

From this, Kitty understood that her sister was a hopeless case indeed. There was no help for it but to go down and comfort poor rejected Mr. Tollemache.

Ten

Sitting down to a light meal, Kitty was delighted to take the hostess' role, although her pleasure in this was diminished by the knowledge of Fran's follies. Discretion fought with an impulse to tell all to her husband, regardless of Mr. Tollemache's presence. Impulse was the victor in this battle, so Mr. Tollemache discovered the identity of his rival promptly and was suitably shocked.

How a woman of Miss Wilbraham's sterling judgment and character could have allowed herself to become entangled with a seducer of Lazenby's type defied explanation. It also angered him. He did not blame Miss Wilbraham. She was a sheltered and gently bred woman and the weaker sex were notoriously susceptible. But he did blame the earl for queering his pitch. There were plenty of women to whom the earl could have made up to with no infringement of Mr. Tollemache's plans, but no, the one woman who he had been able to identify as suitable for his matrimonial aspirations must be got at by this Lothario. It did not cross the mind of the Honorable Lionel that Miss Wilbraham might have rejected his proposal even if she had never met the earl. It was more convenient and more plausible to blame the earl entirely for his lack of success with the lady.

But he had at hand a tool for his revenge. He did not reveal, when Kitty spoke of the imminent scandal that was to descend on Lazenby, that he knew all about it. He disclaimed all knowledge of Mrs. Featherton when Kitty asked if he had not encountered her at The Crown.

"It is a large establishment and of course, you have been so generous with your time and hospitality here that I am scarcely there. No, I have missed the lady and can tell you nothing about her."

"It's just as well the scandal has arisen, Kitty, otherwise this Lazenby would be sniffing around your sister still. As it is, he must leave Nantwich straight away." Sir Arthur hooked his thumbs in his waistcoat and patted at his stomach as he spoke. "Perhaps it has worked out for the best. Lionel may come and stay with us after Christmas and we shall renew our suit in his favor. What do you say, cousin?"

"I say that it is most kind of you to suggest this."

"Of course cousin Lionel is welcome at any time, to stay for as long as he wishes. But I must tell you, once Fran has made up her mind, there is little hope of changing it. If she has refused Mr. Tollemache now, I do not think a few months will make any difference." Kitty continued. "It is also most unfortunate that there should be this scandal. It is just the thing to make the earl seem even more romantic, however immoral. It would have been much better if she could have worn out her attachment to him by seeing him flirt and make up to other women. That would have given her a true disgust of him."

Lionel Tollemache could not help acknowledging the truth in Kitty's words. A love which encounters unsurmountable obstacles was bound to last longer than an attraction worn thin by exposure to the earl's rakish ways in society. None of the Tollemaches doubted that the earl would have continued in his rakish ways: leopards do not change their spots and old dogs do not adjust easily to new regimes.

He wanted to make the earl's life difficult. He wanted to make the earl pay for ruining his prospects with the Wilbraham girl. He wanted revenge, but could not think of how to secure it just yet. Then it came to him. He must make it seem as though the earl had cast off Mrs. Featherton. In offering Mrs. Featherton his protection, the earl was behaving as well as he could do in the circumstances. But what if Miss Wilbraham (and all of Nantwich, and all of society) could see him spurn her? Or harm her? Even better. What he needed to do was to secure an interview with the fallen woman and pay her off. He might even persuade her to write an incriminating letter accusing the earl of heinous crimes prior to the apparent rejection.

Acting swiftly was key. He must secure an interview with Mrs. Featherton before evening. And he must also go and see this house the Tollemaches had found.

"Let me collect a sketch-book and my chalks before we set off. It will take me only a few minutes to stop in at The Crown and I should so like to send a sketch of your new home to the family." This notion appealed greatly to Sir Arthur and Kitty, who always liked to have their doings drawn to the attention of their more exalted relatives.

At The Crown, Mr. Tollemache sat at his desk and penned a swift note.

> *To Mistress Featherton:*
> *You may learn something to your advantage concerning*
> *Earl Lazenby if you come to the weir on the River*
> *Weaver at six o'clock this evening.*
>
> *A friend.*

He threw sand over the paper and shook it off, then re-read the note. She had sounded venal, this Mrs. Featherton, and this was the sort of letter that might appeal to a venal woman. Certainly if he received such a missive, he would respond. He gave the note to a chambermaid with some pennies and strict instructions that it should be delivered immediately. He then joined the Tollemaches to inspect their new home. He had hoped that Miss Wilbraham might be brought to join them, but she was not in the carriage when he returned to Dysart House.

The chambermaid carried out her commission with alacrity. Sally Featherton took the note and read it in wonder. She had been quite careful both at the Assembly and at the inn, so it surprised her that anyone might think she was especially interested in the earl. But she was never one to turn down an opportunity for more information. Or money. Could the word "advantage" mean money? She was extremely short just now, for Mr. Featherton had turned her out with nothing more than her pin money and she had had to spend nearly all that on travelling across the country. The earl would certainly settle her account at The Crown, but it would be nice to have a little extra tucked away.

Her room being chilly, Sally left for this meeting early. Better to be out and about than freezing away under the eaves of the inn. It was not a long walk from The Crown to the weir, but the shift from the activity of the streets of the town to the quiet of the riverbank was marked and, initially, restful. Sally Featherton had never been one to take much notice of nature's glories, and no wonder, for in the gathering dusk the shadow of the great horse chestnut trees and elms, their dying leaves rustling in the slight breeze that came off the river, began to seem gloomy and oppressive. There might once have been river traffic but a canal had been built nearby and now the river was deserted, not even a boy fishing as far as she could see. As she approached the weir, she heard the rush of water.

She stood under a tree and watched as the evening light deepened, wondering what would become of her. She wished her husband had been more complaisant, for she was quite fond of him when not bored to tears by their life together. A child might have improved things. But he had already started complaining about how her reputation was affecting business and he would never be able to keep this scandal from the townsfolk and people all around Edenbridge. Whether it was a sense of remorse for the pain she was causing her husband or whether it was simply the chill of the autumn evening seeping into her bones, Sally began to feel cold. She paced about, moving from tree to tree because as darkness gathered, she felt increasingly uncomfortable and the trees provided at least some shelter and defence. She spotted a stray glove and picked it up. Someone had dropped it, a man, she thought from the size. It was made of fawn kidskin, a supple, delicate material. Distractedly, she shoved it in a pocket of her cloak.

The prospect of living in quiet seclusion with the earl was daunting. She knew full well that he had never loved her, simply dallied with her to pass the time. She had expected him to repudiate her and in some ways, it might have been easier if he had. She certainly did not love him. She had liked his fine looks, she had imagined that he would shower her with jewels and pretty dresses, she had wanted to meet his racy companions. She had believed he would provide her with excitement, an alternative to the stifling round which was the lot of provincial wives of some standing. But he had not. Beyond the thrill of flirtation and the danger of assignations, there had been nothing, for the earl had been casually careful in keeping her separate from the rest of his life. His response to her pleas for parties or excursions had been to agree carelessly enough without ever actually exerting himself to make any firm arrangements. He was a slippery customer.

At last, she heard someone approaching. In the dim light she saw a gangling figure in an olive shooting jacket and maroon waistcoat coming towards her. She remained in the shadow of the tree as he came to a halt and looked around him.

"Mrs. Featherton?" he called in a low voice. She waited. He called again.

"Who are you?" she asked. He came toward her.

"My name is Lionel Tollemache."

"What could you possibly tell me to my advantage?" Her voice was sharp, edged with nerves, for she did not like being here, alone, away from the light and the bustle of the town.

Tollemache spoke bluntly. "I come from the earl. He has changed his mind, he does not wish to be burdened by you or the child."

"That, even if I were to believe it, is hardly to my advantage." Sally Featherton sounded imperious. Underneath, it felt as though the ground were giving way beneath her. But she would not let this stranger see that.

"He loves another woman. Imagine if this woman ever found out about you. She would repudiate him." Tollemache extemporized wildly. "Write to him. Explain you will reveal all to this lady unless he pays you."

"Why are you telling me this? How do you know so much of the earl's affairs?"

"I am related to the lady. And I am horrified by his treatment of you. He does not deserve the happiness of her fortune and her person."

Sally was still suspicious. "How does any of this help me? What do you have to offer me?"

"I'll take you to London and establish you there. Believe

me, the earl wants nothing more to do with you. I am your only hope."

"Do you know, sir, I don't believe you. Not for a minute. I shall go back to the inn and send a messenger to the earl at Dorfold Hall to discover whether this is true or not." She made to go back, but Tollemache lost his head and grabbed her.

"No, you can't." He held onto her. She tried to shake him off.

"What do you mean by this, sir? Unhand me, if you please."

"I won't. You can't contact the earl. He's left already." Sally struggled in his grasp and they were carried a little towards the river. He shifted his hold on her, his arms encircling her from behind. "I won't let you go until you promise to do as I say."

Sally panicked and started kicking out, wriggling furiously in his arms. "No, I don't believe you, and if you hurt me, the earl will find out. Leave me be, let me go." She writhed and squirmed, and Tollemache, not being quite strong enough to keep her entirely under his control, found himself being carried along by her movements. He couldn't let her go, nor could he quite force her to do as he pleased. Unused to physical exertion, he was surprised to discover the extent of this woman's strength.

"Stop it, stop struggling. I don't wish to hurt you. Just do as I say and all will be well."

Sally misunderstood entirely. "Never," she screamed and started calling out for help, convinced that this man was about to assault her. Tollemache tried to stifle her cries by covering her mouth, but as he moved his arm up, she wrenched out of his grasp, lost her balance and careened into the river itself with a great splash. In shock, Tollemache stood open-mouthed as she rose once and called for help again, thrashing at the water. Then she sank down beneath its depths and disappeared.

What should he do? He stood frozen by the bank, watching the dark water rushing past on its way to the weir. Would she come up again? He strained to see, but by now night had fallen completely. There was only the sound of the water and the trees. Surely it was too late to get help? He backed away from the riverbank hesitantly. No one knew he had come out here. There was nothing to connect him with this woman. Perhaps no one would even notice her disappearance.

He returned to The Crown. He had come straight from Dysart House to this meeting, telling Sir Arthur and Kitty that he would dine this night at the hotel. He made it clear that this was a mark of his sensitivity towards Miss Wilbraham, who was clearly still overset by the earl's wanton ways.

Tollemache retired to his room and sent his man down to fetch him some dinner. He checked his appearance in the cheval glass in the dressing room. He looked a little ruffled about, but nothing out of the ordinary way. Mrs. Featherton, for all her struggling, had not left a mark on him, as far as he could see. Thank heavens.

At first, he did not think he would be able to eat, but then, the pie smelled so fragrant, and the beans looked so very fresh and the gravy so very rich that it seemed a shame not to taste them. And once he had tasted them, it would be an insult to the cook not to finish them. The claret that Bloxham had sent up was not of the highest quality, but it certainly drowned (perhaps an unfortunate choice of words) the memory of Mrs. Featherton's face sinking beneath the—another glass obliterated that train of thought. A spot of trifle did wonders for the digestion.

As he sipped some port and warmed his feet before the fire, Tollemache wondered what the earl would do about Mrs. Featherton's disappearance. Perhaps he would simply think it opportune and forget about her. That, of course, was what he himself would do. Would she be washed up? If her body did appear again, perhaps it would simply be dismissed as an accident, a slip of the foot. Well, it had been an accident, he had certainly not intended that she fall in the river. He wondered about the note he had written. What if her room was searched and it was discovered? Well, no one knew his writing. Perhaps he should try to find out her room and retrieve the letter. Or perhaps she had brought it with her, in which case it would probably be destroyed in the water.

One moment, he found himself calm and sanguine, the next, agitated and full of questions. But Tollemache strove to appear without a care in the world to his man and such servants of the hotel as he saw that evening, and if he turned and tossed in his bed, there were no witnesses to see it.

The earl had a far less comfortable night. He had sat on the riverbank, sketching first Miss Wilbraham and then the scene itself, the trees, the reeds, the river, both above and below the weir, until after three. He had not eaten all day. Finally, he levered himself up on his stick and set off for Dorfold Hall, nearly three miles away. Normally, he could have walked this in well under an hour, but he found himself stopping and resting his leg more often than he liked, and when a carter came up, he availed himself of the opportunity to ride with the man for the last stretch of the road. It was in the cart that he discovered that he had dropped one of his gloves somewhere along the way. The carter offered to take him back, but though he knew Soames would nag, the earl was conscious that he could have lost it at any point from leaving

Dysart House, and to retread all that ground was too time-consuming. The glove would have to remain lost. A stray glove was hardly a major calamity in the grand mess he had made out of his life.

On arriving at Dorfold Hall, he asked a footman if Lady Dorfold was free. He dreaded the interview, but he might as well get it over with. He was shown into her private parlor, easier to keep warm now that autumn was upon them than the more imposing public rooms. She gestured to a chair, then continued with her stitching.

"You have done well today, walking back much of the way from Nantwich, I understand. Progress indeed." Her needle flew in and out of the canvas. She did not comment on how very weary he looked.

By now, the earl was accustomed to her slightly roundabout method of interrogation. He did not wait for her to ask what he had been up to in Nantwich.

"I was called into Nantwich by a young woman of my acquaintance. You may have seen her at the Assembly the night before last."

"I didn't notice. I was too busy watching the Tollemaches promoting the Honorable Lionel to Frances. I did not know you had any other acquaintance in the area." Lady Dorfold quirked an eyebrow.

"I do not. Mrs. Featherton is from my home. She came in search of me."

"Ah." She held out the tapestry and checked its colors.

"I will have to escort her away from Nantwich, and I must inform you that there is about to be an unholy scandal." The earl could not carry on. Lady Dorfold folded up her work and turned her full attention to the earl.

"Has she run away from Mr. Featherton?"

"Worse. He has turned her out."

"Oh dear. On account of you?"

"Yes. There is more. She is with child."

"Does Frances know all this?"

"Yes. I went straight to her after I saw Mrs. Featherton at The Crown." The earl sat back in his chair and closed his eyes as though to ward off the memory of this encounter. Lady Dorfold bit her lip.

"That is something. It would have been very terrible for her to find out at second or third hand. What are your plans now?"

The earl straightened in his seat. "I shall pack up and take Mrs. Featherton away. We will settle somewhere quiet in southern France, on the coast. Nice, perhaps. Or Italy. But I shall leave here tomorrow morning."

"Well, we shall weather the storm." Lady Dorfold did not mention Fran again. Still less did she give way to her impulse to give the earl a good shaking. She should have foreseen that some obstacle of this nature might arise and protected her friend better from this man. Instead, she had given way to a romantic dream of reforming a rake and bringing together two people who did seem entirely right for one another. It was the last time she would attempt to make any matches.

The earl withdrew and went to his room, his limp more pronounced than it had been for some days. Soames was already there, laying out his evening wear. The valet looked up as Lazenby walked in.

"What have you been doing to yourself?" he exclaimed.

Lazenby smiled wryly. "Nothing that you would approve of." He sat down and stretched his leg out, massaging first the thigh, then the shin he had so grievously wounded. "I must ask you to start packing. We leave first thing in the morning."

"What trick is this? I thought you meant to stay on for the shooting here. At least another couple of weeks, maybe even a month. That's what you were saying only yesterday."

"Yes. Well, circumstances have caught up with me, as you have long been predicting. My life is about to alter quite dramatically, Soames, and you may wish to part company with me altogether. Rest assured, your references will be of the very highest, though whether they will be worth anything when it is known that they come from me, I doubt."

"For God's sake, what are you talking about?"

"You have warned me often enough. My sins have caught up with me, Soames, and I must pay the piper. Mrs. Featherton has found me."

The earl unfolded the whole sorry story to his manservant and once again offered to release him. "You could do very much better than me, and if you do not wish to accompany me to the continent, I will understand perfectly."

"Have you spoken with Miss Wilbraham?"

"Lady Dorfold asked me the same thing. I have, as a matter of fact. She knows the whole. I have no secrets."

"How did she take it?"

"She didn't hurl me from the house crying 'Get thee gone, foul fiend,' if that's what you mean. But not well."

"Only to be expected." Soames fidgeted once again with the clothes. "I'll come with you. I'm not leaving you to make a greater mull of things than you have already. Italy is pleasant enough."

Slowly, the earl dressed for dinner and went down to speak to Sir Richard about his imminent departure. Of course, the baronet had already been briefed by Lady Dorfold, not that he thought that it was his place to make any comment on this debacle. But after the meal, over the port, Sir Richard expressed his regret that the earl was not able to stay longer.

"We've enjoyed your company. I'm not one for writing letters, but we should be glad to hear from you from time to time. Lady Dorfold will want to know how you get on."

"I am honored that you do not wish to cease all contact with me. Once I am settled, I will write." The tacit implication that by keeping in touch with the Dorfolds, he might have news of Miss Wilbraham did not escape him. Some crumbs would be better than no sustenance at all.

That night, once he had retired and lay in darkness, the earl could not escape from the memory of Miss Wilbraham standing in the glasshouse, taut with tension and mute fury melded with longing. It was poetic justice that he should not be allowed the one woman he could love, but it seemed a cruel fate that had caused her to give her heart to so unsuitable a man. It may have been only weeks since they met, but he knew her now and was well aware that she was not fickle. She loved him and she would not easily be able to love another.

It was an honest, clear-sighted love. What had she said? "Surely she's like all your paramours." She had no illusions about him. She loved him despite his flaws, not because of them. There had been so many young women who had thrown themselves at them because they wished to change him or because they sought their own corruption. There had never been a lady like Frances who loved him against her better judgment, who shared his interests and turned the full force of her intellect on his opinions and views. She did not meekly agree to his every notion, she did not accept his every dictum, but she showed respect for his brain and demanded that he show equal respect for hers. She scorned the customary games conducted between the sexes. Before the arrival of Mrs. Featherton, he had felt hesitant enough about his desire for her. Now that all his hopes were blighted, he could no longer deny the force of his feeling. He had not wept since he was a boy, but now, in the dark, first one tear and then another trickled from his eyes.

Eleven

The first stage and mail coaches came through Nantwich one after another of a morning, between half past seven and nine o'clock, hard on one another's heels. First there was the Union, then the Telegraph, then the Defiance, then the Bruce, heading for Birmingham, Bristol, Liverpool, and Lincoln. With every arrival, there was bustle and furor. But an arrival on the quarter past eight from Stoke-on-Trent caused the greatest uproar. An etiolated man in his early thirties climbed down from the coach, devoid of baggage and haggard in face. He entered the inn and waited until the coach had pulled away before seeking out Bloxham who was busy in the taproom, serving regulars and those on the stage with tea, coffee, bacon, beef and bread.

"Is there a Mistress Featherton staying here?"

The innkeeper was cautious in giving out particulars to a stranger. "Who wants to know?"

"I am her husband. I wish to see her immediately."

Bloxham sent a girl up to Mrs. Featherton's room. She came down in agitation some minutes later. The patrons of The Crown were all ears as she spoke.

"I knocked and knocked, sir, but there was no answer, so I peeked in. She's not there and her bed's not been slept in."

The little color in Featherton's face drained away, leaving him pallid, his eyes rimmed with red. "Where can she be? Did she have any acquaintance in the town?"

"A gentleman did come to call on her yesterday." Bloxham spoke hesitantly. "Earl Lazenby, I believe. He's staying up at Dorfold Hall. Afterwards, she told me she'd be leaving today and to ready her account."

Featherton appeared to stagger and was clearly on the point of complete collapse. Bloxham was well aware of the curious glances directed at the exhausted man, and the sound of the post horn of another coach pulling up to The Crown reminded him of his other duties.

"You may sit and rest in the corner, sir, while you decide what course of action to take." Bloxham was aware of a sense of disappointment emanating from the assembled company, which had expected him to demand that the husband pay his wife's debts on the double or leave the premises.

The gentleman asked for some coffee to be brought to him and sat in the corner of a settle, his head thrown back, his eyes closed, drained of the capacity to make any decision. He had been travelling through the night and had endured innumerable sleepless nights before then, wrestling with the chaos that his wife had visited on him. He had come all this way, abandoning all his business on what now seemed like a wasted chase after some elusive prey. No one dared approach him, but he received surreptitious glances from most of the company.

As soon as he had turned Sally out, he had regretted it, not because their home was in any way a comfortable one, but because he found that her departure left an even greater chasm than the state of armed neutrality in which they had been living for so many months. And now he discovered she was not suffering as he suffered but would be taken up by the earl and protected. Between them, the earl and Sally had heaped injury and indignity on him and they continued to do so. It was hugely unjust.

The coffee came and he sipped it distractedly. He could send a message to Dorfold Hall. He could wait here to see if Sally came back. He could get on the next stage and return home without making any effort to see her. His mind was befuddled with lack of sleep. What harm would there be in going up to Sally's room and resting?

He called Bloxham and told him he wished to wait in his wife's quarters. The innkeeper was hesitant until Featherton hauled out his wallet and warmed his palm with a guinea.

"Tell me the full amount owing."

"That covers the cost entirely, sir. She's been here but two nights. It's not one of our best rooms."

Featherton could well believe it when the maid showed him up the stairs to the poky chamber. And here, he was baffled, for he found Sally's clothes scattered about the room, nothing packed ready for her departure this morning. He sat at the dressing table and looked over the pot of cream, the bottle of eau-de-cologne, the ribbons, and hair pins. She had been wearing her jewellery, he thought. And then he found in a little purse her wedding ring and finally, grief and weariness caught up with him. He cradled his head in his hands and gave way to the confused rush of emotions that had been threatening him for so long. Great racking sobs shook his body. Where was she now? Why could he not see her and slip this ring on her finger once again?

It was thus that the earl discovered the unfortunate lawyer. He had come to the inn in search of Sally, to warn her that they would be leaving as soon as he had completed the hire of a carriage and collected the bays from Dysart House. Bloxham, looking most shifty, explained that Mrs. Featherton was absent, but that her husband was upstairs in her room. The earl frowned in confusion. What the wronged husband was doing in Nantwich he could not imagine, but clearly he could not spirit the wife away without dealing fairly and squarely with Featherton.

His gentle tap on the door sent it swinging open and he saw the man, hunched on the stool, misery personified. Here was another creature to whom he had brought suffering quite carelessly. How the lawyer would react to his presence he could not guess.

"Mr. Featherton?"

The man looked up, his face streaked with tears, his pallor pronounced.

"I'm Lazenby. I—I'm here for your wife."

"I thought she was already with you," replied Featherton. The men exchanged confused glances then looked round the room as though she would suddenly appear before them as if by magic.

"I told her she needed to be ready to leave by eleven o'clock. But it doesn't look as though she's even begun packing."

"She hasn't been here since yesterday evening. The maid said the bed hasn't been slept in. I just assumed she was with you."

"This is most curious. I'll summon Bloxham. We don't want to quiz him in public, but he may know if she's had any other meetings since arriving here."

The earl peered out of the doorway and called for a servant. A girl came almost immediately. "Fetch Bloxham for me, if you please. I need to see him at once. Tell him Lazenby requires him."

The girl pattered down the stairs and while they were waiting for the innkeeper, the two men looked over Mrs.

Featherton's possessions once again. Lazenby was baffled but not unduly perturbed by her absence, but her husband was nervy and agitated. He fluttered about the room, shifting things from the dressing table to the bed, from the bed to the bedside table. He picked up the book that he found there.

"She took *Castle Rackrent?* What on earth possessed her to elope with *Castle Rackrent?* She is the oddest creature!" Out fell a slip of paper. Featherton read the note and passed it to the earl.

"Who could this be from? What other friends did she have here?"

Lazenby looked it over in complete puzzlement. "None so far as I know. She arrived the day before yesterday, she came to the Assembly Hall that evening and I spoke with her yesterday morning. I am not aware that she knew anyone else in Nantwich."

"So she must have gone to the weir yesterday evening."

Just then, Bloxham came upstairs, puffing at the exertion. Lazenby turned to him. "Mrs. Featherton appears to have received a note from an anonymous source. Do you recall seeing her speak with anyone other than me?"

"By no means. She kept to her room. We scarcely saw her. I was a little concerned, truth be told, about a lady travelling alone. Then she told me that she would be leaving today. She did not say it was with you, my lord."

Lazenby thrust the note at the man. "Do you recognize this writing?"

Bloxham took the paper and read it. "No."

"We shall go down to the river and see if we can find any trace of her." Lazenby gestured to Featherton and the lawyer rose up slowly, as if every bone ached. "In the meantime, perhaps you could ask your maids if they remember anyone delivering this message to Mrs. Featherton. It seems to be the last clue we have as to her whereabouts."

It was with increasing foreboding that the earl accompanied Featherton down to the weir. "I was there myself yesterday until half-past three or four."

"If anything has happened to her, I shall hold myself responsible. If I had not turned her out, she would be safe home with me now." Featherton's anguish was palpable. The earl hesitated.

"Surely we'll find her safe and sound and laughing at the pair of us when we return to The Crown."

Featherton shook his head. Unable to speak further, he walked steadily and heavily along with the earl, who retraced his steps from the previous day. As they progressed, the incessant roar of the water over the weir grew louder and louder, drowning out all other sounds.

There was no sign of Sally at the weir. The ground was dry and dusty on the path beside the weir, leaving no trace of footprints. The two men looked around, under the trees, and called her name. There were two men fishing further down the path and the earl made his way towards them, his leg beginning to twinge.

"Good afternoon, gentlemen. Have you seen any trace of a woman of twenty-six or so? Dark, with blue eyes?"

The men shook their heads. "We've seen no one this morning. It's quiet round here since the canal took all the traffic away from the river. That's why the fishing is good. Tasty perch round here."

"The best of luck to you. If you hear of a lady called Sally Featherton, get a message to Bloxham at The Crown Hotel. There'll be money in it for you or anyone else with information about her."

Lazenby and Featherton made their way back to The Crown, where there was no Sally waiting for them.

"Will you allow me to consult with Sir Richard Dorfold? He is a local power and may have some advice for us."

Featherton listlessly agreed. Lazenby suggested he rest

and once again the lawyer, driven to a point of complete compliance, sat heavily on the bed where his wife should have slept. The earl helped him off with his shoes and coat and pushed him into a prone position.

"I'll come for you as soon as I have any news."

Tarbuck had brought the two greys over to The Crown. Lazenby went down to the stable yard to inspect them and the curricle he had hired from Bloxham. They were already harnessed and champing at the bit, eager for some exercise.

"You don't look as though you're off," commented Tarbuck. Lazenby explained that his companion was missing.

"That's a rum do. You can't really cause a scandal unless you run off with her, can you? I hear the husband is here."

"Does everyone know my business?"

"Well, it's a small place and you're a big name here. Not like London or Liverpool where you'd scarcely stick out."

"You may tell the world and his wife that Featherton is asleep, and I am off to consult with Sir Richard. I can scarcely leave without the woman and she may change her mind now her husband has come after her. What an infernal mess!"

It occurred to Lazenby that he must also warn Soames not to leave by the afternoon coach. He climbed into the curricle and tooled off, feeling most unsettled by Featherton's arrival. It was curious to be going on an errand essentially on behalf of a man he had cuckolded and from whom he planned to steal a wife. The whole day seemed to be descending into high farce. Of course, if Featherton and Sally could be reconciled, it would be best, although he did feel that they might have to move away from Edenbridge and all association with the earl. He'd be happy to provide assistance in some way—not pecuniary, that would smack of paying them off. But he could always find a law firm which Featherton could join, he supposed.

Where would that leave him? Back where he had been, free to woo Fran, provided his financial state permitted. It was all very well, but he could scarcely expect her to greet him with open arms. He had damaged her trust severely, he was sure. She had known that he was a rake, but she had not been confronted by the evidence before this. Now she would be forever wondering what further skeletons from his past would suddenly take flesh and reappear in his life.

He had been more careful in the past. He was fairly sure there were no other bastards to create havoc in his life. However, if Featherton and Sally could be reconciled, there was the issue of what role he should play in the life of this one. Almost certainly Featherton would not accept any money. What if he demanded that the earl have no contact with the child whatsoever? Featherton would be perfectly within his rights. That would be that; he could play no part in his child's life. The full force of his reckless negligence struck him then. Whatever happened now, his locust days were over.

In some respects it would be a relief to lead the life of a reputable citizen. The effects of prolonged debauch were beginning to make themselves felt: it took longer to recover from the after-effects of a night of cognac and port; there was no thrill at all from the turn of a card or the roll of the dice and as for the liaisons—the appeal of waking with a woman he scarcely knew had entirely dissipated.

The curricle rolled down the drive of Dorfold Hall and he climbed out gingerly, his leg still aching from the walk he had taken earlier. One of the footmen he had earlier tipped looked at him in surprise but led him without comment to Lady Dorfold's Yellow Room.

All faces were turned expectantly toward the door at

the footman's knock. Lazenby saw at once that Fran was there and recoiled slightly, as did she. Lady Dorfold noted the action as she rose and came towards the earl to greet him.

"The last person we expected. Do you take a seat?"

"No. I do not think so. I need to speak to Sir Richard. Mrs. Featherton has gone missing. Her husband and I have sought her out, but there is no sign of her."

"Her husband?" inquired Sir Richard. "Her husband is here?"

"Yes, which complicates things, clearly."

"Clearly," commented the baronet dryly. "Would you like me to institute some form of search for her?"

"I would. She received a note last night, from an anonymous source, requesting her to go to the weir on the river. She did not sleep in her bed last night. We went to the river to search for her."

"Have you tried any of the other inns in town?"

"We haven't. I don't believe she would have deserted The Crown though. She never struck me as such a light-skirt." The irony of the earl's words was not lost on the company. "I mean . . ."

"Best not to say anything further," suggested Lady Dorfold. "I do not believe you will get very far today. We'll tell Soames to unpack your things. You may keep your horses and curricle here. Let us hope we locate Mrs. Featherton quickly and sort out this imbroglio."

"We'll return to town, I'll summon the watch and we shall send to the other inns. Perhaps get a party to check the river past the weir. My excuses, Miss Wilbraham."

Sir Richard led Lazenby away, asking, "How far down the river walk did you go? What did this note say exactly?"

Fran and Lady Dorfold were left with Matilda in the sitting room.

"Matilda, my sweet, go and practise your scales." The

girl opened her mouth to say she had already practised that day, but caught the glint in her mother's eye and obediently went away.

"What a turn-up! I wonder whether she has made off with some new lover."

Fran felt shocked and somewhat oppressed. "I wish he had been able to leave without further fuss. I cannot feel that her disappearance is without consequences."

"What do you mean, Frances?"

"I fear some accident has befallen her. I do not believe she is safe and however much she may have been a fool to chase after the earl, I do not feel she would be such a fool as to run off with a third man at this point."

Lady Dorfold could not help but agree: an accident seemed the most likely outcome. "It is most curious to think of Lazenby assisting the husband in his search for this woman."

"The whole business is becoming a public show." Fran's distaste was evident.

"Yes. I feel for Lazenby, even if he has brought this on himself. This search is bound to become widely discussed. There is no way of concealing any of the features of this affair. But scandals are forgotten eventually."

"I could not forget it. How many more incidents of a similar nature will afflict him? How many more spurned mistresses and wronged husbands and illegitimate children? It was abundantly clear that his conduct has been thoughtless and wrong. I don't know what I was thinking. That he was capable of change, that there could be forgiveness and healing. That he could escape from the coils of his past." Fran stood and paced. "I am such a fool."

"We cannot always govern where we give our hearts. It is not foolish to love."

"I should have avoided him, I should have heeded

Kitty, but my own pride prevented me from listening to her."

Lady Dorfold felt chastened. She had not helped matters by throwing her friend together with the earl, certainly in part to spite Lady Tollemache. She went to Fran and held her hands. "I'm sorry. I should not have encouraged you in your partiality. I knew better than you what sort of man he is, but I too deluded myself that the past was the past and could have no bearing on the future."

Fran gave a wan smile. "You would not have done that without some indication from me that he was an acceptable suitor. I was in the wrong. Whatever happens, there can be no good outcome for me. I have written to Papa's friend, Mr. Simeon Foulkes. He and Mrs. Foulkes have asked me to stay with them in London and to travel with them to Paris and Rome on numerous occasions before and since Papa's death. I have asked if I may go to them as soon as Kitty and Arthur have moved. I need to be away from home and all the reminders of my own folly."

Soon after, Miss Wilbraham returned to Nantwich. The town was in an uproar as businesses of one sort and another were disrupted by the calling of their men to search for Mrs. Featherton. Sir Richard had commandeered all three of Bloxham's stable boys to go round the other hostelries in the town and enquire after the lady, and when that had elicited no result, he had reluctantly called the watch. The baker was roused, the smith called from his forge, the miller and carpenter summoned, a couple of the cheese makers and old Evans, who had known the river for all his sixty-six years. All equipped themselves with stout sticks and poles to prod the riverbed. Only eighteen months before, a local child had fallen in the river and been washed over the weir. They'd found his body a day or so later.

Featherton was fast asleep when the earl returned to The Crown. Lazenby judged it best that he be left undisturbed for the moment. There would be time enough to call him if the search did locate Sally in the river. He himself joined the search along with Sir Richard, checking the reed beds and the shallows while some of the watch went in flat-bottomed boats, steadily punting from bank to bank.

The sun was beginning to set, casting long, golden shadows on the water, when a shout came from the east bank of the Weaver, nearly two miles out of the town. The men managed to haul the body onto the bank. She looked bloated and discolored. Lazenby had seen bodies before, far more disfigured than this, but the sight of her still made him retch.

Sally Featherton's body was laid in canvas and placed in the back of a cart and carried into Nantwich. She was taken to the carpenter's workshop and Featherton came from The Crown with Sir Richard and Lazenby to identify the body formally. He was very quiet, subduing all inclination to cry or rant or rave. The impulse was there, but he could not give way to it before prying eyes. He looked over his wife, nodded and turned away.

They took him back to the hotel and sat him down in a private parlor. Sir Richard ordered brandy and when it had been served, closed the door and sat beside Featherton.

"Sir, drink this and then we must decide on your next course of action."

The lawyer sipped at the spirit. He put his glass down. "I think it best to have her buried here as quickly as possible. I do not wish to take her back home. Nothing can put right what was wrong between us." He stared dully into the fire.

"That simplifies things a little. But I would like an

opinion on whether her death was purely accidental or whether some person contributed to it. The earl mentioned a note."

"I have it here about me." Featherton felt in his pockets and passed the note to Sir Richard. "You do not believe she simply slipped and fell."

"I do not. But I wish to have your permission before investigating further. I noticed that her dress was torn."

"Who could have harmed her? She was a rash girl. Do you think she was attacked?"

"I cannot say. I am sorry to burden you further."

Featherton shook his head. "It makes no odds. If someone was responsible for her death, I only hope we can bring them to justice. My poor girl." He broke down finally and wept, racked with aching sobs. Lazenby and Sir Richard sat with him until he had calmed down somewhat. Finally, he drew himself up. With dignity, he stood, bade them goodnight and withdrew to the room where his wife had lain.

"Do you really believe that she was killed?" asked Lazenby.

"I am afraid I do. I cannot imagine who would have done such a thing, but I do not think she threw herself into the river. There was no need. You had offered to care for her and the child, her future was safe." Sir Richard hesitated. "There will be people who say you did it. You did not wish to be burdened by her and disposed of her, attempting to make it seem an accident. There will be talk."

"A fair warning. But you know that I had nothing to do with this." Lazenby strove to remain calm.

"Of course I do. And we may offer you an alibi, since you were with us at six o'clock, explaining why you would be leaving today."

"This is the most melancholy business imaginable. If

only Featherton had been earlier. There might have been some prospect of reconciliation. I did not think of it myself, Sally seemed so certain that he had washed his hands of her. But the poor man seems devastated."

The two men returned to Dorfold Hall late that night. Lady Dorfold was waiting for news as they entered the hallway. Sir Richard shook his head.

"It's bad news. We found her in the river late this afternoon."

Lady Dorfold blanched. "Was it an accident?"

"We cannot tell for certain. If only we could find out who this note was from. It might clarify matters considerably."

But Bloxham had asked his girls who had delivered the note and none of them could remember it at all.

Twelve

The Tollemaches had spent most of the day with lawyers and notaries, drawing up the contracts for the lease of the house they had inspected. Fran mentioned briefly at dinner that a search was under way for Mrs. Featherton, but there had been no further news that evening. It was not until Lionel Tollemache came in a bustle to Dysart House the following morning that Fran heard of Sally's death. Kitty was agog.

"She was found in the Weaver! And Sir Richard is investigating further? There must be something shady in the death then." She paused. Mr. Tollemache rushed to fill the silence.

"There is talk that the earl had an assignation with her and finished her off."

Fran was sickened. She rose and excused herself, knowing full well that any protest would be greeted by Kitty and her companions as spoiling their sport. She left them to speculate and gloat. Heartsore and beset by her family, Fran longed to be able to leave at once for London, before any further revelations or incidents could emphasize the impossibility of her attachment for Lazenby. She was desperate for escape and distraction and some opportunity to forget the folly of the past few weeks.

But worse was to come. By dinnertime, the news was

out: a man's glove had been found on Mrs. Featherton's person. Her dress had been torn. Foul play was suspected. Roundell had inspected the body and there had been bruising. Once the owner of the glove was identified, it was thought that Sir Richard might make an arrest.

Lionel Tollemache relished his role as news-carrier between the goings-on at The Crown Hotel and Dysart House. Naturally, he did not mention his own exposure to Mrs. Featherton or the existence of the note. He was anxious, for no one had mentioned the note again at The Crown. The chambermaid he had paid to deliver it had disappeared for the moment, where to, Bloxham had no idea. She came from a notoriously feckless family, and it was likely that she had either been called home to minister to their needs or shaken the dust of Nantwich from her heels for good in an effort to escape any further involvement with them. There had been talk of her courting, but none of the other girls knew any concrete details about the man in question. He was not local, he was not gainfully employed, and he was not the sort to settle down. He was variously thought to be a tinker, a gypsy, a peddler, and a journeyman smith. The long and short of it was that the man had vanished and Becky with him.

Lady Dorfold came to see Frances, since Lazenby was still at Dorfold Hall, as was Featherton himself. The Dorfolds had invited him to stay, for remaining at The Crown, the object of curiosity and false sympathy, would have been intolerable.

"It is a most peculiar situation to have both lover and husband under the same roof, one comforting the other."

"They must be very upset."

"The earl is more horrified than upset. He is most remorseful and blames himself for Mrs. Featherton's death. There is something more serious, and I wished to let you know privately."

"What is it?" Fran could not imagine anything worse than the current situation.

"This talk of the glove about Mrs. Featherton's person. It is Lazenby's glove. He does not know how she came to have it. He was near the weir on the afternoon she died and certainly lost a glove, but he did not see her."

"I do not see the difficulty."

"If it gets out that she had his glove, it will be assumed that he pushed her in. The talk will be that he wished to rid himself of her and the child, and found this opportunity to do so, luring her with this note, pushing her under and leaving her to drown."

Fran was shocked. "He'd never do such a thing."

"Of course not. But Sir Richard fears that conclusions will be drawn. You know what people are, Fran, they will leap to accuse and he has been quite frank about being in the same place where she was found. It may be that for his own safety, Sir Richard must place him in custody until the whole business can be thoroughly investigated. Especially if Becky Chalmers cannot be found. That too begins to look suspicious. Whoever wrote the note is most likely to have been the culprit in this affair, and they may well have done away with Becky too."

Of course, rumors abounded and ever-wilder theories were put forward in all the tap-rooms of Nantwich about the nature of Mrs. Featherton's assignation, the identity of her killer, and the whereabouts of Becky Chalmers. Women were cautioned against going down to the river and there was a widespread move to revive the watch which had been dormant for some years. Bands of local men collected together, brandishing torches and yelling about the streets until midnight or even later. Fran consulted with Tarbuck, always a reliable barometer of feeling in the town.

"There's plenty of talk about the earl getting away with

it. He's a toff, he's a bought off Sir Richard, and will escape without even coming to trial. Half the men say that he should be put in the gaol house, the other half say he should leave now and we could all be at peace then."

The atmosphere worsened when Becky Chalmers's shawl was discovered in Delamere Forest. It was widely concluded that she had been brutally butchered and buried in the forest, and search parties were sent to comb the place for shallow graves and bloodstained groves. None was found, and the search was called off when it was discovered that she had given the shawl to her little sister before leaving for Liverpool with her lover. Young Susie Chalmers had feared to say anything about it because her mother would tan her if it got out that Becky had run off without banns of marriage being read.

A week had gone by since Sally Featherton's body had been retrieved from the Weaver. Fran had heard nothing from the earl and expected to hear nothing, for his horses were now stabled at Dorfold Hall. There was no reason at all for any contact between them. So she was surprised when Lady Dorfold called again in some agitation with a very specific mission.

"My dear, I must warn you, Sir Richard is about to place the earl under arrest for the murder of Sally Featherton." Lady Dorfold paused. "I did not want you to hear by second or third hand. I know what grand inflations of the facts occur and it seemed better that you should know the truth."

"But he has committed no crime! You know that as well as I do."

"Of course he hasn't. But there is a good deal of unrest and you know how delicate things are now in the area. There are rumblings about how if he weren't a peer he'd have been taken into custody last week. There is talk of giving us some rough music at Dorfold Hall unless some action is taken."

"So the earl is to be offered up as a sacrifice?"

"He suggested it. Meanwhile, we are making every effort to track down the wretched Becky Chalmers. The thing is, we have the Assizes coming up very soon. The whole business can be tried here in Nantwich. As magistrate, Sir Richard can commit the earl on a Bill of Indictment and we shall be seen to be doing our duty."

"It's true, the town is filling up already with people eager to see a hanging. Would you do this if the Assizes were held elsewhere this year?"

"I don't know. But Lazenby is prepared to do anything to deflect criticism away from us." Lady Dorfold reached inside her reticule. "He also asked that I act as messenger. He has written you a letter. He said that if you did not wish to read it he would understand."

Fran looked at the paper which Lady Dorfold held out toward her. There was no question of what she should do. But she found herself reaching her hand out.

"I shall leave you to read it in peace. He does not expect any answer, I believe."

Lady Dorfold left and Fran gingerly opened out the parchment.

Dorfold Hall, —November 1823

Miss Wilbraham

  I was presumptuous enough to suggest not so long ago that if my affairs could be set in order, I would aspire to your hand. Subsequent events made this out of the question, and now it seems that misfortune is dogging my every action. Any attachment you might have felt for me must by now have withered. I know that if I

*were a better man, I would not write this letter, but I
find I must speak one last time.*

*With or without the intervention of Mrs. Featherton
and her subsequent death, I have always known that I
was not worthy of your affection or your interest. I have
never been a great believer in redemption, but meeting
you suggested to me the possibility that I might be
redeemed from a worthless and empty existence. You
never sought to judge me or to amend my behavior. But
your generosity, your compassion, your spirit have
inspired me to improve my ways and break from the
deleterious course on which I have for so long been set.*

*Whatever the outcome of the investigations into Mrs.
Featherton's death, I wish you to know that the impression you made upon me was deep and lasting. If I am
released, I will strive to lead a life worthy of your example. If I am convicted of her death, I shall face my own
quietus with resignation and I hope some dignity. In either case, I shall not cease to esteem you, to love you. I
had imagined that I had loved, but since I have met
you, I have come to understand that until now, I never
truly knew what love might be.*

*You will always be in my heart and in my mind. It is
unlikely that you will ever need to call on me in any
capacity, but if ever you need my assistance, be assured
I am at your disposal.*

Lazenby

Fran folded up the letter and gazed into space. She
could not write back. She could do nothing. It was not
permissible for her to visit Lazenby during his incarceration, it was not possible for her to voice any real interest
in his predicament at all, for other than nursing him for
a time, her exposure to the earl was by and large a secret.
The servants at Dorfold Hall and Dysart House did know

that she had spent a good deal of time at Dorfold Hall, but as Lady Dorfold had pointed out, no more than she had before Kitty had come back to live at home. The true level of her attachment to the earl had been concealed from prying eyes.

It was fixed that the Tollemaches would move into their new home just before Christmas and that Fran would join the Foulkes family in London in the new year, ready to engage in preparations for a trip to France and Italy. This left a month before Kitty and Sir Arthur departed from Dysart House. One month in which Fran determined that she would do her utmost to uncover the true identity of Mrs. Featherton's assailant. She stood and paced the room, trying to work out what needed to be done. The first priority, it seemed to her, was to find out all she could about the attack. Then she must find this Becky Chalmers. Once she had discovered as many facts as possible about the state of the body and the last hours of the deceased, it would be easier to prove that the earl had had nothing to do with her demise.

Fran went to the window, folded her arms and tapped her foot as she gazed out on the people of Nantwich going about their business. Suddenly she jumped, as though hit by lightning, and left the room in search of her cloak and bonnet. The doctor's trap had passed the window, and of course, he had been the last person to examine the body.

As she hurried to the doctor's house, Fran tried to think up some ailment serious enough to warrant an emergency visit but not so serious as to lay her low. Perhaps he would be able to assist her in some tale if Kitty should get wind of this visit.

Roundell came at once on hearing that Miss Wilbraham wished to see him. He took her into his office and closed the door carefully, inviting Fran to take a seat.

"How can I help you? I hope it is nothing serious." He flicked his coattails out of the way as he sat behind his desk, then steepled his hands, ready to listen.

"I believe it is serious, Doctor, but not for me." Fran bit her lip, then continued. "I wish to assist the earl and I want to hear from you the exact state of Mrs. Featherton and whether there is any proof other than the glove that he had anything to do with her death. We didn't work so hard, you and I, to save him simply to see him falsely accused of murder."

Roundell stood and came round the desk. He took Fran's hands and said, "I've watched over your health since you were a child, and I've seen you grow into a fine young woman. This will be the hardest thing you have ever done, and if it comes out, your involvement will be closely questioned."

"I am ready for that. But I cannot stand idly by and see the earl falsely accused of so terrible a crime. It is terrible that this poor woman should have been killed and it appears the act was most callously performed. But the earl did not do it and no one else seems to think it necessary to delve into the facts."

"Aye, facts are in short supply and those few we know are being ignored in favor of melodramatic tales. But Miss Wilbraham, are you prepared to uncover unpalatable truths unsuitable for a maiden's ears?"

"I know the truth about the relations between Lazenby and Mrs. Featherton. I did wonder whether she had been molested in any way. I do know about such things, although Kitty and her married cronies would prefer to imagine that we single women know nothing about the baser aspects of life."

"Very well. She was not molested in that way, poor creature. I have her clothes still and her body. I can tell you that she was wearing a dress with a good deal of lace and that lace was torn and wrecked before she went into the water."

"How can you tell?"

"No other aspect of her dress was in much disarray. That suggests to me that very little disturbance was caused once she was in the water. Her garments were so heavy and so waterlogged she would have sunk quickly. Her husband told me that she had never known how to swim, so I believe there would have been little opportunity once she was in the water for her to tear at her own garments."

"So her clothes were torn before she fell."

"Yes, probably in some form of struggle. But there is no sign of any tearing around the skirt or undergarments. Her arms and shoulders were a little bruised, where it looked as though someone grappled with her, tried to hold her still. There are no marks on her legs or buttocks. Forgive me for speaking so frankly."

"If you do not speak frankly, Doctor, we shall never get to the bottom of this." Fran considered what she had heard. "Show me how she and her attacker would have had to stand."

Roundell came to Fran and stood behind her. "I believe that her killer was trying to restrain her in some way and that she must have slipped or broken free of his grasp and fallen then into the river." He grasped Fran in a bear hug. "Like so. She was pulling away, he was holding onto the fabric of her cloak and inadvertently the dress, which is how the lace came to be torn about the bodice." Fran wrestled out of his grasp and saw how momentum could have carried her away from the doctor.

"She must have barrelled into the river. But what sort of person would simply leave her to drown without seeking help in such circumstances? Surely he should have come running for help and then we might have saved her."

"I believe that whoever did kill her wished to deny any connection with her at all. If only we could find out if there was someone else who knew her in Nantwich."

"It is imperative that we find this chambermaid from The Crown. If we can discover who wrote the note arranging the assignation by the Weaver, I believe we will uncover the identity of the miscreant who killed her."

Fran remembered something about the assembly. "What is the time, Doctor?"

"Not yet eleven."

"Thank you very much for your assistance in this matter. I must go and consult with another person who may have some light to shed on this matter. I do not have to ask for your complete discretion."

"Of course not." Roundell escorted Fran to the door and bowed as she left. She was a formidable character when roused, he mused as he shut the door behind her. If anyone could save the earl from a lynching, it would be she.

Fran made her way then up the street and round the corner to the house of the Appersetts. She had never before made a call there, falling as she did between the mother and the daughters in age, knowing of the family, but not familiar with any of them. However, she was determined to get Amy alone as soon as the formalities were performed. She had not forgotten the young lady's sharp eyes and canny comments at the assembly. If anyone had noticed something out of the ordinary, it would be Amy Appersett.

Once admitted, she was ushered into a quiet room at the back of the house, clearly little used. She waited there for some minutes until Mrs. Appersett bustled in, followed by Amy and her younger sister Della.

"Miss Wilbraham! We're very pleased to see you."

"Forgive me for breaking in on you this way, but I come

drumming up business for one of my staff, Hannah Evans. She is setting up as a dressmaker, and I promised her I would recommend her to all my acquaintance. I have sketches of hers at home, and she is adept at recreating the latest fashions. I have been wearing her creations for over a year now, and hope that you will consent to visit and inspect her designs in the next day or two. She is hoping to build up a select clientele of only the most stylish ladies in Nantwich."

Mrs. Appersett simpered, but Amy looked at Miss Wilbraham in puzzlement. Mrs. Appersett was known for her rather wild taste in clothing. While it would be a major achievement for any dressmaker to persuade the lady to wear tamer clothes, she provided a challenge and would not necessarily be a good advertisement for anyone starting up in that sort of business.

Miss Wilbraham caught Amy's glance. "Perhaps Amy might wish to come today, now even, then she may report back to you."

The prospect of having her daughter taken up by Miss Wilbraham was too good an opportunity to miss. Mrs. Appersett had bustled Amy into her pelisse and outdoor boots in a trice, and the girl was accompanying Fran back to Dysart House before she knew it. As they walked along, Fran engaged Amy in meaningless chitchat, leaving the girl feeling increasingly bewildered. It was not until they were safely in a private parlor in Dysart House that Fran felt confident in broaching her true motive in extracting Amy from the bosom of her family.

"Miss Appersett. I noticed how observant you were at the dance last week."

"Unwarranted curiosity, my mother calls it." Amy's rueful demeanor suggested that she had been nagged more than once for doing too much watching and insufficient flirting or dancing at such affairs.

"Did you notice anything or anyone strange?"

"There was the lady who was murdered. Well, everyone says murdered, but surely it could have been an accident?"

"Why do you think that?"

"If it was the earl who met her by the river, it must have been an accident. But I believe it was the other stranger who was staying at The Crown Hotel who met with the lady."

"Which other gentleman? Why do you say that?"

"The one you danced with. The Lancers, I think it was. I was not introduced to him. Mama thought he was much too elderly and set in his ways for any of us to merit his attention. Afterwards, he danced only with Lady Tollemache. He would not stand up with anyone else. But when the earl was speaking with Mrs. Featherton—that is her name, isn't it?" Fran nodded in response. Amy continued: "Well, then he was watching most closely. I think he must have seen how agitated the earl was by Mrs. Featherton's appearance. Anyone would have."

"Just watching hardly constitutes an assignation. And that is what it was, according to Sir Richard. Mrs. Featherton had a letter asking her to come to the river at six o'clock." Fran waited for Amy to speak. This was going more easily than she had imagined possible. But Lionel Tollemache! It was scarcely credible.

"That is why I think it must have been him she met. You see, I saw him. I saw him coming into Nantwich. We had been out and were late back from visiting friends. He was on the bridge across the Weaver, I'm sure it was him, looking quite agitated, ruffled, almost. You know Josiah, our coachman, is nearly blind, but we can't turn him off, it would be too cruel. Josiah nearly ran him down, and I thought that was the reason he looked so frightened, but what if he had just watched Mrs. Featherton drown? I just saw a glimpse of him, and my brother hung out of the window and shouted an apology. I don't believe Charlie would recognize him. You know what boys are, they scarcely notice anything unless it's directly under their noses."

"So you saw Mr. Tollemache coming back from the west bank of the Weaver at what time that night?" Fran wished to establish quite clearly what Amy had seen, and the girl's account was still a little tangled.

"It must have been before seven, but well after six, for we did not leave the Farnhams' until six and it never takes more than an hour to get home from their house." Amy frowned in thought. "I do not think anyone else recognized him. But I did and I wondered what he was doing wandering about when The Crown usually serves dinner."

Fran rose from her chair. "You have helped a good deal, but we will need more concrete proof than this that Mr. Tollemache is the culprit. You will have heard that the earl has been arrested?"

"Yes. But that is simply because of the glove in Mrs. Featherton's pocket and who is to say when she had that? He might have left it at the inn when he went to see her and she picked it up meaning to return it to him at the next opportunity. Everyone knows they met at The Crown on the morning of her death."

Fran wondered who "everyone" was—all of Nantwich or simply the young ladies of Amy's acquaintance? Amy watched Miss Wilbraham.

"The evidence we have against Mr. Tollemache is equally circumstantial. Why do you believe it was he and not the earl?"

"Of course, I do not know Mr. Tollemache, but he

struck me as chilly. He watched everyone dancing but he was on his high horse and disdained all the ladies there. When he did dance with you and Lady Tollemache, he was careful in his steps and kept watching himself whenever he passed a mirror. He struck me as a man of great selfishness and quite capable of wrongdoing if he felt it served his purpose."

"It had not struck me so, but I believe you are quite acute in your reading of his character. Is the earl right? Have you been writing stories about us all?"

"I have been writing stories, but I hope I have disguised all the people of my acquaintance who have been included. I have found a publisher who wishes to produce my stories in a magazine every month. But this is something different. I never thought my powers of observation might help in a matter of real importance."

"They will help, Amy, but there is much to be done." Fran was grim with resolve. The Chalmers girl had to be found.

"Is there anything more *I* can do?"

"I am not sure. I believe that Becky Chalmers, the chambermaid from The Crown, is the key to all this. She apparently delivered the note to Mrs. Featherton, so presumably, she might know who wrote it."

Amy brightened. "I can assist in that case. Our maid knows Becky Chalmers and has been talking non-stop about her for months now, ever since Becky started courting with Ned Minto."

"You know the name of her lover! Sir Richard must be told at once. We are seeking them high and low. Do you think there is anything else your maid can tell about Becky and her plans?"

"I daresay. I shall pump her myself. Miss Wilbraham, wouldn't it be the finest thing if we could find Becky before anyone else? And I feel we should, you know, for this Mr. Tollemache may not scruple to see that harm comes to her."

They made their plans accordingly. Amy would speak at once with Minnie Powell, her maid, Miss Wilbraham would speak with Sir Richard, and if Minnie could divulge any additional information, Tarbuck should be sent in search of Becky Chalmers with instructions to bring her back. And, thought Fran, a good handful of money to ensure that she and her lover did not fear to return to Nantwich to testify on the earl's behalf. For the more that Fran considered Amy's information, the more likely she felt it to be that Tollemache had been instrumental in sending Sally Featherton to her death. He had coldly sent one woman to her death and seemed quite happy to contemplate the prospect of an innocent man standing trial for the crime. Another death might not matter a great deal to him. But why he should behave in so callous and cruel a fashion, Fran could not understand.

Thirteen

The gaol house at Nantwich was an elegant and commodious building, belying its grim function. The earl's cell was near the top of the building. Below, there were communal cells where petty criminals and those remanded in custody before their trials were held, but those with a little money could easily secure for themselves accommodation which was private and even spacious. While there was no fireplace in his rooms, Davies, the head gaoler, did permit the use of braziers, and learning how to keep the one in his cell stoked and functioning occupied a good deal of the earl's time.

Soames had volunteered to keep him company, but Lazenby felt that his man had gone through enough on his behalf, and additionally, might be in a better position to ameliorate the worst discomforts of imprisonment if he were at liberty. They swiftly established a routine. Soames would come early each morning to assist the earl with his breakfast and his clothes. He would leave at eleven or so, then return in the evening with news of Sir Richard's hunt for Becky Chalmers and any other gossip from the outside world.

Although they did discuss the possible identity of Sally's killer, both men were at a loss as to who could have performed the deed.

The day after the earl's arrest, Featherton was his first

visitor, much to the astonishment of the gaolers and Nantwich in general. He was ushered into Lazenby's quarters with great unctuousness, and the door was left open while he was present, all the better to hear what passed between the two men.

"I am so very sorry to see you here," said Featherton. "It is most unjust, even I recognize that. Sir Richard has ridden to Liverpool, so I am here as his deputy, to keep you abreast of the efforts made to clear your name."

"It is good of you to come. May I ask what arrangements have been made for Mrs. Featherton's interment?"

"I am having her buried here. I do not wish to take her body back home."

"It's not the expense?" enquired Lazenby.

"No, no. I could easily afford to have her transported back to Edenbridge. But I must stay here until her killer is uncovered."

"What about your business?"

"I do not know that my business will recover from these sad events, but I do not think I wish to return to Stamford in any case. It holds too many memories for me. I have legal friends in London; it may be that I can find work there. Certainly, I cannot give due attention and care to the interests of my clients in my current state."

The earl stood and came over to Featherton. "I cannot begin to express my shame and regret for what has happened. There is no excuse and the only explanation I can offer for my behavior is a wayward and childlike habit of giving way to every impulse, however much that might hurt others about me."

"You have been fortunate indeed in being able to give way to your impulses. Most of us do not have that luxury. But you are paying for it now, and I do not like to see an innocent man stand accused of a crime he did not commit. However much you might wish to blame yourself for

Sally's death, remember that you did not lure her down to the riverside, nor indeed, did you chase her from her home nor request her to come haring halfway across the country in search of you. This tragedy is composed of many strands and she and I are as much to blame as you."

"I am not sure I would take so charitable a view of matters if I stood in your shoes. It may be true that Sally was the author of her own downfall, but I do not know that she would have strayed without a relentless siege on my part."

"It is done. It is too late now. If I ever take a wife again, I will study to please her better and if we can acquit you fully, I daresay you will study to avoid other men's wives. Let us speak no more about it."

Featherton's calm, dignified demeanor impressed Lazenby greatly. It was clear that the man had loved his wife dearly, although he admitted himself that he had neglected her in favor of building up his legal practice. But he bore no grudges and was happy to apply his methodical mind and legal training to the earl's predicament. It was unusual for the earl to be so beholden to others—once again he found himself dependent and trapped, this time behind iron bars as opposed to tied down by bandages and pain. If Sir Richard could not track down Becky Chalmers, he would be in a sad case.

Soames recognized this all too clearly, but did not know what to do about it. He frequented The Crown, collecting gossip and talk, and it was there that Tarbuck found him two nights later.

"Miss Wilbraham wishes to speak with you. Will you come tomorrow, via the stables?" Tarbuck spoke softly. "She wishes no one to know of her interest in the earl's case, but she is deeply concerned by it."

Soames agreed on a time and found himself at Dysart House, speaking with Miss Wilbraham in the kitchen gardens the following morning. She looked elegant but weary, a faint strain playing about her eyes.

"I hope you did not mention our meeting to the earl. He and I can have nothing to do with each other."

"I have said nothing. There did not seem any reason to speak of it until I knew your reason for asking to see me."

"I am trying to piece together exactly what happened on the day of Mrs. Featherton's death. We need to find an alibi for the earl. I find it astonishing that no one appears to have asked his whereabouts at six o'clock that evening. Surely either you or the Dorfolds can account for him?"

"We can, but we are biased. That is what the townsfolk are saying. But in answer to your question, in the morning, he came to Nantwich. At midday, he purchased sketching materials from the stationer's shop. He went down to the riverbank between half past twelve and half past three, then headed back to Dorfold Hall. His leg was giving him trouble and he cadged a lift from a carter passing by Dorfold Hall. Of course, we don't know this man's name or destination, so we cannot find him, although Sir Richard has asked his people to keep their eyes and ears open."

"Good. I have spoken with Roundell about this whole business and he tells me that he does not believe that the earl had the strength to hurl anyone into a river in any case. His arm and leg are both still weak and would have displayed signs of disturbance if he had been struggling with anyone, however slight."

"Mrs. Featherton was not slight. Petite but not insubstantial."

Fran did not wish to hear any more about Mrs. Featherton. "Now, I wish to consult you before presenting any further evidence to Sir Richard."

"What do you mean, Miss Wilbraham?"

"I have found out the name of Becky Chalmers's young man. Now, to whom should I pass this to achieve the quickest result?"

"Not Sir Richard's men, if you'll forgive me for saying so, for a slower more bumbling pack I have yet to meet outside the boards of a theater. They make even the basest mechanicals seem witty."

"That is what I suspected. Now, of you and Tarbuck, who has the best knowledge of Liverpool?"

"I believe it would be better if Tarbuck went. My absence from my lord's side would be noted, whereas he may slip away on business and no one would query it. Also, he must know Miss Chalmers, which I don't. There's a chance he may spot her where I could have no such hope."

"This was my reasoning also, but I did not wish to send him off without your knowledge. But I hope you will keep this from Sir Richard. He would not be pleased to hear that I am making any independent investigations."

"And the earl? May I let him know?"

"As you please. If it will irk him to think no progress is being made, then tell him, but if you think it might displease him to know that there are those who still have his interests at heart, then conceal it from him."

"He does not say so, but I believe that hearing from you would make a good deal of difference."

"I received his letter. Tell him I have read it."

Soames bowed in agreement and left for the gaol.

The earl was sitting at a table, reading and making notes when Soames arrived there. He made sure the door was properly secured before coming to stand before his master.

"Sit, for God's sake. You look pregnant with news."

"I believe there is some hope for you. Miss Wilbraham is taking an interest in your case."

Lazenby looked at Soames in bemusement. "What can you mean?"

Soames reported his conversation with her, including her final comment.

"How did she look?" The earl's tone was diffident.

"A little weary. A little fidgety. If she could, I believe she'd be in Liverpool now scouring the streets herself for the little madam and her fancyman."

Lazenby leaned back in his chair, closed his eyes and shook his head. "There is no point in dreaming about what might have been."

"You won't spurn her assistance?"

"I have no right to do such a thing, even if I could. Do you really imagine it would make any difference if I said I didn't want her help?"

Soames grinned. "No, she'd ignore you. I've new respect for her. It'll be good to see you ridden over roughshod. Taste of your own medicine."

"I doubt you will see it. She and I can have nothing further to do with each other. Whatever happens, I shall be an outcast now. It's all very well washing dirty linen in public, but you aren't expected to have it exposed and murdered. One or the other, but not both."

"You know such things make no difference to her. She'd stand by you if you'd let her near you."

Lazenby was left to consider this verdict once Soames had disappeared for the afternoon and was forced to admit the truth of his words. Miss Wilbraham was a formidable ally and she had shown no desire whatsoever to become a part of the glittering world of London society, unlike her sister or indeed, Mrs. Featherton. If she could clear his name, would it make any difference to their situation?

For the first time in many years, the earl started to contemplate the possibility of a future. Until he had met Miss Wilbraham, he had never thought much more than a week in advance, and his concentration had been taken up by the demands of gaming and arranging assignations. Now, even if he never saw her again, which was the most likely outcome, he must consider how best to live up to the promise he had made her in his letter, to live an exemplary life. To create some meaning from his life.

Lazenby imagined that he would have plenty of time in which to contemplate how best to achieve this now that he was incarcerated and solitary. However, his isolation was illusory. In addition to Soames, he was regularly visited by Sir Richard and then Lady Dorfold, who liked in any case to keep an eye on the unfortunates in the communal cells. Often the families of miscreants needed additional assistance and she was ready to provide it so that no further crime might be committed simply to feed wife and children. Lady Dorfold even brought Matilda, a step which was widely criticized. Kitty took great delight in disapproving of this particular action in front of Frances.

Fran was careful not to rise to Kitty's gloating pleasure at the earl's downfall. Neither sister had again referred to Fran's attachment for the earl: Kitty put it out of her mind as she did with all inconvenient things that might disappear if she did not think of them, while Frances wanted nothing less than to engage in a postmortem of her emotions with the sister who was bound to misunderstand them. However, Kitty, in common with most of the rest of the county, seemed to believe that Lazenby was guilty and took great delight along with Sir Arthur in chewing over the circumstances of the death with every meal. Of course, the local newspaper was full of the business, recreating poor Sally Featherton's last afternoon in luridly imagined detail and digging up all sorts of salacious stories about the earl's past misdemeanors and suggesting that he must hang if found guilty.

One morning, just over a week following the earl's imprisonment and nearly a fortnight since the discovery of the body, Kitty was mulling over the lack of news at breakfast.

"I cannot understand why things are so slow. What is the procedure, Fran?"

"He will be brought before the Assizes next week and the justice will decide whether the Bill of Indictment must stand, in which case he will be tried before a jury. I daresay he can avert it by requesting that he be tried by his peers and the whole affair must be transferred to London." Fran did her best to conceal her increasing concern for Tarbuck who had left for Liverpool several days before.

"I am surprised you have not joined with your friends the Dorfolds in visiting him. I understand it is becoming quite the fashion to visit convicts since they have taken up with him."

"You know I have never liked to follow fashion." Fran took up her copy of *The Times* and pointedly turned the page and buried her nose in the Court Circular, a section of the paper she generally eschewed.

"Yes, you were a constant visitor when visiting regular criminals, but now you avoid the place. You are so contrary, Fran, I know not what to think."

"Lady Dorfold and I simply wished to avoid the sight of entire families sinking into a morass of crime and punishment. Most criminals only become so through hardship and a sense that there is no alternative. If shopkeepers like

Mr. Parry and Mr. Jones were not quite so assiduous in chasing the theft of every last apple and pear, I daresay Nantwich's gaol would be empty for most of the year. If in addition they gave half as much effort and money into charitable deeds about the town, they would have no thefts at all."

"You are too soft, Frances. There are always those among us who would steal and cheat in preference to making an honest living."

"What do you know of such things except what you pick up at Parry's? There are many families proud of their traditions and their honesty, but the salt-trade is decreasing, our cheese-makers are suffering and all the area is experiencing hardship. When there is destitution, crime must follow. It is up to those of us who are more fortunate to ease the way for those who have less."

"Your crusades are so tiresome. I do wish we could find you a husband who would occupy you more fittingly."

"Let us turn the subject, Kitty. You have stirred these waters before and no doubt will again, but I wish to keep peace with you." Fran returned to her newspaper pointedly. But she was soon to be interrupted. Reed came to the dining room bearing a crumpled piece of paper.

"This was delivered by Miss Evans's young sister. She says it is quite urgent and begs you not to delay."

Fran scanned the note and her eyebrows shot up in dismay. Tossing the note to Kitty, she stood up. "Here is a case in point. Parry has accused my Hannah of stealing ribbons and if ever there was a more hard-working, honest young woman, I have yet to meet her. But he is jealous because she wishes to offer a dress-making service that will scarcely affect his business, and indeed might have led to an increase in sales of his materials. He is short-sighted, mean-spirited, and sneaking. Well, we shall see about this."

Fran stormed from the room, leaving her sister open-mouthed behind her. She picked up the note, which was a plea for assistance from Hannah Evans who had been imprisoned that morning. Soon after, the front door slammed and Miss Wilbraham was marching down Churchyardside with a purposeful stride and a martial glint to her eyes. She went first to speak to Mr. Davies, the head gaoler, demanding to see Miss Evans, who was brought before her. Hannah looked utterly distraught.

"I did go to Parry's, miss, to fetch some bombazine that old Mrs. Murdle had ordered for her mourning clothes. But I never took any ribands, whatever they say. I came away, and was half-way down the street when Mr. Burden, who heads the watch, came after me saying that Parry saw me take some ribbon, some printed grosgrain, very precise he was in his description. I've never been so shamed in my life, miss, Mr. Burden took me into the tap-room at The Crown and there he made me turn out my reticule and my pockets and there was the ribbon."

"Where exactly, in your pockets or the reticule?"

"One length in my cloak, one in my reticule. I was going through the materials when I laid my things down. I might have taken the lengths by mistake, but never on purpose, I swear it, miss."

"We've enough witnesses to swear to your character, Hannah, but what we need is some proof that Parry himself or one of his assistants put the ribbon there. For that is what I believe happened, quite deliberately. Who were you dealing with?"

"Mr. Parry himself. He was cool, but not rude. Mrs. Parry was behind the counter and their girl Molly was in the shop."

"It must have been Molly who did it, but she will have been told to by Mr. and Mrs. Parry. Don't you worry, Hannah, I shall have this sorted out by lunchtime. In the meantime, here are a couple of shillings for food, and I shall speak to Mr. Davies and see if we cannot find a cleaner place for you to lodge until you can be freed."

As she left the gaol, Frances did think about Lazenby somewhere in the building above her, so near and yet so unattainable. She quashed the impulse to turn back and demand to see the earl, turning resolutely instead toward the haberdashers, determined to sort out this mess, which at least, unlike Lazenby's drama, did have the potential to be easily resolved. And so it proved, for what with Fran's threats to remove her business and that of several Nantwich ladies, including Lady Dorfold, the Appersetts, and Lady Tollemache, not to mention her clear willingness to fund Hannah's legal expenses, the Parrys found themselves eager to withdraw their accusations, furnishing a handsome apology and a promise to recommend Miss Evans's dressmaking skills to both regular and new customers at the shop. Fran accompanied Mr. Parry back to the gaol house, where they spoke with Davies, and Hannah was soon freed.

This time, Miss Wilbraham did not leave promptly. She waited until Mr. Parry and Hannah were clear of the premises before speaking with Davies.

"I wish to visit Earl Lazenby. Take me up to see him, please."

"But Miss Wilbraham, he is accused of murder. He may be dangerous."

"He is still relatively weak from his accident. I do not believe him to be dangerous in the least and I have a message for him from Lady Dorfold. I believe she is coming later to visit him?"

"Yes, indeed. But I shall have to lock you in with him lest he make an attempt to escape."

"Very well, although I believe that he is neither a murderer nor so dishonorable as to run from his captors.

You will allow me ten minutes with him, no more, and I shall have a guinea for you when I have finished."

Davies led Miss Wilbraham up the steep stairs to a locked door. He drew out a mass of keys and muttered to himself as he sought out the correct one. He carefully locked the door behind him before leading her down a corridor to another locked door. Once again, Davies unlocked it, ushered Miss Wilbraham through and then locked it behind them. At last they stood before the door leading to the earl's rooms. Davies knocked before opening the door to the room where the earl sat by the barred window, warming his hands over the brazier.

He looked up as the door opened and his face gave his feelings away entirely. He could not conceal the joy and wonder which filled him as he saw Frances in the doorway, tall, slender, and serious. Then he stood and it was as if shutters had closed over his soul.

"You should not have come."

"I know." Fran waited until Davies had turned the key in the lock, trapping them both in the cell. Both she and the earl listened out for his footsteps fading away and the clank of his keys as he locked the outer doors. "We have ten minutes. I do not know whether Soames has told you my news."

"About Tarbuck going to Liverpool in search of the girl?"

"Yes. But I don't believe that Soames has heard that Tarbuck has spotted the man, Ned Minto. I had a letter from him yesterday afternoon. There is no indication whether he will be able to lure the pair back to Nantwich, but I have high hopes." Fran undid her bonnet and unbuttoned her cloak. She handed them to the earl who dropped them onto a chaise longue in the corner.

"Miss Wilbraham. Frances. What are you doing here? You know you should not be here. I never expected to see you again." He stayed by the chaise longue, as if hoping the distance between them might calm his reaction to her.

"I know. Nor should I be expending any effort in clearing your name. I should simply leave you to rot and suffer the punishment you so richly deserve." Fran smiled and went up to the earl, holding out her hands. "But I could not. I was here on other business, and the temptation was too great. I had to see you."

"What about your reputation?" He took her hands and drew her close, gazing into the depths of her dark eyes as though drinking from an oasis.

"I shall not be about long enough for the biddies to destroy it. I am leaving for London in a month, or less, I believe. As soon as Kitty and Sir Arthur have moved out of Dysart House, I shall close it and go to London. I shall spend the rest of the winter with friends there and then accompany them to Paris and Rome in the spring. By the time I return, if I return, any whisper of outrage will have dissipated entirely." She disengaged from his grasp and went to the table, where she fidgeted with his pens and ink. Lazenby followed her.

"Do you go with a respectable family?" He too idly played with the papers scattered about the surface.

"I do. Friends of my father's, scholarly folk, not tonnish at all. Respectable, modest, and reasonably well-heeled." She picked up a book and flicked through it.

"Do they know your reasons for travelling?" He took the book from her hands and firmly replaced it on the table.

"The public reasons—Kitty is off my hands, I am seeking new interests and horizons. They know nothing about you. Kitty does not correspond with them, and she is the only one who would tell them."

"You are rash and impetuous and foolish to come here. But I am so glad to see you, darling Fran." He raised her hands to his lips and kissed each one, then reluctantly pushed her away.

"And I you." She caught his hands again. "I know that you believe that there can never be any association between us, but perhaps in time. Perhaps if you came to meet me in Rome or Florence, next spring, no one would raise an eyebrow. The world will have forgotten this great furor."

"What about Mrs. Featherton?" He did not look away as he asked.

"You were wrong to take up with her, but you tried to behave as honorably as possible in the circumstances. I am deeply sorry she has died, and I hear from Lady Dorfold that Mr. Featherton is devastated. But that is in the past. I do not believe that now you would ever treat anyone so casually. Would you?"

"No. If nothing else, this whole grim episode has taught me to value my fellow humans. And I think, myself. I know you deserve better. Fran, how can you love me?" He turned away from her and went to the barred window. Fran did not follow, but she did speak.

"You are fallible. So am I. I have made mistakes and spoken harshly where I should be kind. I have a tendency to arrogance, a conviction that I am always right, and a managing streak. How can you love me?"

"Because you are a source of perpetual fascination to me. What you say, what you think, what you feel, I want to know all of the answers to these questions on every subject under the sun. I love to watch you and when I do not see you, I am thinking of you constantly. I've never wished to discover every secret of another human before; it is novel and terrifying. I cannot tell whether this is the love of which poets rhyme and singers wail, but I think it is love."

Fran went up to Lazenby and slipped her arms about

his neck. "I think so too. I know no better than you what love might be, but I believe that this is the closest one can be to love. I do not know how or why I have come to love you, but I do." She kissed him then. A gentle, light kiss on his cheek. He turned his head and met her lips with his. He deepened the kiss and her arms tightened about his neck and his arms came round her waist to hold her steady, or himself, he wasn't sure because the world seemed to have tilted on its axis.

Fourteen

The panting of Davies and the clinking of his keys in the distance shattered the cocoon of passion which seemed to have enveloped Fran and Lazenby. They broke apart in a daze, gazing into one another's eyes for a long moment before turning away and shifting to opposite sides of the room.

"He's come too soon, it can't yet be ten minutes." Fran was breathless and dismayed.

"If anything, it is longer." The earl looked carefully at Fran. "Stand still." He came over and smoothed out her hair, straightened her necklace and earrings and stepped back. "Perfect." He went over to the chaise longue and picked up her cloak and bonnet. He handed the bonnet to her and watched as she hurriedly adjusted her headgear. He found himself unable to take his eyes off her. "Frances, you mustn't come back. Please don't. You know I want nothing more than to see you, but it's no good for your reputation if it gets out, and it is bound to get out."

"I won't. I shall try not to. I didn't mean to this time. It just happened." She sighed as the key turned in the lock and Davies came in. Fran gathered her wits and spoke formally. "Good day to you, sir. I hope the message from Dorfold Hall brought you some relief."

Lazenby bowed. "Much relief, I thank you, Miss Wilbraham."

She looked back once, then turned and followed Davies with a steady, controlled step. The earl turned his back and went to the window. In the distance, he could see the trees along the river, turning from the brilliant flames and ochers of autumn to drab brown, some branches baring themselves in preparation for winter. In a month, Fran would be gone from here, and he could not imagine where he would be. He did hope that Tarbuck could track down this girl, but he held out no great hopes. It was likely that he would stand trial for this murder, although Featherton assured him that the evidence against him was far too flimsy for a trial to progress far.

One kiss. That would have to sustain him. She could not afford to be associated with him and he cared for her too deeply to make a wreck of her life as he had so thoughtlessly done to so many other women. This repentance was an uncomfortable business.

On her return to Dysart House, Reed greeted Fran with the information that Mr. Tollemache was waiting in the front room on the first floor.

"Are Sir Arthur and Lady Kitty here?" She undid her bonnet.

"Yes, ma'am, they are just changing. I understand they will be down directly."

"I shall go into Mr. Tollemache briefly, but if I have not been able to leave him after a quarter hour, come and find me, if you please." She handed him her outdoor clothes and started up the stairs to the drawing room.

"Certainly, ma'am." He bowed and withdrew below stairs with a complicit twinkle in his eye.

She slipped quietly into the drawing room where Tollemache was standing by the mantelpiece, weighing in his palm a silver statuette of a sleeping spaniel which Mrs. Wilbraham had given to her husband to commemorate a particularly fine gundog over twenty years before, then examining a Dresden figurine with some disdain. Fran stood there, tamping down her fury at seeing this dangerous and arrogant creature fingering the ornaments she prized as though evaluating their worth at auction. She must give no indication of her suspicions.

"Mr. Tollemache?"

The Honorable Lionel jumped and nearly dropped the little shepherdess he held. "Miss Wilbraham! Have you rescued the deserving poor from the prison gates?"

"I have." She advanced into the room. "My father gave that to me to commemorate my eighteenth birthday. Do you like it, Mr. Tollemache?"

"The colors are exquisite. The glaze is perfection. Dresden?" He replaced it on the mantel with some care, realigning it with precision.

"Yes. Have you been offered refreshment?"

"I have, but I am waiting for Sir Arthur and Lady Kitty." Fran indicated that Tollemache should sit down. He took a seat with a flourish. "How fortunate I am in my relatives. So kind, so welcoming. But soon, I must leave Nantwich and find my way in the world."

"We shall be sorry to see you go, but of course, the wider world must call." She took her time arranging her skirts and avoiding his gaze. Then she looked up. Tollemache's eyes glinted and he smiled, revealing a rather wolfish grin. "Will you be truly sorry? Will you, Miss Wilbraham?"

Lying was bad enough without the lie being seen through. Fran blinked at Tollemache's effrontery. "We shall all be saddened with one less gentleman at our disposal."

"Ah, Miss Wilbraham, so careful." He stood and approached her seat and went down on one knee. "I assume it is not worth reopening my suit? It would be such an inspiration to me in my search for gainful employment if I were assured of your role in my future."

Fran felt teased and worried at. Knowing of Tollemache's duplicity and cruelty made it difficult not to recoil from him physically. He was doing his best to hem her in but to stand would be to give way to his bullying, making it obvious that he affected her. She looked him directly in the eye.

"I must make myself plain, Mr. Tollemache. There is no prospect that I would ever accept your suit."

He stood and withdrew from her. "You prefer your earl. You will make yourself a pariah for this man but you will not entertain an honorable offer from an unblemished source. Truly the ways of womankind are mysterious and unfathomable." His hands were clenched behind his back as though without such restraint he might take her up and shake her.

"I see my sister has been sharing my secrets. I may prefer the earl, but I will be making myself a pariah for no one. I am well aware that there is no likelihood of any alliance reputable or otherwise between me and the earl." Fran rose and went to the bell. "Mr. Tollemache, I do not believe there is anything further to be said. You are my brother-in-law's cousin and as such, welcome here until such time as you leave or the house is closed. However, you will be stretching that welcome should you continue to press this proposal. Let me be frank. Your attention is flattering, but fruitless. You must abandon any expectation of my agreeing to marry you."

"Very well. There is no need to send for the footman to escort me out. I shall be dining at The Crown tonight, which I am sure will be a considerable relief to you."

"I hear their food is excellent," responded Fran through gritted teeth. "Surely you wish me to ring for your coat and hat? It is getting chillier and chillier."

"I daresay Reed will have them ready for me at the foot of the stairs." Tollemache made one last sally. "Isn't it curious how the earl's glove came to be in Mrs. Featherton's pocket? There seems to be no other evidence in this case at all. Still, I daresay he will get off. Though not without a blemished name. Or rather, another layer of tarnish. Just as well he is the last of the Ferrars family. They must be spinning in their graves. They used to be so respectable. Good evening to you, Miss Wilbraham."

"Good evening to you." Fran did not voice her hope that she never saw the man again, but as he shut the door, she felt the strain of being in his presence dissipating from her shoulders, her back, her legs. She took a seat. He had frightened her, and she knew that even if he was not her prime suspect in this terrible case, he was a cold-hearted creature more than capable of the viciousness required to watch a woman drown.

She was still sitting, gazing into the flames of the fire when Kitty and Sir Arthur came into the room.

"Why Fran, you are not yet dressed for dinner. We sit down in twenty minutes, do we not? Unless we put the hour back. It would be more fashionable, though I know you do not care for such things. Will it incommode Cook dreadfully?"

Kitty's flow of chatter finally eased and she looked around. "Where is Lionel? I thought that he would wait and share a drink with us before repairing to The Crown. Have you chased him away, Frances?"

"I fear I may have done so. I find that you have told him a good deal more about my affections than I would wish to be known outside my immediate family."

"He is immediate family," replied Kitty sharply. "He could be even more immediate. How many men would be constant in their affections even when facing a rival such as Lazenby?"

"Kitty, he is not immediate family. He is not related to me in any way, and he will never be related to me. The only constancy he is capable of is his determination to seek funding for a life of leisure, and let me clearly state, as I have already twice explained to Mr. Tollemache: I am not prepared to fund him in any capacity, least of all that of wife."

Kitty was puce with fury. "Arthur, you cannot let her speak to me so."

Sir Arthur stood there, his mouth agape, his eyes darting from sister to sister. Fran came to his rescue. "We should not cross swords, Sir Arthur." He looked at her in some relief and then back at his wife who was still glowering. Fran continued, "Nor should we, Kitty."

Kitty harrumphed and Fran considered voicing her suspicions of Lionel Tollemache. But Tarbuck had not yet completed his mission, and Kitty's lack of discretion was so ingrained that Tollemache was bound to discover that the hunt for Becky Chalmers was on the very next day. To endanger the girl further would be utter folly. She excused herself to go upstairs and change for dinner.

The meal was excruciating, with Kitty putting on her haughtiest airs and graces, Sir Arthur striving to agree with both ladies, hopping from contradiction to contradiction and perpetually picked up in his errors by his wife, while Fran simply simmered, delivering occasional frigid utterances in response only to direct questions or requests. Kitty levelled ever-wilder accusations against the earl, uttering dire warnings that this was likely only the first of many bodies to be uncovered. Fran dismissed this scathingly as complete nonsense, and Sir Arthur was caught between the two, agreeing with everything that was said until Kitty told him he was behaving like a demented robin and he must cease his fence-sitting and take her part. Fran refused to sit with her sister, withdrawing to her bedroom rather than exchanging another word with her.

This did not help Fran in the least, for her night's rest was exceptionally disturbed. She prided herself on sleeping well, but she heard the clock chime three o'clock before she slept and woke intermittently after that, the earl's predicament, her sister's intransigence, and Lionel Tollemache's predatory behavior whirling about her brain like a ceaselessly turning carousel. In the morning, she woke feeling worn and haggard. She had not seen Lady Dorfold recently, and decided to ride over to share the information that Tarbuck had amassed. At least that would keep her out of Kitty's way.

Fran sent down to the stables so that her chestnut hack would be ready once she had finished her last pieces of correspondence. Perhaps there would be another letter from Tarbuck. But the head groom had not written, so just before ten, she went down in her favorite habit made of dark green velvet with black frogging and a top hat with a matching feather. There was Star, still sprightly despite his twelve years, aching for exercise. She mounted up and trotted delicately out of Nantwich, spurring her mount on to a gallop as she passed the town's limits and its prying eyes.

The ride to Dorfold Hall was over all too quickly. It had blown some of the cobwebs from Fran's brain, but she was still unsettled as she was shown by one of the Dorfold footmen to Lady Dorfold's parlor.

"Fran my dear, it has been days since we've seen you." Fran kissed Lady Dorfold on the cheek and took a seat beside her. "I hear you saw Lazenby yesterday."

"As usual, your finger is on the pulse of Nantwich gossip."

"Well, the earl confessed, although Davies was a little baffled as to why I should send a message through you when I was visiting him yesterday afternoon." Lady Dorfold looked down at her embroidery and knotted a thread intently before continuing. "My dear, I am not sure it was wise to visit him. You won't take it amiss if I advise you not to do so again?"

"Of course not. And I shall not be doing so. I was there on account of my poor Hannah."

"And you were seized by a great compulsion." Lady Dorfold was sympathetic. "I understand perfectly. Are you very worried?"

"I am. And I've come to tell you something in confidence, something I should have told Sir Richard but did not. But time is running so short before the Assizes." Fran explained about Tarbuck's hunt for Becky Chalmers and Amy Appersett's observations. "I didn't tell Sir Richard initially because his men are spread thinly enough as it is, and I wasn't sure that this was worth pursuing. But perhaps he can spare someone to assist Tarbuck."

"That may well be the case. I know he has had thin enough pickings here. But do you really suspect Mr. Tollemache?"

"I wouldn't have without Amy having seen him on the bridge. I hesitate to say it, but I genuinely dislike him. Of course that does not make him a murderer. The difficulty is that there is nothing to connect him to Mrs. Featherton other than Amy's evidence, which is even more circumstantial than this beastly glove in the wretched woman's pocket."

Lady Dorfold patted Frances's hand. "Featherton assures me that it is too slight a piece of evidence to make it worth taking to trial. Especially if anyone else could be brought to stand as a witness that he fully intended to take Mrs. Featherton away and was resigned to his responsibilities."

"Anyone else? Who will give witness to this in the first place?"

"Sir Richard is prepared to take the stand in Lazenby's defence. But there is this feeling that we are partisan."

Fran closed her eyes, imagining what Kitty would have to say once she heard what her sister had volunteered to do.

"I could do so also. He came to see me on the morning of her death. He came to thank me for taking care of his horses. He told me he was unexpectedly called away and must retrieve them."

Lady Dorfold quirked an eyebrow at her friend. "How convenient it would be if you could see your way to making this public."

"Of course I will do so. I shall never hear the end of it from Kitty, but I will do it. Are you sure I must bear witness before the magistrates?"

"I am not sure. We must consult Featherton. It may be that we can escape with a written communication. But your name would be bandied about in court, and you might be requested to come forward for questioning." Lady Dorfold made a moue. "Not very savory for a gentlewoman, I am afraid."

"So be it. Lazenby is innocent and I will not see an innocent man traduced when my testimony might have made a difference."

"I shall inform Sir Richard of this and of your suspicions where Tollemache is concerned. You know, the more it has time to sink in, the more likely I think it is that he did commit this atrocity. How vile!"

This visit did improve Fran's spirits somewhat, and she found herself humming as she went home, wondering if the earl would be able to see her crossing the bridge across the Weaver from his rooms in the prison, hoping that Kitty and Sir Arthur would be out when she arrived home and generally considering how best to frame her testimony for the earl.

When she arrived home, she found Sir Arthur waiting for her. He was crisply dressed, sporting a natty maroon waistcoat, an olive jacket and immaculate pantaloons which did perhaps too much justice to his slightly corpulent figure.

"My dear lady, may I beg a word with you?"

"Of course. Is Kitty out?"

"She is. We have completed our contract for the house and she has gone there with our cousin to discuss furnishings and so forth. They expect me to join them shortly, but I had some business to attend to here." He trailed off, aware he was beginning to babble.

"Of course, Sir Arthur. What was it you wished to say to me?" Fran was still standing. Sir Arthur indicated that she should take a seat, then flushed in embarrassment at having been caught out dictating to his hostess. Fran suppressed a smile and meekly sat. He adjusted his coattails and settled himself on a love-seat facing her.

"My dear sister." He paused and gathered his strength. "I do understand that Kitty may be a little pressing, but it is only because she is deeply concerned with your well-being. She desires nothing more than your happiness."

"I do understand, Sir Arthur."

The knight stood and clutched his lapels as a sinking man might clutch a branch. "She is deeply distressed that you will not entertain any question of marriage with our kinsman."

"I am aware of it, brother." Fran's tone chilled noticeably. Sir Arthur winced, but carried on.

"My dear lady. It is so regrettable. She does not understand your objections. Indeed, neither do I."

"Sir Arthur, I thought I had made myself perfectly

clear. I cannot marry where I do not love. Mr. Tollemache, being your cousin, is clearly most estimable. But
I find he is not a man I am able to love. How can I make
you understand?"

"But love is no sound foundation for marriage. I am
fortunate of course in having met a woman whom I esteem and worship with all my heart. But surely it is most
important to bestow yourself on a man of standing?"

"Sir Arthur, I have explained over and over to Kitty that
I see no reason to marry. I am my own mistress. I am exceptionally fortunate in being in sole command of a
respectable independence and I am subject to no caprices
and whims but my own. I see no need to marry anyone."
Fran strove to maintain a pleasant tone in the face of Sir
Arthur's incomprehension.

"It is most unfortunate. Every woman needs a man to
guide her. I did beg your father to entrust me with the
burden of acting as your guardian, but no, he must wil-
fully settle his whole fortune on you and who knows how
you will dissipate it."

Understanding at last that the Tollemaches would
never rest until they had appropriated her fortune and
reappropriated Dysart House which they had so casually
disposed of years before, Fran sighed.

"Is it so very difficult to acknowledge that I am a competent manager of my own affairs? I have been in charge
of the family finances since before my father fell ill. I
have not wasted the fortune on cards or racing, drinking, whoring . . ." Sir Arthur started at his sister-in-law's
blunt speaking. "I have seen the capital at my disposal
increase, my home is in good order and until very recently I intended leaving all this to Kitty and her
children. But the more she presses me, the more inclined I am to find some alternative beneficiary. A home
for indigent women, an orphanage, a campaign against

slavery, all these could draw on my money so usefully. Sir Arthur, I must counsel you, I am nearing the end of my patience with my sister."

"Dear Frances, I only did as my wife requested. She begged me to speak to you out of the purest of motives, I assure you." His agitation could not be suppressed. He jumped up and paced the room. "You who are so delicate, so sensitive, so full of sensibility for the plight of others, would not wish to wound your sister so deeply."

Frances also stood and went over to the fireplace. She watched Sir Arthur with a sensation of detachment that was quite new to her. "You must discuss this with Kitty, of course, but I feel I should warn you both that if either of you raises the subject of marriage with me again, whether to Mr. Tollemache or any other individual, however highly you may esteem them, I shall take the very next opportunity to alter my will and leave everything I possess away from my family."

"Oh, sister, poor Kitty will find this very harsh. Very harsh indeed."

"Sir Arthur, do I have to spell everything out as though to a three-year-old? I did not say that I would do this, only that I might if I chose. I do not yet choose to do so and it lies in your hands to prevent Kitty from teasing me half to death with this incessant talk of marriage."

"What will please you? Shall I send cousin Lionel away?"

"If you desire it. Perhaps if it would grieve you to see him leave Nantwich, you might invite him to your new home. All I ask is that you cease badgering me to accept him and that you make it clear to him that there can be no hope of success with me." Fran saw her chance and grasped it firmly. "I would also be obliged if Kitty could keep any confidences that I might share with her. You may wish to point out to her that I am exceedingly unlikely to share any confidences with her if she is to spread them so liberally amongst the Tollemache family. I am sure that both you and she would feel far happier knowing my intentions, my hopes and plans, but if she cannot keep these to herself, then I will have no hesitation in keeping them secret from her."

Sir Arthur watched his sister with increasing panic. He did not relish in the slightest the prospect of relating the details of this interview with Kitty, who would rail against him and rail against her sister and rail against the world for its injustices. But the truth was, one had to admire Frances. She was a controlling woman, such as few men would wish to marry, but she did not mope or nag. She simply stated how things would be and abided by her decisions. Her determination not to wed Lionel Tollemache was a blow, but she was certainly consistent, and Sir Arthur had more confidence in her than Kitty, who firmly believed that she would marry the dreadful Lazenby as soon as the opportunity presented itself.

"My dear sister, I shall convey your sentiments to my good wife. We shall oblige you insofar as we are able."

"I am relieved to find you so reasonable. It may be some consolation to Kitty to think that you and your children are far more likely to benefit from my fortune if I do not marry Mr. Tollemache. He seems to me a very expensive sort of individual and not the most selfless of men."

Sir Arthur withdrew. Fran pitied him a little. He was only now learning his own wife's idiosyncrasies and seemed already quite under Kitty's sway. She wondered how successful he would be in delivering his message. If Kitty did listen to him, it would be a considerable relief to Frances, and something of a victory. Still, in only a few weeks, they would be free of each other for months, which might allow for a calming of hostilities. It was a pity to be constantly at outs with Kitty, and the prospect of accusing the admirable Lionel of murder or at the least, manslaughter, was not guaranteed to improve matters between them.

Fran shivered. Tollemache had to be uncovered. Hopefully, Tarbuck would succeed in his mission. It was tempting to ride hotfoot to Liverpool and take over the search herself, although in her heart of hearts, Fran knew that she was entirely unfitted to do such a thing. She could only sit and wait—perhaps the hardest task of all.

Fifteen

The Assizes were usually held in Chester under the supervision of Judge Henry Fairfield, who had been one of the Cheshire circuit judges for nearly twenty years. But if the Chester gaol house was over full and there were enough indictable cases to be heard, Sir Henry was prepared to travel. This year, as Nantwich's chief magistrate, Sir Richard had cases of bigamy and systematic sheep-stealing which he had felt were too great a burden for the Quarter Sessions. And now there was this murder, if murder it truly was. Sir Henry had been invited to Nantwich well before Sally Featherton's death, but it was just as well he had agreed to come.

Along with the sheriff's men, barristers, bailiffs, and plaintiffs came a fair and an accompanying hike of the prices at all the inns and taverns of the town. The prospect of public executions also swelled the town's population, for there were those who would travel miles to see such a thing. Consequently, there were fisticuffs and brawls, there were impromptu dances, races for men, ferrets, and pigeons, competitions for swallowing the largest number of eggs or drinking yards of ale and, late at night, for the men only, pugilism. The October fair was particularly busy, for not only had the usual peddlers and craftsmen come in from darkest Wales with odd wares, but also it was the time to buy geese and pigs to fatten up for Christmas.

This year, a troupe of showmen came too, causing a great additional furor. There were contortionists, jugglers, acrobats, and tightrope walkers, a strong man, a whole bearded family, two fat men, a fire-eater, and two Italian sisters, one with trick monkeys, the other with performing dogs. There was great rivalry between the young men of Nantwich, all of whom wished to squire the sisters about town.

Fran habitually gave her people time off while the fair was in town. Chores were pared down to the bare minimum, menus were simplified, and once all the work was done, her servants could attend the festivities. The court itself was as much an attraction as the entertainers, for Sir Henry Fairfield was sharp-tongued and the lawyers before him had to be quick or risk being made to appear foolish before all the audience. The Assembly Hall, so recently a venue for subscription balls, was transformed into a courtroom. The Assizes would last a good three weeks, perhaps more, with Sir Henry's first task to hear the list of Bills of Indictment and determine which cases would be placed before a jury. Then he and Sir Richard must supervize the appointing of a jury. The first cases would not be heard until the Wednesday after the court arrived in Nantwich.

Sir Arthur paid to secure good seats for the proceedings, and his party, including Fran and Mr. Tollemache, took their places early on the Monday morning. They were near the Dorfolds and Mr. Featherton. Fran caught a glimpse of Amy Appersett in the crowd, accompanied by her mother and brother. The girls exchanged glances. Amy raised her eyebrows as if to ask what progress Fran had made in uncovering evidence against Tollemache, and Fran responded with a slight shrug and shake of her head. There had been no word from Tarbuck these five days. Nor had Fran quite got round to admitting to her sister that she was prepared to give evidence in Lazenby's favor. Fran looked round also for Soames, who was sitting with some of Sir Richard's men looking somewhat gloomy.

In came Sir Henry, and the whole court stood while he arranged his robes and adjusted his wig before taking his seat and nodding at the clerk who called for silence in court before bowing to the judge.

"What cases are before us this time?" Sir Henry's voice was resonant and slightly impatient. He knew perfectly well which cases were before him, the usual litany of trespass, poaching and wilful destruction of property, robbery with violence, grievous bodily harm, and a little more interesting, a case of bigamy. Oh, and the death of this woman, of course. But the clerk read through the list in a droning voice and the judge sat with his head cradled on his hand with an air of great boredom, turning to the clerk to confirm that he would hear a case or dismissing minor cases for the next Quarter Session. Even when Mrs. Featherton's possible murder was announced, although the rest of the court received that with an intake of breath and an anticipatory muttering, Sir Henry remained impassive and unimpressed. The judge banged his gavel and glared around the premises.

"We shall appoint the jury now, then start with the bigamy. Provided we move steadily through the catalogue of exceptionally tedious burglaries and affrays, we should reach the murder early next week. That should be enough time to clear the business up." There was a collective sigh of disappointment, then a great shuffling and shifting as people began leaching out of the doors, for the appointment of the jury was a lengthy and fairly dull business. So the drama subsided as did the press of bodies in court.

Trapped by their public position in court, Fran and the Tollemaches were not able to leave until the first recess. They struggled through the press of people and out into the fresh air, both Kitty and Fran burying their noses in their wilted posies in an attempt to avoid inhaling the pungent reek of the crowd around them.

"What a shame! I thought he would have insisted on hearing the Lazenby case first. You would have thought he would not wish to inconvenience the earl any more than necessary, and if he is to be acquitted or sent away to trial in London, surely that could be done at once?" Sir Arthur seemed genuinely affronted by the judge's delay, although he had not hitherto expressed any interest in the earl's rank or comfort.

Kitty and Tollemache produced various theories to explain Fairfield's apparently incomprehensible behavior, but Frances was simply relieved. She had another week's grace, and surely Tarbuck, who knew the date of the Assizes perfectly well, must have found something by now. She did wonder whether Sir Richard might not have discussed this with Sir Henry. The two men had known each other for many years and while not the best of friends, shared a healthy respect for each other. At all events, there was no opportunity to ask either Sir Richard or Lady Dorfold if this was the case.

Lionel Tollemache made his excuses, muttering all the while about the increased discomforts of staying at The Crown. "The service was lamentable enough, but now that Sir Henry and his entourage have colonized the inn, it is thoroughly atrocious. I shall be lucky to secure a decent cup of claret, let alone a palatable meal."

Frances studiedly ignored this undisguised plea for an invitation to Dysart House, despite Kitty's frantic eye contact, and bade the fellow farewell as civilly as she could before taking Sir Arthur's arm and propelling the baronet and his wife towards Churchyardside at a healthy pace.

"Why wouldn't you invite cousin Lionel to supper? It would have been only civil. You may be determined not to marry him, but must you bar him from our home?"

"Kitty my darling, I am sure that Frances is sensible of the difficulty our cousin must have in coming to Dysart House now that he knows his suit is fruitless." Sir Arthur was prompt in heading off another explosion between the sisters. "We shall be installed in our own home in ten days or so, and we may invite Lionel to stay as soon as you wish."

Kitty opened her mouth but caught her husband's eye and subsided. Frances noted this with some interest. It seemed that Sir Arthur was not such a doormat for her sister as he had appeared. She wondered what he would make of her suspicions of dear cousin Lionel. But there was no point in voicing them unless some word had come from Tarbuck.

Fran had to wait another three days to hear from her head groom, three days which seemed agonizing in their length, despite the abundant distractions offered by the fair and the travellers. Lady Dorfold recruited Frances to accompany Matilda to see the freaks and the sideshows.

"You know how she is! She will want to set up her own troupe of performing ponies or some such nonsense, and any objections I might raise will be greeted with a great rolling of the eyes and deep sighs. Whereas you will be able to deflect her from any rash plans with some judicious and timely observation of the disadvantages of taking on any such activity." Lady Dorfold had read her daughter correctly; the girl was entranced by the dogs and monkeys and insisted on visiting them daily to work out how their tricks were done. It was on the third such visit that Fran's fears for Tarbuck were finally relieved.

The travelling entertainers had been issued a license which allowed them to set up tents on the south side of the market place. The performances of the Tagliolini sisters took place every two hours, allowing trainers and animals a little rest. Having escorted Matilda there on Tuesday and Wednesday, Fran was a little reluctant to frequent their tent yet again on Thursday afternoon. In the event, it was just as well that she did, for as she and Matilda were preparing to enter the tent, Tarbuck appeared at her elbow.

"Miss Wilbraham, I must talk to you urgently."

Frances looked round frantically. "I cannot leave Matilda." She sought some familiar face in the crowd—surely there was someone reliable with whom Matilda could stay while Tarbuck spoke with her outside the tent. With some relief, she caught sight of Farr, with Hannah Evans and her little sister in tow. She handed Matilda into Hannah's care and asked them all to keep a seat for her.

The hubbub of people eased at the edge of the market square and Tarbuck quickly led Frances to a quiet spot.

"I've found them and I've hidden them. I don't trust Minto, not in the least. He'd give Becky up to the highest bidder so I need some money right away. The dratted girl's besotted with him, can't see through him, so I can't part her from him."

"I don't have much with me now, but Reed can give you what you need. He's at home, he said he'd seen enough fairs to last a lifetime and that the house shouldn't be left deserted."

"Quite right. Don't know when I've seen such riffraff fill the town." Tarbuck stared about him in disgust. Fran could not contain her curiosity.

"Where have you left them?"

"Here lying low in amongst the market traders and the

acrobats. I thought it best to keep her away from the house, seeing as how Sir Arthur may feel some family loyalty to his cousin. Becky swears it was him that gave her the note."

"Mr. Lionel Tollemache? Definitely?" Her eyes sparkled with relief. Lazenby might yet be spared an appearance before the court.

"She's certain. Didn't think much of him, truth be told. I still haven't explained why it's so important she be here. Minto has an idea. I reckon he'll take the money and do a runner, though."

"Poor girl. He won't desert her straightaway, will he?"

"Not if he sniffs any more guineas coming her way. Don't worry, I think I can manage him and his greed. But the lass is in for a shock. Just so long as she's not with child; that would finish it with Minto."

"Thank heavens you've found them, Tarbuck. As you say, we must keep them safe until we can get her to Sir Richard or Sir Henry Fairfield."

Tarbuck headed for Dysart House and Fran sat through the Tagliolini sisters' show, itching with impatience, desperate to get home and summon Sir Richard and the justice to her house, hoping against hope that Tollemache could be arrested before sunset. She did not dare let her mind wander toward what might happen next. She had a feeling that Lazenby, repentant as he was, would never offer for her. But that was a different dilemma for another day.

At last, the finale of the show, where monkeys rode dogs and jumped through flaming hoops, was done and Fran took Matilda back to Dysart House. Tarbuck had been and gone, according to Reed.

"He took twelve guineas, Miss Frances. Twelve guineas! Of course I gave him what he asked for, but if he isn't set upon and loses the whole sum, I shall be surprised. One shouldn't go out in these crowds without expecting that sort of trouble."

"Thank you, Reed. Have you sent to Sir Richard yet?"

"I have. They are all still in court, and he is to come here to collect Miss Matilda as soon as the day's proceedings are complete. But Sir Henry, he's a stickler, he won't let up until he feels ready. I've heard of other judges who end the day prompt at four o'clock, or even earlier if they choose, but he'll work straight through until six or even eight. Why, I've even heard of a sitting lasting past ten o'clock."

But before either the magistrate or the judge appeared, Fran's brother-in-law appeared in considerable agitation, bursting into the drawing room where Frances and Matilda were comparing novels.

"I've no idea what to do!" He looked first at Fran, then at Matilda. "I beg your pardon, Frances, but I must have a word with you in private, if Miss Matilda will excuse us?"

"Of course she will. Matilda, go up and wash your hands, we shall be having some refreshment very soon, tea and cakes, I believe." Matilda curtseyed politely to Sir Arthur and left.

The baronet hurried to the window and gazed out on the street, anxiously inspecting the passers-by before turning to his sister-in-law and hissing, "I know not what to do. I have the most terrible suspicions."

"Of what?"

"Rather say of whom. To which I must reply, my cousin! I cannot believe it, I hesitate to voice my thoughts at all, it seems so improbable."

Fran was alert and on edge. "Explain yourself, Sir Arthur."

"We were at the market, Mr. Tollemache and I. Kitty had disappeared with some acquaintance or other, telling me not to wait, she would make her own way home, we would not wish to assist in the purchase of all her frills and laces. So we were walking away when cousin Lionel went pale and rigid. He hauled me through the crowd in pursuit of whatever it was he had seen, but man, woman or beast, we could not catch it up. Then he took me back to The Crown and tried to fix that he was with us on the evening of the murder between five and seven. But I believe it was one of the first nights on which he went back to The Crown to dine, having been recently rejected by you and consequently a little delicate in coming too often to join us for his meals. I kept telling him that I could not remember precisely, but he became more and more insistent, and it crossed my mind that it was he who met this woman and sent her to her doom. Of course such a notion is ridiculous, but he was so vehement and even a little forceful."

Fran looked carefully at Sir Arthur. He might be pompous and somewhat stuck-up, but he was a fundamentally honest man.

"I too have had my suspicions. There are several things that have led me to this conclusion, Sir Arthur, and your experience only confirms it. I believe he caught a glimpse of the girl who carried the note to Mrs. Featherton, the note which instructed her to meet with her killer at the riverbank at six o'clock." Fran rang for Reed and continued, "We must send someone to Tarbuck to be extra vigilant in watching Becky Chalmers. If your cousin has carried out this deed, he is likely to make some attempt on Becky to prevent her from testifying that it was he who wrote that note and passed it to her."

Reed came in, unhurried and dignified as ever despite Fran's frenzied ringing. "Reed, I must extract Sir Richard from the courtroom at once. Do we have anyone we can send? And as soon as Tarbuck is back, he must be sent to me. It is of the utmost urgency."

"Farr is returned, Miss Frances. I could send him to the court. As for Tarbuck, I shall wait for him myself. The rest of the household is . . . gallivanting." A pained expression crossed his features as he spoke.

Frances and Sir Arthur paced the room in silence as they waited for Farr to bring Sir Richard to Dysart House. The minutes ticked past, both inhabitants of the room starting as the quarter hours chimed first once and then twice before they heard the door open and the murmur of masculine voices, followed by the firm tread of a man coming upstairs.

It was Sir Richard. "Frances. Sir Arthur. How may I assist?" He was cool, still somewhat irked by Fran's failure to reveal that she had sent Tarbuck in search of Becky Chalmers. He had been grateful for Amy Appersett's observations, but also skeptical about their worth without any solid evidence to support them.

Sir Arthur spoke, then Fran explained that Tarbuck had tracked down Minto and Becky Chalmers. "He has brought them here and concealed them somewhere in amongst the folk come for the fair. But now Mr. Tollemache has spotted Becky, I fear for her safety."

Sir Richard nodded gravely. "We must keep her closely guarded. We need to get her before Sir Henry. Even out of court, once he hears her evidence, he will probably declare that Lazenby has no Bill to face and the charges will be dismissed. Of course, there will then be sufficient evidence also for a Bill to be drawn up against Mr. Tollemache. I suppose we had better arrest him, regardless of the state of Lazenby's case."

Just then, Reed admitted Tarbuck, who looked coolly at Sir Richard and Sir Arthur. But he was concerned when he noted Fran's agitation.

"Miss Wilbraham, is anything the matter?"

"Tollemache has seen Becky at the fair."

"Damn the girl. I told her to lie low. I might have known she could no more do that than fly to the moon. She wished to show off Ned Minto to all her friends, but I did think I'd impressed upon the pair of them how important it was they keep hidden."

"Lead us to them, Tarbuck, and I can provide her with shelter and a guard of some sort," said Sir Richard.

Despite the disapproval of all three men, Fran insisted on accompanying them in search of Becky Chalmers. "She will feel easier if she sees me. She will feel she is in dreadful trouble if she sees only a gaggle of men and very likely try to evade you. I might be able to talk some sense in her." She called for her cloak and Tarbuck went in search of a lantern. Sir Arthur was less keen to brave the fair again and having ascertained that he was not needed, volunteered to remain at home and watch for Kitty and Tollemache.

Evening was drawing in, but the fair was as busy as ever, every corner of the Market Square lit with torches. Tarbuck wove his way through the crowds, Sir Richard and Fran trying to keep up and remain as unobtrusive as possible. The uneven flickering of fires and flaming brands made the shadows seem darker and Fran kept imagining she saw Tollemache first here, then there, behind them, ahead of them, a taunting smirk on his bland face to tease her.

Tarbuck led them through the square and across to the field where the fair folk and the troupe of travelling entertainers were camped. It was darker and quieter here, only occasional lanterns illuminating the shadowy silhouettes of tents, carts, and two or three caravans. Here and there, women were stirring cooking pots in front of their homes and in the distance came the shouts and music and yelling of the crowd, somehow intensifying the quiet in this temporary village.

At last, Tarbuck came to a halt outside a darkened tent. "Becky?" he whispered. "Becky? Are you there?" There was no reply. "Minto?" he said once. Then, bending forward, he opened the flap of the tent and shone his lantern within. It was clear the tent had been vacated and in something of a rush. Or perhaps with a struggle. There was bedding there and it had been tumbled, but there were no clothes, no food, no washing hanging dry, no cooking utensils or plates or even a table as was the case with the other tents.

There was a neat caravan nearby, apparently dark, but then Fran looked more closely and saw that there was a faint light from behind the curtain in the window. Tarbuck and Sir Richard were muttering in conference and turning over the few bits of blanket left in Becky's tent. Fran turned away and went up the three steps to the door. She tapped on it.

"Who's there?" A deep, disembodied voice responded. It was impossible to tell if it belonged to man or woman.

"My name is Frances Wilbraham. Please, could you help me?"

"Depends."

"I have money."

The door to the caravan opened and a dark face peered out. "Come in quickly."

By the dim light of a single candle, Fran saw an impassive face with hard planes, sharp cheekbones, and deep-set eyes. It seemed to be a woman, wearing a turban and a tightly bound shawl about her chest. The caravan reeked of blood and a sweet, herbal tobacco. She could not quite stand upright in the enclosed space.

"What help can Yolanda give to the woman?"

Fran looked into her eyes and then neatly piled five

single shilling pieces on the tablecloth. "What happened in the tent next door this evening?"

The woman threw back her head and laughed. "You're another one after the little slut. My, she's a popular missy."

Fran repeated the question calmly. The woman reached for the money and counted it.

"There's more for you if I think you're telling the truth. Another five shillings." Fran chinked the money in her palm, well aware that if this woman chose, she could wrest the coins in a trice from Fran's hand.

"Minto's been looking to get rid of the girl. You weren't the first to come looking for her. There was another man, well-spoken like yourself. She wasn't there when he arrived, but he waited and he watched, he watched and he waited. When Minto came back, he'd had too much to drink. They talked. The man was angry, but too weak to fight Minto. He paid him instead and Minto packed and left. Then the girl came. When she saw the fine-speaking man, she gave a shriek and she ran. She ran like a rabbit when it meets a weasel."

Fran handed over the coins and then took out two more. "Which direction did she take?"

"Down to the river. That's where the girls always go. Down to the river and into the river she'll flow."

Fran recognized that she had received as much information as Yolanda was willing or able to give. She gave the woman the final two shillings and eased out of the caravan, trying not to knock anything or bang her head.

Tarbuck and Sir Richard were waiting.

"We've no time to lose. She's gone down to the Weaver. I think Tollemache was hot on her heels. Let's hope she can run fast." Fran paused, then issued her orders. "Tarbuck, you'll be quickest. Run as fast as you can in search of her while Sir Richard and I fetch help."

Tarbuck turned on his heels and took the fastest way to

the river, while Fran hauled Sir Richard back to Market Square in search of some assistance. He was somewhat bemused by this forceful, determined aspect of Miss Wilbraham. She was not going to allow Tollemache to get away with this crime. Not if she had to hunt him down and corner him herself.

Sixteen

With the huge number of strangers in town, the watch was alert and active. It took only a few minutes for Sir Richard to summon five men to accompany him down to the Weaver. They assembled in the High Street and he turned to Frances.

"I don't suppose I could persuade you to go back home?"

Fran shook her head. "You may yet need me. She may come with a woman more readily. I can keep up, you know that, and once we have found her, we can take her back to Dysart House and keep her safe there until Sir Henry can be summoned. But we must hurry now."

Away from Market Square, the crowd was much sparser. There were certainly more people about than was customary for a Thursday evening in Nantwich, but these were occasional gaggles of children reluctantly meeting their curfew, the odd courting couple, and some of the legal officials attached to the Assizes with no interest in fairs and other such amusements.

The lanterns and lighting also thinned out until there was simply the darkness of the countryside. Fran wondered what on earth had possessed Becky Chalmers to run, and whether she had really gone down to the river. Then she remembered where the Chalmers family cottage was, on the west bank of the river, to the north of the bridge. That is where the maid would be making for, with Tollemache following. The Chalmers cottage was nearly a mile from the bridge, near an old ford which had been for cattle and other livestock but was scarcely used since the bridge had been built.

The search party reached the bridge and paused. Sir Richard sent a couple of men southward along the west bank, just in case Tollemache had caught up with her early and decided to take her to the weir where he had already so successfully disposed of one woman. That left four men and Fran to make their way downstream.

"Should we call her?" asked one of the men.

"No," declared Sir Richard. "If we do, it may alert her attacker, he may hide. We must be quiet as possible and try to surprise them." They doused their lanterns and waited the minute or so it took them to accustom their eyes to the dark. There was a moon out, not full, but it shed a little light, and Fran could just make out the path they needed to take. Sir Richard led the way, familiar enough since boyhood with the river, where he had often attempted to tickle trout. Fran was sandwiched between the three members of the watch. Her petticoats rustled in the grass, but she had stout boots and like Sir Richard had spent enough afternoons escaping from one governess or another by the riverside to know the path well.

Five minutes along the path, the only sound to be heard was the soft panting of the men and the swishing of their movements against the long grass and reeds. They paused and listened every hundred yards or so. The path took them into denser bushes and trees, slightly away from the water's edge. Now underfoot they stepped on leaves and tried to avoid dried twigs that might snap and give away their position.

Ten minutes along, they paused again and this time,

they heard something. At first it seemed to be only the sound of leaves in a bush. Then the sound of rustling and crunching seemed more frenzied and furious and then there was a yell, a man's yell and a woman's shriek, abruptly cut off. Sir Richard blundered towards the sound, and his party broke into a clearing where three shapes were wrestling in the dimness. Fran could just make out that there were two men and a woman. She realized that Tollemache was holding the girl while Tarbuck tried to wrest his arms away from her. It was only a matter of time, for Tarbuck was far stronger than Tollemache, even if he was a good four inches shorter. Becky was struggling too and managed to break free and hurtle into the woods. Frances gathered up her petticoats and followed her, calling now, "Becky, Becky, come back, you're safe, we're here to help you."

Becky turned back and looked for one second, then carried on into the woods. Fran gave up shouting and ran after, determined to pin this elusive girl down once and for all. There would be five men against Tollemache, which should surely be enough.

For all that she was a country girl and sturdy, Becky's stamina was limited and Fran soon caught up with her, leaning against a tree trunk, panting and sobbing.

"Becky, don't run away, you're safe now, I promise."

The girl sank against the tree and then slid down until she was huddled at its roots. She looked up, her face streaked with dirt and tears. "Am I?"

"Yes. There are enough men to hold Mr. Tollemache."

"I've caused a deal of trouble, haven't I? Will I be punished for it, do you think?" She spoke slowly, her voice low and defeated.

"No. I see no reason for punishment. " Fran sank down beside her and put her hand on Becky's shoulder. "You must have been frightened out of your wits."

The girl started sobbing again. "I was. I was. But where's Ned? Where are all Ned's things? Has he left me? Why wasn't he looking out for me?" And she fell into a fresh bout of sobbing, not yet able to believe her lover's perfidy, yet bereft by his absence.

"I am afraid that Mr. Tollemache may have paid him off. I think he is gone for good, my dear. I'm very sorry." Fran hugged Becky to her as a mother holds a child distraught that its favorite toy is broken. The girl's sobs intensified and it felt as though her whole body might break. Fran tried ineffectually to comfort her, stroking her hair and murmuring "There there, there there."

"But I love him so. How could he treat me thus? I'd have done anything for him, Miss, anything." Becky's breath came in great pained gulps. "I didn't want to leave Nantwich, but he said he must, and if I wanted him, I must go along with him. And I went, though I knew it was wrong. Oh, what will become of me?" A fresh sobbing racked the strapping girl. Fran waited until the girl's cries subsided. Finally, shuddering slightly still, Becky wiped her face and searched for a handkerchief. Fran reached in her cloak and handed over her own fine cambric cloth. Becky wiped her eyes and blew her nose, then sat, her arms hugging her knees, her head resting there, exhausted but still shuddering with emotion.

"I don't know yet, Becky, but we must face the music." Fran stood up and held out a hand to the girl. "Come with me now to Dysart House. We must call up Sir Henry and you must speak to him. There may be a reward in it for you. I know that is small consolation."

Becky took Fran's hand and hauled herself up. Fran put her arm about the girl's waist and led her toward the clearing.

The men had subdued Tollemache, who stood now, his arms behind his back, one of the watch on either side. He watched as Becky and Fran came forward, but said nothing.

"We'll take them both back to Dysart House if you'll allow it, Miss Wilbraham. Then we can summon Sir Henry. It will be more pleasant than the gaol house for all of us." Sir Richard waited for Fran's nod of acquiescence before setting off for town, Fran with her arm about Becky Chalmers. From time to time, Tollemache swore as he was jostled and pushed, his hands still bound, over the route which he scarcely knew and found next to impossible to navigate in the dark without falling over his own feet.

Fran was astounded to find that it was only half past eight when the party reached Dysart House. Reed was ready to report that Sir Arthur and Lady Kitty were still out, and that Farr was present. It was fixed that Tollemache should be guarded by two men from the watch and Tarbuck in a small room off the dining room. The rest were dismissed with some extra shillings for their trouble. Fran, Sir Richard, and Becky Chalmers sat in the front parlor, waiting for Farr to rouse the judge. Becky was still very shaken and Fran tried to put her somewhat at her ease so that when Sir Henry arrived, she should not be utterly cowed by his presence and able to give coherent testimony.

Sir Henry arrived promptly. He had known Mr. Wilbraham slightly, but Fran had never seen him without his wig and robes, so it was a shock to her to find that he was a trim, small man with a firm handshake and brisk manner. He was all business.

"What's this then, Sir Richard?"

"We believe this man Tollemache to be the true culprit in the case of the death of Mrs. Featherton. He gave this girl Becky Chalmers half a crown to deliver a note to Mrs. Featherton, a note which arranged a rendezvous with the lady on the riverbank. We have the note, it was in Mrs. Featherton's effects, and we must test his handwriting against it, but otherwise we are convinced that it was he who wrote it. The additional proof is that he hunted down Miss Chalmers when she returned to Nantwich and made an attempt on her life."

"Serious accusations. Of course, I must question the fellow. I take it he is here on the premises."

Tollemache was brought to the judge by Tarbuck. He entered the room slowly, looking first at Sir Richard and then Fran and realizing that he had no allies there. Becky cowered against Fran as Tollemache came closer.

"Mr. Lionel Tollemache?" asked Sir Henry. He was standing, his thumbs in his waistcoat, as he might well have done in the days when he was a barrister cross-examining a witness.

"Yes." Tollemache looked pointedly at a chair, expecting to be asked to take a seat. Sir Henry ignored this and continued.

"Can you explain to me why you were caught attempting to harm this young woman this evening? She still bears the bruises about her neck."

"There has been the greatest misunderstanding. I went in search of this young lady because she had run some errands for me while at The Crown and I did not feel I had sufficiently rewarded her. I wished to give her an additional sum."

Tarbuck harrumphed but at a glare from Sir Henry, fell silent.

"What errands did she run?" The judge paced as he questioned.

"She starched my collars and cravats, she fetched things for me."

"Did she deliver a note on your behalf to Mrs. Featherton?"

"I do not know a Mrs. Featherton, so I believe it unlikely that I would have written a note to her."

Sir Henry smiled. It was not a friendly smile, more like the grin of a shark when it catches the scent of a meal. "I see. I need a sample of your handwriting, if you please, Mr. Tollemache. Would you be so obliging as to write a note for me? I shall dictate the content."

"I do not see why I should, Sir Henry. I am deeply affronted by this whole business. I am assaulted, taken captive, force-marched, and held prisoner."

Fran could see that Tollemache was working himself up into a frenzy. There was a way to shortcut this. "Sir Henry. If you will allow, I have a note from Mr. Tollemache inviting my sister and me out for a drive. It is upstairs in my study, if you will permit me to fetch it."

"You meddling witch." Tollemache spat the words out before he could help himself and looked as astonished by the outburst as the other men in the room. Fran quirked an eyebrow at him. "I always wondered what you truly thought of me, Mr. Tollemache." She left the room and hurried upstairs for the note.

When she re-entered, it was clear that Tollemache had taken refuge in stolid silence. Sir Henry and Sir Richard were now seated, while Tollemache continued to stand, guarded by Tarbuck. She handed a piece of paper to the judge. He perused it thoroughly and said, "I'll keep this if I may, Miss Wilbraham." Then he folded it and tucked it in a pocket.

"Oh, very well, I can see I must confess." Tollemache was defiant. "I did write a note to the Featherton woman. I did meet her as suggested in the note. But I did not kill her. She slipped. I—I do not know how to swim."

"Interesting. But it does not explain how she came to have her clothes ripped and how you failed to alert anyone to her fall. It is a case of manslaughter at the very least. And then there is the question of the assault on this girl. There are charges to be answered." The justice stood. "Sir Richard, you may take this gentleman to the gaol and release your other suspect. It is clear that this Lazenby has no charges to answer."

"There has been a great deal of ill feeling in the town over this case. If we release Lazenby without a hearing, there may be a reaction in some quarters." Sir Richard, while delighted with the result, was reluctant to cause any additional ferment in the town.

"Very well. Take this gentleman to the gaol house, and bring Lazenby before me first thing in the morning. I shall then dismiss the charges against him and we may lay the Bill of Indictment for this fellow before the court. Will that avert riot and mayhem?"

"I believe so. Thank you, Sir Henry, and my sincerest apologies for interrupting your evening."

The judge bowed and withdrew. Sir Richard turned to Fran. "Now that Tollemache is in custody, will you take care of Miss Chalmers?"

"Of course. Reed will find her somewhere to rest and someone to rest with. I know not all of the maids have gone to the fair, and I imagine that she will want some company still."

Tollemache could not contain himself. "You show more care for this serving wench than for my predicament."

"You have brought it on yourself, Mr. Tollemache." Fran spoke coldly, her fear and dislike of this man finally gaining ascendance. "You have shown yourself to be a thoroughly dangerous individual with no feeling for your fellow humans. How you came to push a woman into a river and leave her to drown is something for the courts and your conscience. But it is beyond me to conceive how you can expect anyone to feel any compassion for you."

"This is all your fault," shouted Tollemache. "If you had simply accepted me, none of this would have been necessary. But no, you must set yourself against your family and against what is proper and tease us all with your independent ways and your money." He spat the words out, then made to lunge for her, but was held back by Tarbuck. Struggling, his eyes wild, saliva dotting his chin, he wriggled and squirmed as the groom forced him from the room.

Fran looked at the door, utterly bemused. It was clear that Tollemache was beyond reason. It might yet be that he would end his days in an asylum rather than a prison or on the gallows. She rang for Reed and had him escort Becky away, leaving her alone with Sir Richard.

"You may be needed in court tomorrow, Miss Wilbraham."

"I would not miss it for the world. Nor, I daresay, will Kitty and Arthur. He seemed almost unhinged just now."

"I must escort him to the gaol and speak with Davies. It is very full at the moment, there may be no way of securing a private room for him. But I shall see what I can do. I believe he will disintegrate entirely if we have to place him in a communal cell. You are not upset by his outburst, I hope."

"Not unduly. I am relieved that the earl will finally be released."

"Yes. So long as we have some culprit to take the blame for this death, I believe we may avoid unrest in the town. But with the salt-trade dwindling and other trades suffering, people seem very volatile at the moment."

"What shall we do with the Chalmers girl? Should I bring her to court tomorrow?"

"I see no need for that. She will need to be a witness in Tollemache's trial, of course, but I don't think her presence is necessary unless she wishes to be there to see him indicted. As to her future, we must do something, or she'll end up on the streets. Bloxham won't have her back, but I should think she's learnt her lesson and if she is in a more secluded spot, perhaps she'll be less open to temptation in the form of stray peddlers. Perhaps you and Elizabeth can put your heads together."

"Of course. I shall see you tomorrow morning in court then. I feel sure that Sir Arthur will wish to attend tomorrow morning."

Sir Richard took his leave and Fran picked up a book and sat by the fire, intending to wait up for her sister and brother-in-law. They were not long in returning home. Reed showed them into Fran's drawing room and closed the door.

"What is it, Fran? Reed was most mysterious." Kitty yawned as she spoke.

"Please be seated. I have some news that may shock you." Sir Arthur and Kitty exchanged perturbed glances and sat. "It is Mr. Tollemache. He has been arrested."

"Arrested? Arrested? Our cousin?" Kitty leapt up, flabbergasted. "For what? What is he charged with?"

"The death of Mrs. Featherton. And an assault on the chambermaid from The Crown Hotel, Becky Chalmers, who carried his note of assignation to Mrs. Featherton."

"This is impossible! How can this be?" Kitty rounded on Fran. "This is your fault. If you had only accepted him, he would never have been brought to such a pass."

Sir Arthur turned on Kitty. "How can you speak such folly, Kitty? If the man is the sort to push women into rivers, he is hardly the sort one wants one's sister to marry. Good God, woman, if you could only hear yourself."

"But he is your cousin! He is son of the earl of Dysart!" Kitty fought back valiantly, but saw that her husband was quite implacable.

"Yes, I daresay that may help him escape the gallows,

but to kill one woman and assault another is not the act of a gentleman. Heaven knows what he got up to in Italy." Sir Arthur turned to Frances. "My dear sister, we must apologize for bringing you into contact with such a fellow. Mustn't we, Kitty?" He looked meaningfully at his wife, who gathered the tattered shreds of her dignity about her.

"Yes. I suppose so. I am very sorry, Frances, that you should have had to encounter this Tollemache. You know I only did it with the best intentions."

For the first time, Frances felt easy in her sister's choice of husband. She took Kitty's hands in hers and kissed her sister. "I understand." She suppressed the urge to lecture Kitty on not meddling. She turned to Sir Arthur with new respect. "He is your cousin after all. I have come to no harm. But tomorrow, Mr. Tollemache will face the court and I believe Earl Lazenby will be released. I shall attend, and I thought you might wish to also."

"Of course. We shall be ready."

Sir Arthur and Kitty bade Frances goodnight and retired. She doused the lamps and took a candle up to bed. Her maid was still out at the fair with the other members of staff, so she was alone for once and inevitably the thought of Lazenby arose with nothing to distract her from him. As she unbuttoned her dress, untied her laces and ribbons and rolled down her stockings, he was there in her mind's eye. Would he ever see her as she was now? He must be practised in the art of undressing a woman. What would it be like to have his hands touch her? It was immodest, reprehensible, to have such thoughts, but they would not be suppressed, not as she slipped into her nightdress, not as she pulled the tortoiseshell pins that held her hair in its neat chignon, not as she ran her brush through the thick locks and felt her whole scalp relax. Since he had kissed her, she had done her best to put him out of her mind, for there had then been no future for them. Now he would be released, without a stain on his character, or at least with no additional stains.

When he had come to see her, before meeting with Sally Featherton, he had hoped that she would wait for him until he could establish the extent of his difficulties. Perhaps matters between them could return to that point. But that seemed unlikely. Although he had not directly pushed Sally Featherton into the Weaver, it was through his agency that she had been exposed to danger and he would not be able to put that from his mind. He would wish to flagellate himself and make some reparation for her death. What that might be, Fran could not guess, but she was sure that he would regard himself as no more worthy than when he was likely to become a convicted murderer.

It might be that the physical obstacles standing between her and the earl had dissolved: from tomorrow morning, he would no longer be imprisoned, he was regaining his strength and health, he was prepared to repair his financial position. But now that a woman had died, Lazenby might feel that his name was so besmirched that he could not in honor offer himself to her. It was the sort of quixotic idea she was certain the earl would harbor.

If she had been inclined to despair, Fran might now have succumbed to the urge. She could not do something outrageous herself: that would betray the earl's expectations of her own behavior and standards. She could not remain in Nantwich doing nothing. If she left for Europe Lazenby might backslide and return to his rackety life. She had no formal hold over the earl.

One thing was sure. Even if he were released tomorrow morning, he would not be able to leave Nantwich

immediately. He would surely have to testify at Tollemache's trial, explaining his role in Mrs. Featherton's
arrival in town. So he must remain at Dorfold Hall for at
least another fortnight. Kitty might be held off by her
own guilt and by Sir Arthur's connivance. There was yet
hope. She could not see her way through, but she did
have hope.

Seventeen

At first, imprisonment had seemed almost like liberation to Lazenby. He had no decisions to make, no places to go, few people to see. There had been books, there were pen and paper, there was Soames. Perhaps this is what it was like to be a hermit, a condition he had never aspired to but now found somewhat appealing. At least until Frances had come to see him. Since her visit, though, he had not been able to settle back into any sort of routine. He found himself starting out of his sleep, after nodding off over the volumes of Plutarch and Marcus Aurelius which Sir Richard had happily donated from his library, and waking repeatedly through the night. And do what he might, he could not dismiss Sally's pronouncement that he was the father of her child.

He had been quick enough to grasp her meaning. Yet no other woman had ever given him such news. He had been careful and so had the women. Unexpected babies would serve only to embarrass all parties concerned. He thought he had been careful with Sally. He should have been enraged by her announcement, but amidst the dismay, there had been a kernel of pleasure and now he mourned that unborn child.

If it had been a girl, he would have guarded her from men like him. If it had been a boy, he would have taught him never to emulate his father. Now, he would never have a child. Fran might have looked on him with favor, but once he had appeared in court, even if he was acquitted, her relatives would do anything in their power to stop her from making the mistake of marrying him. And mistake it would be. It was all very well hoping one might change one's ways, but the reality was that people did not change. If anything, their characteristics became more entrenched with time. He had been a rake and he would be again. There was no point in making her miserable. And yet he had given his word that he would change his life if he ever left Nantwich gaol.

It was after another restless night that the earl woke to find Soames at his side. It was still dark.

"What time is it?"

"Not yet seven. But we are all a-bustle. Miss Wilbraham tracked down the serving wench and Tollemache has been taken into custody. You are to appear before Sir Henry Fairfield this morning. He's summoning the court early, for nine o'clock. They'll arraign Tollemache and release you. Now get up so I can shave you and make you respectable for the judge, or else they'll have you back in a cell."

Lazenby looked dazedly up at his man. "Come again? Miss Wilbraham found the girl? Tollemache is the one who dispatched poor Sally?"

"Get up. I'll tell you the whole while I'm shaving you, not before. Do you wish to eat first?"

"Of course not. Shave me and speak." Lazenby hoisted himself out of the prison cot and went in his nightshirt, shivering slightly, to a simple chair beside an equally plain washstand. Soames layered his face in hot towels, then started running the razor along the strop as he spoke.

"Miss Wilbraham set her man Tarbuck on the trail of this girl. He found her, brought her back, she ran off,

Tollemache tried to do away with her, and was caught. She confirmed that it was he who'd written the note and they compared the handwriting to some note he'd written to Miss Wilbraham and there you are, he was whipped into a cell last night." Soames lathered up his master's face. "They daren't release you without the say-so of the justice seeing as how the place is in ferment, which is why you are still in prison."

"Lord, how soon will I be able to shake the dust of Nantwich from my heels?"

Soames took his lordship's chin in his grasp and ran the razor down his cheek with smooth, easy sweeps. "At least a fortnight, I hear. You'll be called to give testimony at the trial. So will Featherton. Another comfortable time at Dorfold Hall, the pair of you staring over the dinner table at each other, both hangdog and miserable."

Both men fell silent as Soames rhythmically removed the bristle from his lordship's chin and rinsed his skin down before applying Hungary water. The earl sat back and watched as his manservant laid out fresh linen.

"I'll eat before dressing." He stood and shrugged on a brocade dressing gown before going through to the main room of his quarters. Ham and eggs sat congealing on a plate, but for the first time in some days, the earl found he had a reasonable appetite and ate the whole dish and then some toast washed down with tea.

"I suppose the entire town will be present."

"Aye. And there's even a man from *The Times,* they say. It's on account of how Tollemache is the son of the Earl of Dysart."

"They didn't make such a fuss when I was arrested."

"You've done your best to evade your duties and avoid power. You've no influence and less money. Not like the Dysarts. No one's interested in impoverished nobility, even if your reputation in society is a little tarnished."

"You're harsh, Soames. Harsh, but probably right." Having worked so hard to be a blackguard, it was a little dismaying to be dismissed as a nobody. He stood and made his final preparations. "We should pack up, I suppose. Or is that premature?"

"I've had my instructions. I won't be in court. I shall remove your possessions to Dorfold Hall this morning and see you at lunchtime."

"What shall we do next, Soames?" Lazenby examined his cravat, arranged his watch and fob and shrugged his way into his coat.

"I couldn't say, sir. There's always the hope you might settle down to some creditable pursuit, but I still wouldn't put money on it." Soames knew better than to broach the issue of Miss Wilbraham. She might not want a gaolbird for a husband, though her action in tracking down the girl from The Crown suggested otherwise. Not to mention Lazenby's tiresome sense of honor which would almost certainly prevent him from making her an offer.

They heard the shuffling of Davies approaching. The gaoler took his time in unlocking the doors.

"This way, my lord. I hear you won't be back. But I've a new tenant for your rooms, and it seems he won't be going all that quickly." Davies grinned. He cocked his head and watched as the earl left the cell.

"I hope you're not expecting a tip for your excellent service. Although this has been a better bivouac than many an inn in Spain, eh, Soames?"

"Indeed, sir."

"Tip? Why no, sir, you've been more than generous already. I only hope the new gentleman is so ready with his blunt. But maybe he's less fond of his comforts."

Lazenby was escorted by a pair of guards to the courtroom, where he was shown to the dock. He looked round for Tollemache, but the other man was being kept separate. The earl glanced about the courtroom. It was full, news mysteriously having circulated throughout the town of the great reverses and discoveries in the case of the poor drowned lady within hours of Tollemache's arrest.

The earl saw Fran there, flanked by the Dorfolds on one side and the Tollemaches on the other. Kitty was dabbing at her eyes with a miniscule handkerchief while Sir Arthur kept feeling his collar, then folding his arms, then tapping his thigh. Frances looked imperturbable and distant. Then she caught Lazenby's eye and could not quite look away as she should. He was the first to break the contact. He gazed about the room where he had walked with her to the strains of a minuet so long ago. It was unrecognizable. He kept his eyes firmly on the high window opposite the dock, through which he could see nothing but grey sky and the bare branches of an elm tree.

Everyone rose. Sir Henry entered and gave his permission for them all to take a seat. There was a great rustling and shuffling as the crowd settled.

"Alexander Ferrars, Earl Lazenby, please stand." The earl hopped up, feeling like a jack in the box. Sir Henry clasped his hands and spoke sonorously.

"Fresh evidence has been placed before the court in the matter of Rex versus Ferrars. This evidence clearly indicates that you, Alexander Ferrars, had no role in the death of Mrs. Sarah Featherton. Indeed, we have a confession which clears you entirely of any wrongdoing. Therefore I declare the Bill of Indictment issued against you must be rescinded and you are free to leave this court without a stain on your character. Officers of the court, please release his lordship."

The onlookers gasped and muttered as the guards opened up the dock and indicated to Lazenby that he should step down and into the main body of the court.

He walked forward slowly, and the crowds parted. Sir Richard Dorfold indicated to a seat next to him and Featherton which the earl took, calmly brushing a speck of dust from his almost spotless trousers as he sat down. The judge banged his gavel once more and all attention was again focused on him.

"Earl Lazenby, although you are free, you are still required to act as a witness in this case, so I must request that you remain in Nantwich and available to the court until the case has been fully heard."

The earl nodded his head in assent. Sir Henry continued. "Bring in Lionel Tollemache."

The door from the wardrooms opened once again and this time, a dishevelled Tollemache was wrestled into the dock. "No, no, I protest, this is an outrage. You cannot do this. I demand an inquiry, I demand the right to be tried by my peers." His yells echoed about the assembly halls and he continued struggling even as the judge's gavel cracked against its cup twice and thrice.

"Mr. Tollemache, be so good as to hold your peace. You will be considered in contempt of this court unless you can amend your conduct and listen in silence to the charges brought against you."

Tollemache settled and the charges were read against him. As the clerk completed his reading, Tollemache could no longer hold his tongue.

"Arthur, do something, do not allow this travesty to continue. How can you let them do this to me? I am an earl's son. I demand my rights! I demand to be tried by a court of my peers. I will not submit to this."

"Mr. Tollemache!" roared Sir Henry. "Mr. Tollemache, control yourself. This is your last chance, do I make myself clear?"

The prisoner trembled with the effort of collecting

himself. The judge glared at him. "Mr. Tollemache, I asked you a question. Do I make myself clear?"

"Yes, my lord."

"Very well. The court finds that there is a case to answer regarding this Bill, and this case of Rex versus Tollemache will be brought before us next week. Meanwhile, the prisoner will be held on remand in Nantwich gaol until his case is heard. Remove the prisoner."

This time, Tollemache went quietly, his shudders as the guards laid hands on him clearly visible. There was a great uproar in court and Sir Arthur turned to Fran and whispered:

"Please escort Kitty home. I must visit my cousin and bring him some succor. Heavens, I cannot imagine how this will be taken back at Bentley. The earl will be horrified." Sir Arthur stood, hauled Kitty to her feet and physically handed his wife into Fran's care. Kitty shook them both off, only to continue fiddling with her handkerchief.

"Have you written yet? I will frank any correspondence, of course," Kitty said.

"I have not written, but I will do so as soon as I return to Dysart House after visiting my unfortunate cousin. I do not know where the earl will be. I should think Ham House will be closed for the season and he'll be shooting in Suffolk, but I am not entirely sure."

"Write to both places. I have heard, Sir Arthur, that a scribbler from *The Times* was present today, so it is of the utmost urgency if you wish to be beforehand with this news."

A short recess was declared before the real business of the court began, so Frances led Kitty out of the press and into the street. They were closely followed by Lady Dorfold and Lazenby. As the sisters were about to walk up the street back home, Lady Dorfold hailed them.

"My dears, it is too shocking. Kitty, I am so sorry about Mr. Tollemache. What a blow! But Sir Arthur will sort this business out and earn great gratitude from his family, I am sure."

Lady Dorfold continued her words of comfort and Lazenby drew Frances aside. He removed his hat and raised her gloved hand to his mouth. It was the first time, she realized with some shock, that she had seen him without a walking stick or his arm in a sling. He wore a navy coat, a white waistcoat, and fawn trousers. He seemed taller and broader than she recalled, his eyes more penetrating, his whole manner a little impenetrable and quite imposing.

"May I call on you, Miss Wilbraham?"

"Please do. I shall be at home this afternoon and much of tomorrow."

"It will be my pleasure." He bowed and offered his arm to Lady Dorfold.

Fran linked arms with Kitty and returned his bow with an incline of her head. The sisters watched as the earl escorted Lady Dorfold to her carriage, handed her in and then sprang in to take a seat beside her.

"I had never thought of prison as a rest-cure before. It clearly has had a most beneficial effect on a rake." Kitty hauled her sister along the road, her handkerchief and die-away airs entirely dispelled. "I suppose you are going to accept his offer now."

"I do not believe he is going to make me an offer. I think he is simply coming to thank me for tracking down Becky Chalmers. I am sure that Sir Richard will have mentioned Tarbuck's role. Perhaps he wishes to give Tarbuck some reward."

"If you wish to be deliberately obtuse, that is your right, I am sure." Kitty sniffed as they approached Dysart House.

"I can see that he is very handsome, but be warned, Frances, you cannot change a man, however hard you try."

"I do not think it my place to change him." Fran resigned herself to a lecture. Kitty needed something to get her teeth into now that the sport of urging her sister to marry Lionel Tollemache had worn so very thin.

"Just as well. If you take him, he will lead you a merry dance, spend all your money, and I daresay keep fancy women with the interest. Don't say you haven't been warned."

"Kitty, as usual, you are ahead of the rest of us. Earl Lazenby has not singled me out for particular attentions. He has a perfectly good reason to visit me, and certainly, this will be his opportunity to take his leave of me and shake the dust of Nantwich from his heels as soon as he can." Fran's heart plummeted as she spoke. It occurred to her that this was all too likely to be the truth and it grieved her. She decided to start packing for London and the continent immediately. There was no reason to remain here in Nantwich: the servants scarcely needed her to supervise the closing up of Dysart House, the Tollemaches would be installed in their house within a week or so, and the earl would be gone. He had been in Nantwich just under three months and she could not imagine the place without him. She only knew that to remain in Cheshire would be intolerable once he had gone, so she might just as well go before he did.

Reed opened the door to the two ladies. Fran handed over her pelisse, bonnet, and gloves and said, "I wish to see you and Mrs. Flint as soon as possible, Reed. In my study when it is convenient."

"What start is this, Fran?" demanded Kitty.

"I shall be making arrangements to leave Dysart House. I am going to London to visit with the Foulkes family. I wrote to them last week. I shall stay with them through Christmas and then I shall accompany them to France and Italy. You know that Mr. Foulkes has been several times before to Florence and to Rome. I nearly accompanied them the year that Papa fell sick. This time, I shall definitely go."

Kitty opened her mouth to protest and cavil, but she caught herself for once. Fran's chin was at its most determined. There was also a militant gleam in her eye. At least she would be in respectable, if not glittering, company, and she might get over this unfortunate tendre for the erring Lazenby.

Reed and Mrs. Flint were surprised but unquestioning when they heard of Fran's plans. They knew of old that once she had decided upon a course of action, she wished it accomplished with all possible dispatch and while they might have their suspicions as to why she wished to leave Nantwich so precipitately, they were not inclined to jeopardize their positions by querying her orders.

By mid-afternoon, Fran was deep in lists of things to do and items to pack, her mind quite distracted from the possibility that the earl might visit. She scarcely noticed the doorbell when it chimed and had her nose buried in one of her father's old guide-books of Florence, trying to work out what the weather would be and what type of dress would be most suitable to wear there. Reed had to cough discreetly to alert her to the presence of her visitor. She started and stood up, unaware that she looked a little dishevelled and decidedly distrait.

She wore a woollen gown the color of crushed raspberries, a rich, deep color which brought out the warmth of her hair, the depth of her eyes and the smoothness and pallor of her skin. Errant locks escaped her chignon, framing her face with delicate tendrils. She looked young and vulnerable, like a cornered animal braced for its first wound. Lazenby suppressed the urge to cry out that all was well.

"Miss Wilbraham. Thank you for seeing me."

"You must be relieved to be free." He took her hand and kissed it, then stood, waiting. "Please be seated, Alexander."

He watched as she took an upright chair by an occasional table. There were plenty of items there for her to fidget with—a pen, fresh nibs, an inkwell, paper, a tray of sand, books, a periodical of some sort. He took the seat on the other side of the table. "I've come to thank you for all your efforts on my behalf. Without you and Tarbuck, I should be languishing still in gaol."

"I was glad to have done it. It would have been wrong to stand by when an innocent man was facing such charges." She watched him warily.

"You believed implicitly that I was innocent. That means a great deal to me. Many would have forsaken me the moment the prison doors closed fast upon me."

"Many others would not have had the advantage of knowing what your plans were. You had already made it clear to me that you would not forsake Mrs. Featherton. You had only her best interests at heart."

"Poor Sally. But she was loved. Featherton is distraught. I think that even though I had offered her my protection, she would have returned to him. Better to be loved even where one does not love in return than to be endured."

"Did he know about the child?"

"We have not spoken of it. Sally told me it was the reason he had given for sending her away from his home, but I am not sure he would have done such a thing. When she mentioned the man to me, she depicted him as a tedious fool, but he is neither, and like you, he has stood behind me when he might well have deserted me to a just fate. He is a man of principle and integrity."

"What are your plans now?"

"As you heard, I must stay until the trial is done. If Tollemache appeals and exercises the right to a trial in London, I suppose I shall be obliged to attend that too. Otherwise, I shall return to Edenbridge and deal with my affairs. What about you?"

"I am leaving for London this week. There is nothing to keep me here. Kitty and Arthur are moving soon and the servants are more than capable of packing up the house without my presence. I have no desire to watch Mr. Tollemache's trial, or any of the others." Fran began to neaten the pile of books on the table, squaring the corners and aligning the spines.

"You will then go to Europe?" Lazenby was aware of a sinking, hollow sensation about his stomach. Fran nodded in reply. The silence lengthened.

"My letter stands. Whatever my feelings for you, it would be wrong of me to approach you. I am not a respectable suitor for Miss Wilbraham of Nantwich."

"What about Miss Wilbraham of nowhere in particular?" Fran challenged the earl. "What about a wicked Miss Wilbraham? Would that make any difference?"

"Fran, you might take a hundred lovers and you'd still not be wicked. I don't believe it makes a bit of difference what you do. You're in the same case. You jeopardized everything by coming to visit me in prison, you don't seem to care what I do, you cannot alter your affections."

"But—" Fran stood up and paced the room. "What is holding you back? There are no obstacles between us now. You are whole, you are free, you are unencumbered."

"There are my estates. And this I think you will understand." Lazenby paused, sought for the correct words but could not find them and plunged on. "Call it guilt or atonement, I feel it would be disrespectful not to mourn

Sally in some way, for some time. Disrespectful to you and to her. I am not so light that I can forget her in an instant."

Fran closed her eyes. This she could not fight against. The money, the lurid past, the imprisonment, these she could all overcome, but his own sense of obligation and duty she could not quibble with. She opened her eyes and looked at him, her eyes unguarded and filled with tears.

"I can wait. I will wait. I've waited long enough to love, I can wait until you feel you have paid your respects."

"Even if I can give you no set date? Come, Fran, you should forget me and find some suitable young man in London who will assist you in your good works and feel no temptation to give way to idleness, drink, and gaming." The earl stood in preparation for his departure.

"Why is it that everyone thinks they know what is best for me? Why cannot I be the judge of what will suit me best?" She rounded on him. "I do not want some young prig for a husband, I want you. I am prepared to give you sufficient time to establish your situation, recover from your excesses, and explore your remorse. Why can you not offer me one crumb of comfort or hope?" By now, she was glaring at him, her arms folded, her back rigid.

"My darling Frances, I dare not let myself hope, let alone you. It is unjust that I should be so fortunate where others are so miserable, in this field, where I have dallied and seduced and wrecked." The earl sighed. "It is not just Mrs. Featherton I have to atone for, but all the wives I have misled, all the husbands I have cuckolded. I have deliberately sown misery and dissent. I cannot begin to repair all the wrongs I have done, but I can start at least to lead a life which is worthy of you."

"How long must I wait?"

"I cannot tell. May I write?"

"You may, but I don't believe I will hear from you. Some misplaced sense of chivalry will dictate that you withdraw yourself from my life and you will go about your own world in a monastic habit, complete with hair shirt and a tattoo of *mea culpa, mea maxima culpa* engraved on your breast."

Lazenby laughed. "You may well be right about the hair shirt, but I am not so self-denying as to lose the chance to hear how your travels go. I will write. I promise. I may not send you every letter I write, but I will write."

"I suppose that is a crumb. Very well, Alexander. Go and do your penance, if not with my blessing at least with my understanding. It would be wrong to read the banns when Mrs. Featherton is not yet cold in her grave."

"Thank you, Frances. It is just one more instance where I am in your debt." He came over to her and touched her cheek. She looked up into his eyes. They were solemn and a little fearful. "If you do meet someone else, Frances, do not be afraid to tell me. It would be fitting after all the grief I have caused to lose you to another man."

Frances smiled. "Of course I would tell you. But I hope I am not so fickle." She moved back, away from his touch. "I must get on with my arrangements."

"Of course. I shall come to call when you are back in London." He bowed and walked over to the door. "Take care, Fran. Have fun." Then he slipped out of the room, the latch clicking quietly behind him.

Eighteen

Stresa, Lake Maggiore

The English party had taken a villa on the lakeside. There were two elderly gentleman, an elderly lady, and two younger ladies, as well as a crew of maids and menservants, their guide and translator, and a cook from France. They were a quiet party, no late nights, no drunken revels, something of a disappointment to the locals who had hoped for poets and painters who would liven up the daily round by providing a good source of gossip and disapprobation. But these people were unexceptionable, entirely decorous, and appreciative of local customs. They were delighted by their villa, neglecting to complain about the mattresses or the overall level of cleanliness, pleased by the weather, which was pleasant but not unduly hot, and they spread their largesse liberally.

The truth was after travelling to Paris and then southward to Nice and Menton, on through Genoa, Turin, and Milan, the Foulkes party was glad to spend some weeks in one location. They had originally thought to spend only a fortnight at Lake Maggiore, but the place was so pleasant that they decided to extend their stay. The mountains kept the temperatures down and it was very pleasant to take a boat out on the lake and visit the palace of the Borromeo on Isola Bella.

"I had been told that it was almost impossible to visit the island," said Fran as they organized their first visit. "But now I find that there isn't a single member of the family to be found near the place and provided you pay enough, you can visit at any time you please." So much for Lionel Tollemache's protestations about the exclusivity of the Borromeo.

Although the treasures within the great house were magnificent, its real beauty lay in its gardens, formal, manicured, and positioned on the small island to make the most of views across the lake. There were stone stairs, statuary, and parterres where an abundance of delicate flowers grew—roses, oleander, geraniums, a profusion of camellias, even tulips and forget-me-nots. Although the garden at their own villa was pretty enough, it was a pleasure to take a book and a light picnic and spend the afternoon on the island, surrounded by water, the quiet broken by the occasional cries of fishermen and birds.

The pause in their travels did give Frances time to think back to the events of the past few months. Her travel journal was full of sketches and notes, her eyes had been opened to a variety of landscape, cuisine, and people, and she had learnt that she was equal to coping with a crisis either in reasonable French or rudimentary Italian. There had been instances of misplaced luggage, difficult border officials, and confusions in markets over the bric-a-brac Mrs. Foulkes so loved to collect. Fran had managed to calm all parties involved, and solve the riddles with the assistance of their most competent major-domo.

Nantwich seemed distant and rather faded in retrospect. Travelling in sun-kissed lands overflowing with exotic fruits and delicious shellfish, sharing meals on terraces overlooking the turquoise depths of the Mediterranean, lingering in town squares, exploring aqueducts and amphitheatres at Orange, Nimes, and

Arles, there had been so many extraordinary sights and experiences that Frances had scarcely had time to absorb them all. A week here, three days there, they had seemed to travel at breakneck speed through France, Piedmont, and Lombardy. But, unwritten, unspoken, unacknowledged, the thought of Lazenby colored everything she saw. What would he say about the cherry blossoms at Avignon, or the great stone houses of Genoa and its narrow, vertiginous alleyways and tortuous streets, what would he think of the pretty girls carrying great trays of flowers to market in Nice, or the fishermen mending their nets at Menton, what would he have made of the extraordinary Duomo of Milan? She could scarcely open her eyes without wondering what he was doing and how he might have reacted to the places she had been and the people she had met. Every now and then, her heart leapt as she thought that she had caught a glimpse of him. She would see someone with a similar haircut or an equally jaunty tilt to the chin, or shoulders as broad and think at first that she had seen him, however improbable that might be. The frequency of this dwindled somewhat the longer she had been away from Nantwich, but every now and then she was still fooled.

At times, she was exasperated by the persistence of his presence in her thoughts and her heart. But this, she supposed, was the essence of love: finding it entirely impossible to dismiss from one's mind the object of one's passion. At least, she hoped, she did not bore her fellow travellers with this intrusive spirit.

She was fortunate in her travelling companions. There were Mr. and Mrs. Foulkes, and Mrs. Foulkes's brother, Mr. Edmund Hanbury, and their daughter, some five or six years older than Fran, Miss Sarah Foulkes. They were indefatigable and incurably optimistic, amused by the inevitable delays of travel, always willing to engage in conversation with people of all ranks and position and equipped with introductions to interesting salons. They had spent some weeks in Paris, where Mr. Hanbury had an extensive acquaintance with a lively circle of writers and thinkers, and this had provided them with further introductions elsewhere in France. Doors had been opened to them which might otherwise have been closed, escorts were provided for sights which only the cognoscenti knew about and new acquaintances and friends had flocked to meet them.

The Foulkeses and Hanbury were passionate about Roman architecture and antiquities and they had been in paroxysms of delight over the signs of Roman occupation which dotted southern France. Fran found the remnants of Renaissance life more appealing and redolent of the romance of history. Additionally, she enjoyed the more lurid and violent tales surrounding such relics, tales of poisonings and stabbings and long-running vendettas, either despite or because of the high melodrama surrounding the death of Mrs. Featherton and Mr. Tollemache's subsequent trial.

Kitty had written to tell her that Mr. Tollemache was now incarcerated in an asylum back in his home county of Suffolk. Sir Henry had not needed much persuasion to deliver a verdict of manslaughter while of unsound mind, and certainly the experience of incarceration appeared to have unhinged Mr. Tollemache entirely. Kitty's letters were full of dire warnings of the dangers of Italy, where it was widely thought that Mr. Tollemache had "gone wrong." In her most recent letter, Kitty had revealed that she was increasing and that the great event was expected in November, and surely Frances would be back from her jaunting by then.

Fran did not know whether she would return to England in time for her sister's confinement. The Foulkeses were on the verge of deciding to spend the winter in Italy. The summer was too hot for travel, autumn would be a much more pleasant season for exploring the southern sections of the country, and there was so much to see that a lifetime would not truly be long enough. Both Mr. Foulkes and Mr. Hanbury had introductions to academics at the great universities of Padua and Bologna, there were still Florence and Venice and Rome and Naples to take in. There was no incentive to return to England at all. Despite his fine words, Lazenby had not written. Neither Kitty nor Lady Dorfold had heard any word of his activities since he had left Nantwich.

He had not forgotten her, she was sure. She trusted the strength of his emotions and the truth of his declaration to her. But his estates had been heavily encumbered and so long neglected that the amount of work necessary to repair the damage must be considerable. He could have written, she supposed, but it was more likely that the burden of his financial and moral debts was so overwhelming that he could not bring himself to reveal just how unlikely it was that they had any future together. In which case, what was the point of returning to that arid life when there was so much to distract her here? Kitty's baby would not be a sufficient incentive to persuade her back, and Kitty was now so many hundreds of miles away that her nagging had virtually no effect.

There were mornings when she woke to find her face awash with tears, her pillow wet, in mourning for that grand ardor which had swept over her like a spring tide, but which was now ebbing because it was foolish to spend one's life longing for the moon. It was self-indulgent and wasteful to expire in the name of love. Better by far to rise, to walk, to watch, to learn of new places. Eventually, she might run out of new towns to visit and new sights to see, but for the moment, it was more than sufficient distraction for the essential emptiness of a life without her wicked earl.

Today's distraction was the prospect of a night on Isola Madre, some distance from Stresa, closer in fact to the opposite bank of the lake and the town of Pallanza. It too was an island owned by the Borromeo family, with a small villa and again, extensive gardens, occupied only by albino peacocks and pheasant. The villa was apparently often offered as a guesthouse and it was assumed that the English would wish to see the pride of the island, its English garden.

The servants had gone ahead with sufficient equipment to ensure a comfortable night's stay, and the main party assembled after breakfast to climb into a neat fishing vessel and sail to the island. It was a fine day, with a light breeze, the air on the water fresh. On either side of the lake rose the great slopes of the Dolomites, some still snow-capped despite the advancing of summer. Only the most prosaic of souls could have withstood the beauty of the lake as they passed by the promontory of Isola Bella, and Fran found her heart lightening and her spirits rising.

The lake was busy this morning, small wherries and skiffs thronging the shores and carrying goods from town to town along the shore, a quicker route by far than the road, which was prone to landslips and heavily rutted from winter rains. It was market day in Pallanza and lake people were gathering there with wares to sell or buy until the whole dockside was a mass of little boats. Fran noted with surprise that one boat was setting out from Pallanza and seemed to be heading for the Borromeo islands, perhaps a ferry service collecting people to attend the market. She was distracted from watching any further by her arrival on Isola Madre.

Their translator, a Piedmontese student called Guido recommended to them by an acquaintance in Genoa, leapt out of the boat and greeted the steward in charge of the island and its villa with a cheerful barrage of the local dialect. The gentlemen helped the ladies onto the jetty and they were escorted up to the Villa where they took refreshment, delightful little almond cakes with Marsala. They were shown their rooms, all with magnificent views and after a brief pause, met downstairs to be shown the gardens.

The island was not large, although it was densely planted and full of botanical wonders. The steward gave a lightning tour of the grounds which seemed more sheltered than the spectacular gardens of the palazzo on Isola Bella, and consequently supported an even greater range of planting. There was a great deal to look at, and the Foulkeses, keen gardeners, were full of questions and exclamations. It was clear that they found the island a demi-Paradise and that a day there would be scarcely long enough for all their explorations and questions. Fran, while she was interested enough in the gardens, did not feel the necessity of learning the optimum soil, positioning, and watering regime for every plant in the grounds. When, after lunch, it was clear that the Foulkeses and Mr. Hanbury were intent on extracting from the gardener every last morsel of information, Fran excused herself and said she would prefer to sketch and paint while she could.

A servant set up her easel in a secluded dell where she could choose between a long vista across the lake to Pallanza or more detailed studies of a wisteria-lined pergola leading back to the house. At first, she could not settle, making rough sketches of first the immediate surroundings and then of the lake. She finally settled on a particular composition and set to. She covered her white muslin dress with a voluminous smock, and adjusted her wide-brimmed hat of Leghorn straw, then refined her favorite sketch and started applying watercolor to the

picture with a sure, even touch. Every now and then, she
would step back to examine the composition, but mostly
she was concentrating on her work with an intensity that
encapsulated her as effectively as a bird in a bell jar. She
did not hear any footsteps behind her, or notice the man
watching her every move. He sat then, on a low stone
balustrade and continued to observe her, unable to take
his eyes from her.

An hour passed and then almost another before she
was finished. It was a romantic sight, the picture of the
lake with its jewel-like waters, the sheer, dark greenery of
the mountain slopes, the scattering of houses and
church spires which marked the town in the distance. It
would be a fine memory of the beauty of this day and the
heart-stopping loveliness of the landscape. Fran put
down her brushes, stepped back and looked on it.

"I want it framed and near me always."

She whirled, then folded her arms tight across her
body as though fending off a blow to the solar plexus.
She stepped back. Lazenby stood up.

"I did not mean to terrify you. Forgive me." He
reached out a hand. Fran stepped back again, her eyes
disbelieving. "Frances, it is me. I am here."

"How?"

"I missed you. And I need your money." His prosaic
aside drew a smile from her. He said nothing for a moment, watched as she relaxed her grip on her arms a
little, then continued. "It's true, you know. I've been
back to Edenbridge, and matters there are greatly improved. I have looked into every aspect of the estates. My
concerns there had not come to so desperate a case as I
feared. Indeed, if I can secure some capital, I shall be in
the way of producing a fortune. So I've come to ask you
to marry me, purely for your money."

"Why didn't you write?" She was tense and taut again.

"I did write. I just didn't send the letters. I have them all at home. If you marry me, you may read them."

"I don't understand." She thought she did, but she wanted him to explain himself thoroughly. She was still standing, appearing almost ready to flee.

"That's unlike you. But you may have your pound of flesh." He looked down, avoiding her gaze. "The letters were too revealing. Every time I sat down and prepared my nib and set out my papers, I imagined that I could write a calm, dispassionate, cheerful letter. Every time, I would read what I had written and realize it had become a frenzied torrent of longing for you. If I had sent them to you, you would have come back and it was always too soon. But then, I couldn't bear it any longer. I kept hearing about your itinerary from Lady Dorfold, and then she told me that you had asked after me, asked whether she had heard from me and I couldn't do it any longer. I had to see you." With relief, he saw her relax a little. She sat back on the stone balustrade on the other side of the pergola, her face concealed by the brim of her hat. He approached her and knelt down before her. He tilted her chin upwards so he could see her face and covered her folded hands with one of his.

"Frances, my beloved girl, will you marry me? I don't need the money. I can raise it elsewhere easily enough now that I am seen to be a reformed character. But I do need you. I've worked and worked but it seems pointless unless you are there beside me to share it."

"Really?" She could barely speak.

"Truly. I thought I loved you to the limit but since you have been away, I have thought of you every day, wondered where you were, what you were doing, who you were doing it with, and why I was not there at your side. Whether you are there or not, now I have admitted the possibility of love into my heart, I cannot seem to quell it. It grows. It will not stop growing."

She leaned forward, looking into his eyes as her lips touched his. Her hands came up to frame his face and she deepened the kiss, as though making a pledge. Then she drew back.

"What if I said I would not marry you, but I would live with you as your mistress?"

"If that is the only way I may have you, I will accept it. I know there is nothing you value so highly as your independence." He continued to look up at her. She pulled at his hands and indicated that he should sit beside her.

"Of course I will marry you, Alexander." She threw her arms about his neck and his hands came to hold her waist as they kissed, all barriers down, all constraint vanished.

The wedding took place that September at the earl's seat in the Edenbridge chapel. It was well attended, for the bride was a lady with a considerable, if eclectic acquaintance and, on his engagement, the earl began to be more widely accepted in tonnish circles. When they finally retired for the night, the earl swept his countess into his arms and carried her up the grand staircase to whistles and catcalls and thunderous applause. By the time he reached the door to the master bedroom, the bride was slipping, but he did manage to negotiate the door without injuring either her or himself. He righted her and kissed her.

"My lady. My life." They kissed again. The countess was the first to break the kiss, pulling back with a warm smile.

"I have something for you." She turned and looked round the great bedroom. Leaning against a chair was a large, flat package wrapped in brown paper. She led the earl to it. "Here. It is my wedding gift."

Lazenby ripped the paper. There, beneath, in an elegant walnut frame was the watercolor Frances had been painting when he proposed. He lifted the painting and propped it on the mantelpiece before returning to his bride.

"I believe that was the most frightening day of my life."

"Yes, Alexander, justly so. I accepted!"

He grinned, then the moment of levity passed. "Frances, it has been a year since we met. If you can call our first encounter a meeting. The fear that you would send me on my way has been with me up to this day. You do know there is no going back now."

"I know. But you have wooed and won. I love you, and I always will."

The earl looked at his painting. He was home, he was whole and he had Frances. He took her in his arms and held her close to him, as he would for the rest of their lives.

<u>BOOK YOUR PLACE ON OUR WEBSITE</u> <u>AND MAKE THE</u> <u>READING CONNECTION!</u>

We've created a customized website just for our very special readers, where you can get the inside scoop on everything that's going on with Zebra, Pinnacle and Kensington books.

When you come online, you'll have the exciting opportunity to:

- View covers of upcoming books

- Read sample chapters

- Learn about our future publishing schedule (listed by publication month *and author*)

- Find out when your favorite authors will be visiting a city near you

- Search for and order backlist books from our online catalog

- Check out author bios and background information

- Send e-mail to your favorite authors

- Meet the Kensington staff online

- Join us in weekly chats with authors, readers and other guests

- Get writing guidelines

- AND MUCH MORE!

Visit our website at
http://www.kensingtonbooks.com